THE CORNMASHERS

WENDELL D. OWENS

The Cornmashers
Copyright © 2004 by Wendell D. Owens

International Standard Book Number: 1-929612-56-7
Library of Congress Control Number: 2004092698

PRINTED IN THE UNITED STATES OF AMERICA

HannahJohn Publishing Company
PMB 82
1539 South Mason Road
Katy, Texas 77450

Adams Press
Chicago, Illinois
www.adamspress.com

DEDICATIONS

To my wife Judi, whom I have loved since the day I first saw her standing in line at voter registration in Chicago. Currently, she is working on her master's degree in instructional technology; sits on the Board of Directors of the Katy, Texas, YMCA; and volunteers at John's and Hannah's schools. She's also a world-class chef, a pet lover, and an expert in home repairs.

In the course of writing this book, I also discovered Judi's talents in the publishing arena. She redirected the story line of my book, edited it, designed the cover, designed and built the Web page, and devised a marketing strategy. She has also been thoughtful enough to advise me that she will be collecting all monies from its sale.

Judi is a kind and insightful friend. She is the smartest person I know and has a great sense of humor, yet she remains modest and down-to-earth. I would list all of her other good qualities, but space restrictions simply will not permit it. (Note: My wife also writes my book dedications.)

Cornmashers is also dedicated to you, Hannah and John, to show you that you can do anything you set your minds to. In writing this book, I have been inspired by your discipline as you race to your study desks to commence plowing through your homework assignments without prodding from me or your mother. I have been moved by your encouraging comments, such as, "Are you *ever* gonna finish that book?" and "Are you *still* writing it?"

You have both thrilled me by sacrificing your own private pleasures in order to stick to your bigger goals of making homework and chores the number one objectives in your lives. I tear up as I reminisce about the times you, John, have erupted with an emphatic "No!" to invitations to go to the Skate Park in order to stay home and dance with your dangling participles. And I swelled with pride each time I overheard you, Hannah, screaming "No!" to your friends' invitations to stomp off to the theater to see the newest movie. Instead of gorging yourself on popcorn, you chose to stay home and gouge your eyes out as you voluntarily elected to spend a greater fraction of your precious time learning to multiply fractions.

I am proud of you both, and I hope you continue to exercise this same rock-hard discipline and good judgment that you have demonstrated so far. On the whole, you will both go far in life if only a fraction of these compliments are, indeed, true.

CHAPTER 1

Glory Days

"Nothing in life is certain except that you will never get enough prime quality slop and your troubles will always outweigh your joys."

Looking in from the outside, life at the pig pens was pretty doggone good. However, mixed in amongst the smell of hogs, rotting pine needles, mud and slop was the scent of something quite human. The smell of money.

Down on a drowsy, tranquil farm in Georgia, there was a large pen full of pigs. Every so often, a slew of squealing, pink-eyed piglets with curled up tails raced through the pig pens, shattering the peacefulness. As squadrons of plump flies darted around, buzzing like miniature fighter jets, hundreds of hogs dozed and twitched, as they laid sprawled out in a dazzling array of colors, sizes and shapes. The hefty, spotted-colored sows and the handsome, heavy-eyed boars gazed lazily at each other and grunted periodically, as they slept stretched out every which-a-way.

The hogs didn't have a care in the world, as they wallowed in the powerful aroma of day old slop. Each morning, the sun strolled out and announced the arrival of a new sleepy-eyed day with a stunning thunderclap of warm, brilliant colors.

As a general rule, hogs are a pretty lazy bunch. These hogs were no exception. They lazed peacefully in the blinding morning sunlight, barely breathing, with their eyes glazed over and half-shut. The pigs were fed every day at sundown. George Thomas Brown, the owner of the pigs, fed them slop, which was leftover food scraps that he and his farm hands drove around and collected from local restaurants.

Farmer Brown drove a faded red pickup truck. His farm hands drove big, white trucks with rows of huge, faded green and white barrels rattling around in the flatbeds. These barrels were receptacles for every imaginable type of food scraps left over from the dinner tables, restaurants, local diners and military mess halls in the local Georgia and Alabama areas. The men used large, white plastic buckets with cold gray metal handles to dip the slop out of those humongous, grease-stained barrels on their trucks and dumped some of it into the pig's wooden feeding troughs. The rest of the slop was poured into the permanent barrels that remained at the pig pens.

The slop barrels resembled haunting metal monuments, as they stood there, almost as tall as the rows of magnificent pine trees that guarded the perimeter of the farm. The pigs milled aimlessly around, eye-balling that gorgeous slop piled up in those gritty barrels. Farmer Brown and his men piled the delicious slop on high. Sometimes, it sloshed over the tops of the barrels and spilt out, splashing onto the ground.

The sight of all those bodacious barrels of sweltering slop created the same craving and optical effect on the pigs that the "Golden Arches" have on a hungry child. While a hongry' hog might not sell his soul to the devil for a chance to eat some slop.....he might consider pawning it for awhile.

Every evening around six o'clock, the high-pitched whine of Farmer Brown down-shifting gears in his old red truck ricocheted through the woods. It created a frenzied roaring sound that bounced from tree to tree, then echoed around the woods three or four more times for good measure. This sound triggered the pigs' ritual feeding dance, as they started stampeding towards the feeding troughs, pushing and shoving to secure a spot at the front of the chow line.

By the time Farmer Brown and his farm hands arrived and started pouring slop into the pigs' troughs, those who had successfully secured a VIP position in the front row were lined up, slobbering at the mouth. Pigs were pushing, shoving, grunting and squealing, as they fought to be first in line.

Sometimes the pigs talked amongst themselves about how good life was on their farm. If life was any better any place else, they decided…why…they wouldn't be able to stand it. On cool, breezy fall days, some of the pigs loved to root under the fences and escape. After escaping, they enjoyed tramping around in the surrounding woods until Farmer Brown caught them and returned them to their pens, kicking and squealing up a storm. But mostly, they just lazed around. The hogs had tons of time to kill, since time don't mean nothing to a hog.

Although the scene on Farmer Brown's farm looked peaceful, some pigs wondered if the farm was really as safe and comforting as it seemed. A few of them had noticed some mysterious events that hung over the pig pens like a newly spun spider web. Hogs were flat-out disappearing. Not hide nor hair seen of them again. When you mentioned the disappearances to somebody, the pigs frowned at you with a puzzled look before changing the subject.

*"Life is grand, when your head is stuck in the sand.
Because you can't see your friends being turned into
hams."*

CHAPTER 2

Disappearance of the Cornmashers

"What? Pigs disappearing? Who says pigs are disappearing?" said Livy to her friend, Melanie. "I ain't seen nobody disappearing. Craziest thing I ever heard. Look at me. I'm a Cornmasher. And I'm still here. Ain't I? All they're doing is taking us Cornmashers for a ride. Then they bring us home again. Actually, it kinda' sounds like fun. I'll tell you all about it when I get back. Chile'.....I tell you the truth.....all this excitement about going riding is 'bout to kill me!"

Elmer G. had been the runt of his litter, meaning he was the smallest pig to plop out into the new world that day. However, during the past year, Elmer G. had developed a ferocious appetite. As his natural metabolism slowed down, he wasn't burning off calories as fast as he used to. Elmer G. started filling out his waistline in a handsome manner.

He loved information and was curious about how things worked. Elmer G. never met a stranger. He talked openly about his own secret dreams and fears. The other pigs responded by telling him their life stories. He freely offered advice, even on subjects he knew nothing about. Elmer G. liked to be in control of his life. He got very nervous and fidgety when he couldn't make sense out of things.

Although he had no living family members, he still maintained a positive outlook. Elmer G. was optimistic that a positive change was right over the horizon. He was not an intentional liar, but he tended to throw an overcoat over the truth from time to time. He told stories in a unique way that you could tell *he* believed his tall tales were real. Every snake he saw in the woods was always sixty feet long and thick as a log. He was not a particularly good listener because he believed he had already forgotten more things than the others would ever know.

One morning, Elmer G. crawled through a hole in the pig pen fence so that he could explore the neighboring woods and experience being free for a few hours. A giant splinter of wood scraped his right shoulder, as he wiggled his hefty girth underneath the loose fence slats. The splinter cut a shallow groove that throbbed in pain, as bright red blood began to spread slowly across his shoulder.

Later, Farmer Brown and his farm hands caught Elmer G. and the other escapees and returned them to the pig pens. Farmer Brown used the most awful language as he dragged Elmer G. and the other squealing pigs by their hind legs back to the pig pens and tossed them inside, slamming the gate shut. After his exhilarating adventure, Elmer G. laid sprawled out under a shade tree, enjoying the evening sunset as he rested from being dragged back home. As he laid in the cool evening shade with his eyes slightly closed, his thoughts turned to the mystery of the disappearing pigs.

There was one scene that bothered Elmer G., as it was repeated over and over. He noticed that once every month certain pigs were rounded up by Farmer Brown and his men and herded into a set of smaller, sanitized hog pens that had scented pine wood floors. These pigs seemed to be just as excited as people who move into a new house with hardwood floors. They pranced around their new home and could be heard commenting, "Girl...look at my new floors. Ain't they something to write home about? We may have to eat in one corner so we don't mess 'em up with corn mash and what-not. These floors are so clean you can eat offa' em'!"

Course, once the pigs were herded into these compact pens with the wooden floors, their days of rolling in that squishy, black mud were over. After they settled into their new homes, Farmer Brown fed these special pigs fresh corn pellets and a cornmeal grain mixed with water and a splash of honey, which was called corn mash. Some of the pigs almost choked to death when they got their first taste of corn pellets and corn mash because they were scarfing it down their gullets at such a frenzied pace. They snorted the corn mash up in frantic motions, stopping only long enough to grunt their approval of the taste test. As they greedily smashed the corn pellets between their top and bottom sets of grinder teeth, each pig tried to eat as much as he could before the other pigs beat him to it. The pigs that were herded into these special pens were called "Cornmashers" by the other pigs because they crushed the corn pellets with their teeth and gulped down the corn mash.

When the pigs in the regular pig pens saw the prime treatment the Cornmashers were getting, they fought with each other to be first in line when Farmer Brown started the selection process for a new group of pigs to go live for awhile in the pens with the pine wood floors. Some days, Farmer Brown had to break up fights among the hogs, as they shoved and leaned hard against each other in order to secure a spot in the front of the line to become a Cornmasher.

Although it tasted heavenly and they ate tons of it, their diet of corn pellets and corn mash actually had a trimming effect on the

Cornmashers' waistlines. The Cornmashers gradually lost weight, as this special diet cleaned out their digestive systems and increased their muscle to fat ratio. After a few weeks on the pine wood floors away from the slop and mud pits, they were a clean, lean and handsome looking lot. After their makeover in the Cornmasher pens, many of them now possessed looks......to die for.

After they stayed in these sparkling clean pens for a few weeks, a gigantic, candy-apple red trailer truck driven by Bobby Lee Pain, pulled up to the pig pens. Farmer Brown, Bobby Lee and their helpers herded the Cornmashers unceremoniously into the back of the long, ominous looking trailer truck. The buff, toned Cornmashers were whacked and prodded with long, wooden poles by Bobby Lee and the other farm hands, forcing them to walk up a wooden ramp into the trailer truck. Then, they were driven away, staring silently out between the wooden slats on the side of the truck.

As Bobby Lee shifted gears and guided the growling trailer truck down the winding dirt road, the Cornmashers looked like candy bars swinging silently from side-to-side on hooks inside a vending machine, dressed like pink, black and white colored candy wrappers. Once they were driven away, the Cornmashers were never seen or heard from again. Although Elmer G. tried to find out where they were being taken, none of the other pigs had much taste for discussing what happened to them.

One day, Elmer G. slipped over to the special pens and peeped through the slats to watch the Cornmashers eat. He decided he was going to find out what happened to them because these mysterious activities didn't pass his smell test.

When Elmer G. asked the other pigs what happened to the Cornmashers, he could never muster up a straight answer. He decided to take another turn at bat. Elmer G. decided to ask someone new about the disappearance of the Cornmashers. He asked Scruffy what he knew about the fate of the Cornmashers.

Scruffy, who preferred to be called 'Scruff Daddy', was a gansta' pig who wore a dirty old, red head rag or 'Doo Rag', as he liked to call it, tied around his head. Scruff Daddy had a knot in his Doo Rag behind each ear and a flap in the back shaped like a triangle. He was not one to put on frills. Nobody could spread himself around thick as molasses, like Scruff Daddy. He roamed everywhere he pleased. He knew the answer to any question you could think of. Scruff Daddy seemed to live such a care-free life of lazing around and playing all day. He wasn't scared of nothing. Some of the young pigs followed him around, trying to be like him.

Scruff Daddy and his posse strutted around terrorizing the younger pigs by pushing them out of the way and throwing mud at them. When they got tired of harassing the younger pigs, Scruff Daddy and his gang rooted holes in the bottom of the wooden fence planks, crawled through the openings and scampered away into the surrounding woods. After they escaped, they hid in the shrubbery. From their hiding places, they would jump out and scare other unsuspecting escapees who were enjoying their own afternoon of temporary emancipation.

"Scruff Daddy," said Elmer G. "Do you know where Farmer Brown sends the Cornmashers after they've been locked up in the hardwood pens for a few weeks?"

"Oh yeah," said Scruff Daddy, with his ever-present scowl on his face. He spoke in a tone of voice that indicated he thought the question was easy as pie. "I know where they take the Cornmashers."

"Where?" asked Elmer G.

"That ain't no big secret or nuthin'," explained Scruff Daddy, as he swelled himself up a little bit. He was feeling pretty smart answering Elmer G.'s questions. "They're taking 'em into town to a prison for pigs. The peoples that represent the system.....like Farmer Brown...are putting their work boots on the necks of poor pigs like us."

"How come?" asked Elmer G.

"To make us give up our dignity while they make money and get rich," replied Scruff Daddy, as he started blowing around like he had more important things to do. "You see....."

"Excuse me," interrupted Elmer G. "But I don't understand the connection. I didn't realize the disappearing pigs were related to how much humans care about making money."

"Elmer G.," said Scruff Daddy in his most serious and solemn tone, "when it comes to humans....they always....care about the money. Always! Matter of fact, this whole issue about missing pigs is all about the almighty dollar. 'Course......if you had my inelegance...you would already know these things. But since you obviously haven't had the intell-electrical simulation that I've had, let me break it down for you. Elmer G.....humans love three things. Money. Money. And themselves. They will lie, cheat and steal to get their grubby hands on some more money."

"But Scruff Daddy...surely they wouldn't lock pigs up in prison just to make money," said Elmer G.

"WHAT?!!!" screamed Scruff Daddy. "You think they wouldn't lock a pig up in prison for money? Boy....pu...lease! Gimme a break! Elmer G....I thought you was smart. But I'm beginning to wonder about you. You need to come on in out of the cold storage of ignorance and warm yourself up with a dose of hot reality. Humans will rush down to the local prison and turn in their mama, daddy, children, friends and neighbors if they can collect some reward money for doing it. So you know they wouldn't hesitate a split second before dropping a dime on us pigs and dragging us away to prison in exchange for the almighty dollar."

"You really think they would do that?" asked Elmer G.

"Why 'shore!" said Scruff Daddy. "Do you think a human being with a fist-full of dollars will survive if he walks the streets flashing his money?"

"I don't know," said Elmer G., in a hesitant tone of voice.

"He'd get shot or knocked in the head with a crowbar by another human in about forty—-seconds," said Scruff Daddy.

"Why would someone do that?" asked Elmer G.

"Well let me tell you why," said Scruff Daddy. "They'd do it for the Benjamins! The Washingtons! They'd do it so they could steal his money! Actually, humans attack each other even when there ain't no money involved. But, adding money to the mix seems to really get 'em fired up something awful. Why in the world do you think humans would let a pig live free, if they can make money by locking us up in prison?"

"It sounds like money makes humans crazy," said Elmer G.

"It does make 'em act crazy," said Scruff Daddy. "The only thing that makes humans crazier than money is when they fall in love, or ain't got nobody to fall in love with. That's when things really get crazy."

"But Scruff Daddy," said Elmer G., "how does putting the Cornmashers in prison make money for the humans in power?"

"I'm telling you, Elmer G.," said Scruff Daddy, "pigs in prisons equals jobs for humans. If you wanna' run a state-of-the-art prison, then you need human workers to be guards, cooks, receptionists, construction supervisors, road repairmen and all other sorts of jobs."

"So," said Elmer G., trying to hide his disbelief. "Let me get this straight. You're telling me that you think the Cornmashers are being taken away to prisons made just for pigs. And the humans are doing this so that people can have jobs guarding the pigs? In other words...instead of auto manufacturing, mobile home sales, construction projects, home sales, retail sales, cattle ranching, steel production, and the production and sale of oil and petrochemicals...that it is really hog security that is forming the backbone of the humans' economy?"

"Beautiful ain't it?" said Scruff Daddy. "I mean...you would never expect a lowly, self-edumacated pig like me to figure something like this out. Knowledge...my boy...is a powerful thang'. Mighty powerful. Sometimes...Elmer G....I jus' amaze my own self, with the thangs' I know about."

And on that note, Scruff Daddy cocked his eyebrows skyward and proudly trotted off into the morning haze of lifting fog.

Elmer G. watched Scruff Daddy trot off and thought to himself.... "if Scruff Daddy was representative of the average pig's brain-power....then pigs are in a whole heap of trouble. If brains was ink...Scruff Daddy couldn't put a dot on top of the letter "i"."

"Do you really think they're taking pigs to the slaughter house to kill us? Why...that's the most ridiculous thing I've ever heard! Bunch of nothing! I think that red trailer truck is taking the Cornmashers for a joy-ride," confided one Cornmasher to a fellow Cornmasher. "Some of these pigs are jealous because Farmer Brown puts us Cornmashers in front of them. We are his special pets. He loves us Cornmashers. That's why he puts us in these here nice, clean pens. And he feeds us corn mash. I wouldn't be blown away if one of these days he didn't up and surprise us by inviting us to join him at his supper table. I expect one of these days we'll be right at the kitchen table.... side-by-side with Farmer Brown and the rest of his family."

CHAPTER 3

Clichés By the Bushel

"A pig in the pan is worth two in the pen."

A few days after his conversation with Scruff Daddy, Elmer G. asked a pig named Cliché if she knew what happened to the Cornmashers. Cliché was usually on top of things.

"Cliché," said Elmer G. "What happens to the Cornmashers when they're driven away in that humongous trailer truck every few weeks?"

"All I can tell you," said Cliché, with a heavy sigh, "is that you'd better avoid those Cornmasher pens like they were the plague. Elmer G., you're a babe in the woods. Chile, you just don't know what you're up against. All of us pigs have our backs against the wall."

"I don't understand what you mean," said Elmer G. "Are you saying that something bad happens to the Cornmashers?"

"Let's just say that if something bad does happen to the Cornmashers," said Cliché, "then there's no use in crying over spilt milk. That's just the way the ball bounces. The Cornmashers may think they are living in the lap of luxury, but may find themselves behind the eight ball. Yes indeedy.....up the creek without a paddle. Cornmashers are down for the count. If Farmer Brown cuts 'em to the quick....why the Cornmashers will be crying crocodile tears."

"Stop! That's enough!" shouted Elmer G. in frustration. "I don't wanna' hear no more of your doggone clichés! Can't you just tell me in plain English what happens to the Cornmashers?"

"The Cornmashers," whispered Cliché, "may have to give up their pound of flesh. At the end of the day, they may find themselves dead as doornails."

"Cliché, where are you getting all this stuff from?" asked Elmer G. "I never heard such talk before in my life."

"Elmer G., I heard it all through the grapevine."

"The grapevine?" said Elmer G. "What grapevine?"

"Well," said Cliché, "the grapevine means that one pig tells something to another pig and that pig tells another pig and so on and so on until somebody tells me."

"So you heard all this information through the grapevine?" said Elmer G. "I ain't never heard nothing through no grapevine."

"I heard part of it through the grapevine," said Cliché. "Plus I read a lot. And...I've got Mother Wit."

"Mother Wit?" said Elmer G. "How can you have Mother Wit when you ain't no mother. You ain't even got no piglets. Girl...you ain't nobody's mama. I don't know why I'm arguing with you anyway. I don't even know what Mother Wit is."

"Well now....Mister Smarty Britches," said Cliché. "For one thing, you don't need to have no piglets to have Mother Wit. And for your information, Mother Wit means knowing things because you have life experiences. I've been through some stuff...and I learned from those experiences. You ain't got no Mother Wit because you ain't been nowhere and you shore' ain't been through nuthin'. Where you been Elmer G.? You run away out into the woods with Scruffy and his gang of no-accounts until Farmer Brown drags ya'll back home. That ain't no big deal. Which reminds me...you wanna' know what happens to the Cornmashers? You'll never figure it out because you can't see the forest for the trees."

"I might be able to figure it out if you gave me some better hints," said Elmer G.

"I'll give you a hint, Elmer G.," said Cliché. "Try this one on for size. Farmer Brown may have to sacrifice the Cornmashers so that he can bring home the bacon."

As she tossed out this last bit of advice, Cliché began to laugh at her own joke. As she tried to stop laughing, Cliché said, "I don't wanna' make any bones about it, but I guess I'm really sorta'.......hamming it up!! Get it?! Hamming it up!!!" And she burst out laughing again.

Elmer G. left Cliché splashing around in her own cloudy cleverness. He strolled over to the corner of the pig pens where he slept each night inside an empty, wooden hog-head barrel, with metal straps binding the outside. As he settled down to go to sleep, Elmer G. thought about what he had learned that day. He was scared stiff because he couldn't shake this bad feeling he had about the fate of the Cornmashers. In his efforts to find out what was happening to the Cornmashers, he'd confirmed that something strange was indeed going on at the pig pens. Elmer G. had not figured out the particulars, but he was sure all the cards weren't laying face up on the card table. He decided to continue his investigation tomorrow.

He suspected that some pigs, like Scruff Daddy, had absolutely no clue about the fate of the Cornmashers. On the other hand, he didn't believe Cliché was telling everything she knew about the Cornmashers. But he didn't know how to get the truth out of her. Cliché's habit of talking in riddles frustrated him to no end. Her riddles drove him right up the sides of the pig pen fence.

Elmer G. was tired. So he decided to get some sleep and continue his search in the morning.

CHAPTER 4

Lying ...An Art Form

"Someone said that one day Mrs. Liar and Mrs. Truth were given the same piece of information to spread around the neighborhood. Within minutes, Mrs. Liar was in the next County, straddled across the top of a barstool, slurping on a tall frosty glass of sweetened iced tea, with a lemon wedge floating around the top waves, loudly and boldly spinning falsehoods left and right. She had a peaked look. Her face glowed with excitement as she talked. Mrs. Liar looked strong and healthy as an ox on steroids. Truth is....Mrs. Liar looked like she could live.....and lie forever. Meanwhile Mrs. Truth was still at home, half-dazed, lazily rubbing sleep out of her eyes.... struggling to get out of bed to throw some clothes on. When Mrs. Truth finally got up, she was wheezing, hacking and coughing, as she hobbled out the door to begin making her rounds, looking every bit as if she might fall out dead any second."

Early the next morning, Elmer G. woke up and scrawled the following message on the pig pen fence. This was his attempt to help him remember what he had learned from talking with Scruff Daddy and Cliché the previous day.

"Finding the Truth is 'bout as rare as finding a pig wearing overalls and suspenders."

After he finished writing his message, Elmer G. walked over and joined a conversation with a group of pigs who were busily chattering away.

"Good morning everybody," said Elmer G., as he sat down.

"Good morning, Elmer G.," they sang out, as they scooted over to make room for him.

"Anybody care to 'fess up about what happens to the Cornmashers after Farmer Brown and his men load them into the giant trailer truck?"

"Ain't nothing to 'fess up to," said Nate, as he rooted under a trough to hungrily snap up a piece of aged baked potato. "Nothing happens to the Cornmashers. They're doing fine. To tell you the truth, the Cornmashers are doing better than us. I wish I could live in one of those nice, clean pens with the pine wood floors and all. And eat that there lip-smacking corn mash all day. Somebody run fetch me a napkin to wipe my mouth. I can taste it now!"

"Nate's right, you know," chipped in Vicki, as she struggled to stop laughing at Nate's antics. "The Cornmashers have a great life. Clean pens. Nice soft, tasty corn mash every day. I wanna' be a Cornmasher myself. I think they take 'em for a ride in that pretty candy apple red trailer truck. Later, they bring 'em back home. Now ain't that a hoot?!"

"But Vicki," said a frustrated Elmer G., "we never see any of the Cornmashers again after they're taken away in the trailer truck."

"Who told you that?" asked Jenny. "Whoever said it don't know what they're talking about. That ain't true. I saw Oscar two days ago, alive and well. And he was a Cornmasher. Chile…Oscar looks good too! He 'shore do! All firm, muscular and porked up. Looking like he all that. My boy Oscar got it going on!!"

"You saw Oscar with your own eyes?" asked Elmer G.

"Well.....uhhhhhh.....not exactly with my own eyes," said Jenny. "But I heard from a reliable source that someone else saw him the other day."

Elmer G. decided to test a theory he was thinking about. "Look everybody! Over there! There's Oscar now on his way over here to join us. Look!"

His friends kept talking among themselves. What's funny is that not a single pig looked up to see Oscar walking up. Elmer G. knew what this meant. They didn't look up because they already knew Oscar was not walking over to join them. They knew Oscar was gone for good. But where? Something strange is going on around here.

Elmer G. left the chattering group of pigs after he realized that they didn't know any more than he did about the fate of the Cornmashers. He had a sneaking suspicion that when they left the pig pens in the trailer truck, the Cornmashers were *not* being driven on a scenic tour of the area and brought back home.

As he was walking away, Elmer G. saw an elderly hog, named 'Barley', dozing under a shade tree. Barley was long in the tooth and had been around the hog pens forever. Barley was a serious, gruff, but wise old pig who kind of kept to himself, unless you sought his opinion on a matter. Then he seemed to brighten up, as he explained things. On a whim, Elmer G. decided to ask Barley about the Cornmashers.

"Barley," said Elmer G., "how you doing today?"

"Fine, thank you," said Barley. "Everything's copathetic. Beautiful morning. Mighty fine weather. How you doing, Elmer G.?"

"Can't complain," said Elmer G. "I'm doing good. Barley, I wanna' ask you something. It's sorta' a sensitive subject around the pig pens."

"Go ahead," said Barley. "What's your question? I can't promise you I'm gonna' be able to answer, but go ahead."

"Barley.....what happens to the Cornmashers after Farmer Brown sends them away in the trailer truck?" Elmer G. expected Barley to give him the same run-around response like the others had done.

"Elmer G.," said Barley, "these are grave matters that you ask me to speak about. Speaking of them stirs up unpleasant memories. But you need to know the truth about these matters."

"Does this mean you're gonna tell me what happens to the Cornmashers?" asked Elmer G., trembling with anticipation.

"Elmer G., I can tell you what happens to the Cornmashers, but you won't like my answer. Matter of fact, once I tell you, your life will never be the same."

"Yeah...right," said Elmer G.

"No, I mean it," said Barley. "Once we talk about what happens to the Cornmashers, your life will be turned upside down, inside out and right-side up. It'll take the wind outta' your sails, that's for sure."

Elmer G. was delighted that he was finally going to find out what happened to the Cornmashers. "Please tell me where they take the Cornmashers," pleaded Elmer G. "Even if my life will never be the same."

"Remember," said Barley in an ominous tone of voice, "I tried to warn you."

"Okay old fella'," said Elmer G., in a mocking tone. "Your warnings and weeby jeeby predictions are all duly noted for the record. Now....what happens to the Cornmashers?"

"They drive the Cornmashers to a huge building called a slaughter house," said Barley, in a flat, even, matter-of-fact tone of voice, like he'd told this story a thousand times.

"I ain't seen no slaughter house around here," said Elmer G.

"It's located about six miles outside of town," said Barley.

"What happens to the pigs after they go to the slaughter house?" asked a curious Elmer G.

"At the slaughter house," said Barley, "they place each pig on a conveyor belt and clamp metal cuffs on all four feet so they can't move."

"How come?" asked Elmer G.

"So the pigs can't move around or escape," said Barley.

"Escape from what?" asked Elmer G.

"From the humans," explained Barley.

"Why do the pigs wanna' escape from the humans?" asked Elmer G.

"So they won't get shot with a stun gun," said Barley.

"Shot by a stun gun?! What's a stun gun?" asked Elmer G.

"A pistol that shoots enough electrical shivers through your body to make you fall out in a dead-faint for a little while. When the pigs get to a certain point in the conveyor belt line, the humans shoot 'em in the forehead with a stun gun to knock 'em unconscious."

"What?!" exclaimed Elmer G. "They shoot them in the head with a stun gun!?"

"That's what happens to 'em," said Barley. "Why you so shocked? Ain't you the one that was dying to know what happens to the Cormashers?"

"Why they do that, Barley?! Why are they shooting pigs in the head with stun guns?!"

"To keep the pigs disoriented until they finish with them," said Barley.

"Finish with them?" said Elmer G. "Finish what? Maybe it's just me, but you would think a shot in the head with a stun gun would be enough socializing, don't you think?"

"Well," said Barley, "they are not there to socialize. I can tell you that. This stuff is serious, Elmer G. The next thing they do is....pretty gruesome. Do you want me to stop?"

"Not on your life," said Elmer G. "Go ahead and tell me the rest. You got my interest up now."

"Well, the humans take these razor-sharp knives and slit the stunned pigs' throats from ear-to-ear."

"Okay Barley. I've heard enough. Thank you very much for your time. I'm going home."

"Don't you wanna' know the rest of the story about what happens to the Cornmashers?" asked Barley.

"Nope," replied Elmer G.

"Why not?" asked Barley.

"I know too much now," said Elmer G. "I'm 'bout as full as I need to be, so I'm gonna' push back from the trough and mosey on home. I ain't hongry' for no more information about the Cornmashers."

"Come on Elmer G. Let me tell you the rest."

"Barley, how I'm gonna' sleep at night listening to you talking about stun guns shooting pigs in the head. And humans slicing pigs' throats from ear to ear. I'm partial to a less frightening style of fairy tales."

"You're the one that asked about the Cornmashers," pointed out Barley. "I'm just telling you the facts. Calm down and let me finish. After they slit their throats, the humans dump the dead pigs into a drainage tank so their blood can flow out into a huge drainpipe."

"I can't take this," said Elmer G. "I don't wanna' hear the rest of this story. I feel sick."

"Buckle up boy!" said Barley. "Brace yourself! Elmer G., you need to know this stuff. How else you gonna' understand what's going on 'round here. You ain't even heard the toughest parts yet. All I've given you is a few drops of the truth. I'm 'bout to turn the truth facet on full throttle."

"Why you gotta' tell me all these terrible things?" asked Elmer G. "I don't wanna' hear no more!"

"But you need to hear it, Elmer G. The truth is the only thing that can set you free. And what I'm telling you....is the stone-cold truth. Not that foolishness about putting pigs in prison and taking 'em for joy rides. That's all foolishness these pigs done made up to avoid facing the truth. These pigs are avoiding the truth by feeding offa' 'Comfort Pies".

"Comfort Pies?" repeated Elmer G.

"Yeah!" said Barley. "Comfort Pies are lies pigs tell themselves to make sure they don't disturb their comfortable little ignorant world. Hush up now! And let me finish explaining to you about the Cornmashers. I'm 'bout to finish dropping the real dime on you."

"Dropping the real dime?" repeated Elmer G., leaning forward towards Barley. "What does that mean?"

"Get up outta' my grill and give me room to give you the 411," explained Barley.

"Get up outta' your grill…and you're gonna' give me the 411? I'm not following you Barley. What are you talking about?"

"What I'm saying is that I want you to back up a taste….outta' my face and I'm gonna' give you the real story about what happens to the pigs at the slaughter house," explained Barley.

"I sure would like to know what happens to the Cornmashers," said Elmer G. "The suspense is 'bout to kill me."

"Well," said Barley, "like I was saying, first they drain the blood out of the pigs. Then the humans dump their lifeless bodies head-first into gigantic, gleaming barrels of scalding hot water."

"Why are they dumping the pigs' bodies into hot water?" asked Elmer G. "They're already dead. Why are the humans drowning dead pigs?"

"They're not drowning dead pigs, boy!" said Barley. "They dump 'em into the hot water to soften their hair. After the pigs' hair is softened up by the hot water, the humans run their bodies through a scraping machine that's got these razor sharp edges. The mere sight of these razor-edges is enough to freeze you in your tracks. After they line the dead pigs up to run 'em through the scraping machine, they commence to scraping. And scraping. And scraping. And....."

"Barley!" screamed Elmer G. "I get the point! Please finish the story."

"Oh. I'm sorry," said Barley. "Well anyway, they scrape and scrape until the pigs' bodies are as shiny and pink as an Avon Lady's hot pink Cadillac. Finally, they cut the pigs up into different pieces of meat and sell it to supermarkets."

"They cut pigs into pieces?" asked a shocked Elmer G., as he trembled with fear. Then he involuntarily started shaking and trembling with a cold shock and rage. Without being aware of it, Elmer G. involuntarily started wetting the inside of his hind leg, accompanied by a splashing sound, as it furiously splattered on the ground, creating a puddle.

"Yep," said Barley, as he noticed Elmer G. was getting irritated at all this bad news. Deciding to play it safe, Barley delicately slid away from Elmer G. to drier ground. Then he continued. "They cut us poor pigs up into bite-sized portions."

"Bite-sized portions," repeated Elmer G.

"The humans hack the Cornmashers up with meat cleavers," explained Barley. "Then they commence to whacking the Cornmashers into endless racks of dinner-sized ham shanks, heaping piles of pork ribs and barrels overflowing with sides of bacon. They chop and whack away at the pigs until they have stacks of pork chops. Buckets of pig feets. Foot tubs overflowing with pig ears. Rows and rows and rows of sausage rolls and miles and miles of pigs' intestines that they grind into chitlins. And then they chop........."

"You're joking," said Elmer G., in an exhausted tone of voice.

"Nope," said Barley. "But I wish I was. I really do wish I was joking." He paused, deep in thought, then continued. "Elmer G., the humans even eat our guts, which they call chitlins'. And if there are any leftover body parts lying around, they grind those pieces of meat up to make breakfast sausage. Get this Elmer G. They even sell pigs' blood."

"Is there any part of the pig they don't eat or sell?" asked Elmer G.

"Matter of fact, there are some parts of a pig that humans don't eat or sell."

"Well, that's a relief," said Elmer G. "Which parts do they pass on?"

"The three parts of a pig that humans don't eat is our footprints, our shadows and our eyebrows. It's a sad situation, Elmer G. when the only thing you don't have to worry about losing is your footprint, your shadow and your eyebrows."

Elmer G. had never been this afraid in his life. "Barley," said Elmer G., in a voice trembling and cracking with fright, "are you sure about this? How do you know all this stuff anyway?"

"Boy! It ain't no big secret. Lots of pigs know about the slaughter house. They just don't wanna' believe it."

"But, how do you know it's true?" asked Elmer G.

"Cliché saw it all when she was a young pig. She was playing in the back of the trailer truck and accidentally rode out to the slaughter house. She was too young to be slaughtered, so Farmer Brown brought her back home. She told us what happened to the Cornmashers. Most of the pigs here are in denial about the Cornmashers being slaughtered. They refuse to believe the truth, because they know they can't do nothing to change it. But I *know* it's true. Elmer G., denial is just another way of coping with a destiny you don't like and can't change."

"But, Barley," said Elmer G., "why is Farmer Brown sending us to the slaughter house to be whacked into dinner-sized pieces?"

"At the end of the day," said Barley, his voice dropping a little, "it's all about the money. Farmer Brown gets paid money by the pound for each pig he delivers to the slaughter house. Plump pigs fetch a handsome price, Elmer G. A mighty handsome price."

"Barley," said Elmer G. in a dismal tone of voice, "do the humans raise all the animals just to slaughter them for food?"

"I don't think so," said Barley. "Some animals are expected to give milk and eggs, which are really harmless donations to Farmer Brown's diet. But not us pigs. Elmer G., let me put it to you in a way you can understand. There's an old story that goes like this. When it was time for breakfast one day at the farm, the farmer asked the animals to donate food for his breakfast spread. All the barnyard animals were called in to see who would donate a little something. Clara Chicken cheerfully spoke right up without any prodding. She volunteered her services. She shore' did. Clara volunteered to donate a slew of fresh eggs. All the other animals clapped and cheered at her unselfishness. It was truly a touching scene. Portabus Pig got so caught up in the excitement of the moment that he piped up and offered to donate some ham and a little bacon for the farmer's breakfast."

"What happened then?" asked Elmer G.

"Well, the room got deathly silent," said Barley.

"How come?" asked Elmer G.

"The animals were amazed at Portabus' extraordinarily generous offer," explained Barley. "Suddenly, the room exploded in applause. At first, Portabus blushed with embarrassment and waved bashfully to the crowd. He was enjoying all the praise and attention his friends were heaping on him."

"What happened to Portabus?" asked Elmer G.

"Well, the situation turned grim when the Farmer strolled back into the barn," said Barley.

"Why?" asked Elmer G. "What did he do?"

"It's not what he did, Elmer G. It was what he was carrying."

"What was he carrying?"

"The farmer was carrying a rifle propped under his right arm," said Barley. "And that ain't all."

"Really?" asked Elmer G.

"Really," answered Barley. "The farmer also had a big old butcher knife in his left hand."

"Butcher knife?" said Elmer G. "For what?"

"I'm about to tell you, if you hold your horses a minute. I can't tell you if you keep interrupting me."

"I'm sorry Barley."

"See. There you go interrupting me again. Now let me finish. Like I was saying, as Portabus was about to be slaughtered, his face suddenly took on a solemn, puzzled stare."

"What was he staring at?"

"The farmer, of course," said Barley.

"Why?" asked Elmer G.

"Because Portabus realized he was not going to be making a contribution to the Farmer's breakfast," explained Barley.

"If Portabus was not going to make a contribution to the farmer's breakfast, then what was he going to do?" asked Elmer G.

"Portabus was about to make a *total* commitment by providing the ham and bacon. Do you see my point, Elmer G.?"

"Yeah Barley," said Elmer G., in a stunned tone of voice. "I think I see your point. Us pigs can't make a contribution to the humans' breakfast table. We have to make a total commitment by giving our lives."

Elmer G. staggered home to go to bed, but he was so loaded down with the weight of his new knowledge that he spent a sleepless night, with his eyelids propped wide open.... staring into the pitch black darkness. He kept reaching down every few minutes to feel his shoulders, feet and ribs to make sure they were still there. Now he understood what Cliché meant when she said that Farmer Brown might have to sacrifice the Cornmashers so that he could bring home the bacon.

Elmer G. paused while he collected his thoughts. "So, in a bizarre, twisted sorta' way, Scruff Daddy was right," he thought to himself. "When you get right down to it, the slaughtering of pigs was all about the money."

"Goodness gracious," thought Elmer G. "They're gonna' cut me up, fry me up....and serve me with toast, homemade apple preserves and eggs. Then wash me down with an orange juice chaser."

He shuddered involuntarily at the thought.

CHAPTER 5

Slaughter House Blues

"The search for truth is a tiring and frustrating adventure. Living in ignorance requires no effort at all. Accepting things as they are leaves you tons of time to laze around, waiting to die."

E lmer G. was up most of the night. Tossing around from side-to-side, replaying over and over his nightmares about being sliced into bite-sized pieces. When he finally dozed off, he was so exhausted he slept late the next morning. He woke up refreshed and plumb full of spit and vinegar. He couldn't wait to start his day because he was ready to tackle the world. That is ....until he remembered the horrors of the slaughter house. Then, his energy and excitement just got up and trotted away. Suddenly, he felt exhausted and down in the mouth.

With slumped shoulders and a heavy heart, he walked over to visit a spell with Barley.

"Barley," said Elmer G., in a dejected tone of voice. "They must not be killing all of us pigs."

"What makes you say that?" asked Barley.

"You didn't become a Cornmasher," said Elmer G.

"That's true," said Barley.

"And you're not the only one," said Elmer G. "There are some other pigs here who didn't become Cornmashers. You all didn't get killed at the slaughter house. How come?"

"Well Elmer G., that's true," said Barley, in a low gravelly tone of voice. "Let me tell you a little secret."

"What's that?" asked Elmer G.

"If you don't want to die at the slaughter house, then you..."

"I what?" asked Elmer G., trying to lead him on.

"You have to move some of the odds over in your favor," said Barley.

"How?" asked Elmer G.

"The first step is to learn how to communicate with Farmer Brown," said Barley.

"That's the most ridiculous thing I ever heard!" said Elmer G., in a voice trembling with shock and outrage. "Pigs can't talk to humans!!"

"I'm not saying you need to *talk* to Farmer Brown," said Barley. "I'm saying you need to *communicate* with him. You can communicate with humans in a lot of ways besides talking with them."

"Barley.....what you talking about!? Come on now. You know that ain't true!"

"But you can, Elmer G. There are ways for pigs to communicate with humans. Every encounter you have with Farmer Brown presents a unique opportunity for you to communicate with him. Course...it's up to you whether those communications are positive or negative. Every little thing you do is a form of communication. He will judge you by your actions, both seen and unseen. Farmer Brown sees the results of our actions. He knows what's in our hearts. He rewards the vast majority of us pigs with death. But there are a few that are saved by his grace."

"What do you mean, saved by his grace?" asked Elmer G.

"To be saved by grace," said Barley, "means that a lot of little things you have done in your life are added up by someone else who has power over your destiny. And hopefully, they will show you mercy at that critical time when you need it. But you have to communicate your small acts of kindness to Farmer Brown if you wanna' get credit for 'em."

"How in the world am I supposed to communicate with somebody who is planning on whacking me into little pieces and frying my chops?" said Elmer G. "Barley, you have got to tell me the secrets to avoid going to the slaughter house. You've just gotta' help me."

"Elmer G., I'm old. I been through a lot of stuff. Missed a lot of stuff. Seen a lot of stuff. Overlooked a lot of stuff. Done a lot of stuff. Skipped a lot of stuff. Learned a lot of stuff. Stepped *over* a lot of stuff. Stepped *in* a lot of stuff. Forgot a lot of stuff and remembered a lot of stuff. What I'm going to share with you may, or may not help you avoid the slaughter house. I can point you in the right direction, Elmer G., but you're gonna' have to learn a lot of this stuff yourself. Through experience."

"Teach me, Barley," said Elmer G. "Although this is a lotta' stuff to learn, I'm about as ready as I'm gonna' get."

"That's a good attitude to start off with, Elmer G."

"What's the first thing I need to learn?" asked Elmer G.

"First," said Barley, "you need to understand that everything you do from this moment on will be focused on one goal."

"Barley, I've changed my mind."

"About what?" asked Barley.

"About learning all this new stuff to escape the slaughter house," said Elmer G. "I've changed my mind. I'm not gonna' do it. I won't be able to remember everything."

"What are you belly-aching about, boy?" asked Barley. "I ain't even told you nothing yet. And you're already worried about what you can't remember. Elmer G...... grow a backbone, son."

"It's just too much stuff happening at one time," explained Elmer G. "I can't learn all this stuff you're talking about. I feel like I'm losing control."

"Elmer G., let's get real. You ain't never had no control over nothing. You just *thought* you had control."

"Well, at least I *felt* like I had some control over my life. That is, until you started telling me about that slaughter house."

"You felt like you had some control over your life because you were living in ignorant bliss," said Barley.

"What"?! Ignorant bliss? Barley, what are you talking about?"

"Well, Elmer G., ignorant bliss means you were living your life and feeling like you had control because you didn't know all the facts. You thought Farmer Brown was feeding you slop because he liked you. Now you've found out he's fattening you up to sell you to the slaughter house and you're mad. Like most pigs 'round here, you'd rather hide your head in the sand and pretend like life is great. No worries. No fears."

"There's another problem too," said Elmer G., as he ignored Barley's explanation of the meaning of 'ignorant bliss'.

"What's that?" asked Barley.

"I think part of my problem is that things are just moving too fast for me," said Elmer G., in a reflective mood. "You know what I'm saying? I mean....I need more time to turn these new ideas over in my head before making such a big commitment."

"So you're saying you think things are moving too fast for you?" asked Barley.

"Yeah," said Elmer G. "That's right. There are too many new choices for me to make. I don't wanna' mess up and complicate my life by making snap decisions."

"Well...slow your roll, Player," said Barley. "Slow down and take some time to think things over. I'm not rushing you to decide anything."

"I'm not gonna' be able to do this," said Elmer G.

"How come?" asked Barley. "What's your problem now?"

"I'm not gonna' make it, Barley."

"You already said you're not gonna make it, Elmer G. Ain't

nobody putting up no arguments against you on that point. But just out of curiosity, why aren't you gonna' make it?"

"I'm a little embarrassed to admit this, Barley."

"Spare me the modesty act, boy," said Barley. "Spit it out. What is it that's making you think you can't learn enough to escape the slaughter house?"

"I ain't as smart as you," said Elmer G. "I'm scared to try because I can't remember everything you're telling me."

"That's the beauty of it, Elmer G." said Barley. "You only have to remember one thing. You only have one goal."

"What's that?" asked Elmer G.

"That one goal," said Barley, "is to increase the odds in your favor so that Farmer Brown will show you mercy. The trick is to motivate him to have some positive feelings about you. Especially during that brief moment of time when you're walking up the ramp into the trailer truck that will carry you to the slaughter house."

"Is that all I have to do to be saved?" asked Elmer G.

"Not exactly," said Barley. "But, it's a start. There is no way to guarantee that you won't be slaughtered. The best you can do is to increase your positive odds and decrease your negative odds. The secret is to stack the odds in your favor."

"Well Barley, what are some of the things I can do to improve my odds of avoiding the slaughter house?"

"The first thing I suggest," advised Barley, "is that you learn how to pray."

"Pray?" said Elmer G. "What does that mean?"

"It means for you to talk to someone else and ask them to help you out," explained Barley.

"Who is this someone else I'm supposed to be praying to?" asked Elmer G.

"You have to learn to pray to God," answered Barley. "God is our Lord and Savior."

"Who is God?" asked Elmer G.

"Whatever you believe God to be. You see, Elmer G., God made these pig pens, trees, the woods, wind and weather and everything else in the whole wide world. He controls the past, present and the future. God holds power over life, death and everything in between."

"Where is God?" asked Elmer G.

"All around you," answered Barley.

"I don't see nobody but you, Barley."

"That's because you're looking through the eyes of a non-believing pig," said Barley, "instead of looking through the eyes of faith. When you gain faith in God and humble yourself before Him, then you'll see His works. You can't see God. We can only see His works."

"Will God answer back when I pray?" asked Elmer G.

"Probably not," said Barley. "He's a rather peculiar fellow. God doesn't show up and talk with us the way we talk to each other. But He answers our prayers in other ways. He is a God of action. He does stuff to help us, like nourishing our hearts and souls. God answers us in other ways besides jabbering up a storm. There's enough pigs 'round here doing an excellent job of jabbering. God nourishes our minds, bodies and souls."

"You mean you want me to pray and humble myself to someone I can't see," said Elmer G. "You're asking me to put my life in the hands of some invisible being I never even met? I still don't see why I need to pray to God. Is God a pig? Is God a human or a pig?"

"God is whatever you need Him to be," answered Barley.

"Judging by that wishy-washy answer...I'm suspecting God ain't no pig," said Elmer G. "He can't be a pig."

"Why you say that?" asked Barley.

"If He was a pig," said Elmer G., "he wouldn't be giving the humans bacon for breakfast. Let's say there is a God. Now, I'm assuming He's fair. God may be fair, but He is 'shore more fair to humans than He is to us pigs. I don't wanna make the Man mad, since I ain't even met Him yet. But that's the truth…and I'm sticking by it. Since God is supposed to be in charge of the whole world and He's so mighty and smart and such…why does He go and let pigs grow up to be slaughtered anyway? That ain't terribly smart, now is it? Looks to me like God is listening more to humans' prayers than to prayers that come from pigs."

"God listens to all our prayers, Elmer G. Both humans and pigs. Besides, all pigs don't grow up to be slaughtered. Look at Miss Piggy, she's got her own television show."

"Miss Piggy? Television show? Barley, what in the world are you talking about? Who is Miss Piggy? And while we're on the subject, what is a television show? I never heard of such things."

"I'll explain about Miss Piggy and television later," said Barley. "Let's tussle some more with understanding God. I was telling you that you have to believe that God has a master plan for all of us."

"But the question is," said Elmer G., "does God have a plan for us that makes sense to *us*? What's fair for a pig may be dangerously unfair to someone else, like Farmer Brown. Farmer Brown may think it's fair and reasonable to scare up a score of ham and bacon for breakfast. But, that is very unfair to me because I'm the one making the contribution of ham for Farmer Brown's breakfast platter. What does God do when pigs and people need different things?"

"Even though some things that happen to us don't make sense," said Barley, "we still have to believe in God's wisdom. You have to believe that He will take care of you."

"Why?" asked Elmer G.

"Your belief in God's ability to save you is like a motivator to God to live up to your expectations," explained Barley. "This belief that God will rescue you is called having "faith" in God. No matter how bad things get, and they will get bad….you must continue to believe in God's power and wisdom."

"Yeah. Right, Barley. Even when I'm walking up the ramp to board the trailer truck that will take me to the slaughter house? I'm still supposed to believe that God is gonna swoop down and save me?"

"You must have faith in God all the time, Elmer G., *especially* when you're walking up the ramp to board the trailer truck that will take you to the slaughter house."

"Says who?" asked Elmer G.

"Says the Bible, that's who," said Barley. "Have some respect for your elders, boy! What done got into you? Carrying on like you done lost your mind. Elmer G., listen to me, son. I know this is a lot for you to try and digest in one setting. But you've got to try. Now getting back to this faith thing. Let me explain it another way. When things are going good, you don't need as much faith."

"I'm not following you, Barley."

"What I'm saying," said Barley, "is that you don't need as much faith when the sun is shining down on you and all is going good in your little world. When you're lapping up slop after rolling around in a mud pit all day, you ain't got much need of religious faith. When a pretty sow sashays across the pig pens and bats her eyelashes at you, religious faith is the last thing on your mind. It's easy to believe in God on glorious days like these."

"At last you're saying something we both agree on. I don't need no religious faith if I'm having a day like that," said Elmer G. "So what's your point?"

"My point is that you're not gonna' have these great days every day."

"I'm not?" said Elmer G.

"Nope," said Barley. "We're all gonna' have some dark, cloudy days in our lives. Rainy, lonely and freezing cold days make up part of all our lives."

"And your point is….?" said Elmer G.

"My point is that it is in your darkest hours that you will need God and faith the most," said Barley. "Like in those dark hours when you're locked in the back of a trailer truck rumbling nosily down the road, swaying from side-to-side, heading towards the slaughter house. This is the time when you need a faith as strong as an oak tree trunk and deep as the Chattahoochee River. This is when God's purposes and powers will be made clear to us."

"So you're saying that even in my darkest hour, I still have to believe in God's purpose and powers," said Elmer G. "Like when I'm walking up that ramp to the trailer truck. That's hard to do, Barley. If it's that late in the game, you can understand my concern that God may have forgotten about me."

"I understand Elmer G. I understand that if you don't get yourself together, you're gonna' be hamming it up in a supermarket cooler somewhere. You better listen to what I'm telling you, boy. Don't play with God, Elmer G. And don't make Him mad with all your little mind games. I'm trying to teach you something special 'cause I like you. But you're a hard nut to crack."

"I know, Barley. I'll try to do better. It's just that this is a lotta' stuff to understand and accept. Go ahead and finish. You were telling me about having faith in my darkest hour."

"Oh yeah," said Barley, "like I was saying, it is even more important in our darkest hour that we believe that God has not forgotten us. We must believe that He is still by our side. It is at these difficult moments…when we are too tired to walk anymore.…that God carries us. But there is one condition. Your faith must be absolute and unwavering. God sees everything we do and He rewards our faithfulness."

"Now let me get this straight," said Elmer G. "You're telling me that I ought to say prayers to somebody that I never met and can't see. To top it off, He don't even answer back when I pray to Him asking for stuff. Yet and still, I'm supposed to ask this God of yours to help me avoid the slaughter house."

"Yep. That's what I'm telling you," said Barley.

"I see," said Elmer G. "First, you tell me that God is in charge of everything that happens in the whole world."

"God is in charge of everything," said Barley.

"If that's true," said Elmer G., "then He's the reason humans are killing us pigs in the first place."

"That's one way of looking at it," said Barley.

"But I'm supposed to be cheerfully praying," said Elmer G., "as I strut into the slaughter house to get myself killed. So far, don't none of this make sense. And even though I know none of this makes sense, I'm supposed to have faith that God knows what He's doing. And if He's in a good mood on my day of reckoning...he *may* save me. Barley...don't you have no better plans than this? 'Cause I'm about to get killed using this one."

"Don't be blaming me!" exclaimed Barley. "I never said that believing in God made sense. But, if you believe in God, you don't have to be afraid to die. Farmer Brown can only destroy your physical body."

"Barley, in case you haven't noticed.......all I got is my physical body."

"No Elmer G." said Barley. "All you *see* is your physical body. But, you also have a soul."

"A soul?" said Elmer G.

"Yes. Your soul," said Barley.

"What is my soul?" asked Elmer G.

"Your soul is your inner spirit," answered Barley.

"What is my inner spirit?" asked Elmer G.

"Boy...you 'shore got a lot of questions," said Barley. "You are testing my last nerve! Don't you know nothing?"

"I'm sorry, Barley. But I ain't never heard of no 'soul' and no 'inner spirit'."

"I know," said Barley. "I know. Let me think of a good way to explain what your inner spirit is so that even you can understand it. Okay. I've got it. Let's just say you somehow develop a strong faith in God. Now, your soul is the same as a spiritual body that's inside your physical body. If you have a strong spiritual faith, then Farmer Brown can destroy your physical body. But, he can never destroy your soul, or inner body. Elmer G., when you find your spiritual faith, it will free you up and make you invincible. Or at least it will make you less afraid."

"Well....we all agree that we can't see God." said Elmer G.

"That's right," said Barley, relieved that he and Elmer G. were agreeing on something.

"And according to what you're saying, God 'shore don't sound like the most eager conversationalist I never met," said Elmer G. "It seems to me that having faith in a God that goes out of His way to avoid contact with his servants, is sorta' like climbing out on a thin limb after eating a heavy supper. I mean...you can't see the Man. He don't talk. He don't write."

"He don't call," said Barley, getting into the swing of things. "No emails."

"Emails?" repeated Elmer G.

"I'll explain later," said Barley.

"He don't send smoke signals," said Elmer G. "No flowers. So far, we get zippo communications from God. I mean...from the looks of things...He ain't the easiest person in the world to have faith in."

"But you still have to keep nursing your faith in God," said Barley. "Even though you can't see him and He does not communicate with us in ways in which we are accustomed to. The essence of faith is the willingness to believe in something without a lot of proof that it exists."

"So, what you're saying," said Elmer G. "is that having faith in God means believing in something that I know probably ain't even true.......and hoping I'm wrong."

"Although I have never heard it put quite that way before," said Barley, "I suppose that's one way of looking at it. Bottom line is....you still need to pray to God."

"Now Barley, are you for real? Do I really need to pray to God?"

"Yes Elmer G., you need to pray to God so you can find your spiritual center. You must believe in a higher being than yourself, or Farmer Brown. All of us need to know that there is spiritual order in the universe."

"I don't mean to be difficult, Barley, but I still don't know why you're making such a case for me to find a spiritual center. From the looks of things, chances are, I'm gonna' get shipped to the slaughter house anyway. Then what? If I do get slaughtered, what will God do then?"

"The Bible says you'll go to Hog Heaven if you've been good during your lifetime," explained Barley.

"What is the Bible?" asked Elmer G.

"Remember when you were young and your mama and the other older pigs taught you the right things to do," said Barley. "Like saying thank you when another pig did something decent for you. And they taught you all the bad things you were not supposed to do? You were taught not to fight and how to treat others the way you wanted to be treated?"

"Yeah. I remember," said Elmer G.

"Well, remember how you broke all the rules you learned?" said Barley.

"Yeah," said Elmer G.

"And the older pigs always seemed to be the only ones who were living by these rules?" said Barley. "And they spent most of their time harassing everybody else into living by those same old rules?"

"That's right," said Elmer G. "Now that you mention it, I believe you're hitting the nail on the head."

"Well, religion and believing in God works sorta' the same way," said Barley. "The Bible is a big book of rules with examples that explain how we should behave. Naturally, everybody breaks most of these rules until they're too old to break 'em anymore.

Then, in their old age, religious pigs really hunker down and try to force everybody else to obey these same rules that they didn't obey when they were young."

"Are you sure about that part?" asked Elmer G.

"Yeah," said Barley. "I'm pretty sure that's how it works. I mean…think about it. It's easy to get home at a decent hour after a night of fun, if you're so old you're having trouble staying awake. And look at humans. Humans say grace with bowed heads and clasped hands, as they prepare to cut into a crispy fried pork chop. They thank God for providing the pork chop, so they can eat it. No thought a' tall about the poor pig that was forced to donate his life. But getting back to the Bible. The Bible also tells you all about God and all the people He helped. It talks about how He performed miracles and all kinds of stuff. And it also explains why God said we have to be baptized by water before we can get by Saint Peter, who is patrolling the red velvet ropes outside the main gate to Hog Heaven."

"What does it mean to get baptized?" asked Elmer G.

"Getting baptized is sorta' like being born again," explained Barley. "But this time you are born into a new faith based on your personal relationship with God. You know how when a sow births a litter and she dies in childbirth?"

"Yeah," said Elmer G.

"What happens to her new litter of piglets?" asked Barley.

"Another sow that has birthed a litter of piglets recently adopts the dead sow's piglets and feeds 'em and generally raises them as her own," answered Elmer G.

"This is the same way it works with God," said Barley. "When they dip you in the water, you have to proclaim your faith in God. The water symbolizes your new birth into a new life with God. This is how you start your new life with God. Once you proclaim your faith in Him, He'll take care of you just like you're one of His own."

"Will a baptism in a mud pit do?" asked Elmer G. "I don't know where there is any clean water. Even our water troughs are kinda' murky. Since God made everything, the least He could do is to provide some clean water for our baptism, don't you think?"

"Elmer G., I think the idea is for you to make friends with God and praise Him. Not criticize Him for what He ain't done for you. You are about the most difficult pig I ever met."

"All I'm doing is asking if God will accept me being baptized in a mud pit that He made. I don't see nothing wrong with asking. Can't a pig at least ask Him about the particulars of this baptism thing? That's all I'm saying. You ain't got to blow a gasket over it, Barley. It ain't like it's a life or death sorta' thing."

"Actually, it is a life or death sorta' thing, Elmer G."

"Yeah. I reckon it is a bit on the serious side," said Elmer G. "That's even more of a reason for me wanting to know if I can get baptized in a mud pit. I'd hate to be walking around thinking I've been baptized proper and it turns out that ain't the case."

"That's up to God to make a call on," said Barley. "Who knows if He'll count a romp in a mud pit as a proper baptism. According to the Bible, He's plumb full of surprises. I'm sure anybody that can walk on water and feed thousands of hongry' people with a few paltry fish and a handful of stale loaves of bread can let a little mud pit serve as a proper baptism. But like I said, that's His call to make."

"But you still haven't answered my question about what happens to me if I do get slaughtered," said Elmer G.

"If you've been baptized and adopted by God," explained Barley, "then you'll go to a place called Hog Heaven when you die."

"You know something Barley? God don't care nothing about us pigs. Else he wouldn't let us grow up to be slaughtered."

"That's not true, Elmer G. God loves pigs too. He loves every creature He made. That's why He created a special Heaven for us....called Hog Heaven. Why....in Hog Heaven, pigs are treated like we're diamonds. Diamonds on the hoof. And there are no slaughter houses."

"Where is Hog Heaven?" asked Elmer G. "Is it walking distance?"

"No Elmer G. Hog Heaven isn't walking distance."

"Well then, how am I supposed to get there?"

"You have to die before you can go to Hog Heaven," said Barley.

"Why I got to die to get to Hog Heaven?" asked Elmer G. "Ain't there no other way to get there alive and in one piece?"

"Nope. If you wanna' get to Hog Heaven, you've got to die and pass through the cemetery."

"You've got such a way with words, Barley. I mean...the way you turn a phrase, is so moving. And your positive comments are always so uplifting. Have you thought about hiring yourself out as a motorvational speaker?"

"You can be funny all you want to, Elmer G. But I'm gonna' make you understand this religion thing no matter how hard you try to resist. You need help, boy. I'm telling you the truth. You can't do this thing by yourself. Nobody can."

"I want to understand how Hog Heaven works, Barley. But I do wanna' get there in one piece, preferably without dying."

"Let me tell you a story, Elmer G. There once was a young pig a long time ago. He was just a child. His home was on the other side of a cemetery. There was only one dirt road he could walk down to get to anywhere he wanted to go. He had to walk down this road to go to school. He had to walk down this same old dusty road to go play with his friends. Every time he left his home to go anywhere he had to walk down this one lonely, dirt road that passed through the middle of the cemetery. This cemetery was where all the dead pigs were buried."

"That must have been scary for him to walk down that road through the cemetery," said Elmer G.

"It 'shore was scary," said Barley. "At least it was at first. When he first started going down that road, naturally, it made the young pig a mite nervous. But over time, he got used to it. It was either that, or he'd have to stay at home. But like I said, he got used to it. You know why?"

"Nope," said Elmer G.

"Well, keep listening," said Barley. "And you'll find out. One day, at dusk, as the sky was growing dark, the little pig finished playing with his friends. When he was saying goodbye to his playmates, he started heading off down the dirt road through the cemetery. As he started walking, one of his friends asked him if he was scared to walk through the cemetery where all the dead pigs were buried."

"I was wondering about that too," said Elmer G. "What did he say?"

"He said, "I ain't scared. Ya'll see that light shining in the pig pen on the other side of the cemetery? That's my home over there. And at home, my father is waiting for me. At my home over there, my mother is waiting for me. All my brothers, sisters and cousins are at home waiting for me to join them. But my home is on the other side of the cemetery. I ain't got no choice. If I'm going to return home to be with my family and all the other pigs I love, I've got to go through the cemetery to get there. There ain't but one way for me to get home so that I can be with my family. I ain't scared to walk through the cemetery. Ya'll see it as a walk through the cemetery. But I see it as a stroll down a dirt road to attend a homecoming celebration." And on that note, he marched on off down the dirt road through the cemetery."

"What does the story mean, Barley?"

"It means that everybody you love that's already died, or been slaughtered will be at home in Hog Heaven waiting for you to join them one day. But this home is on the other side of the cemetery. And we've all got to die and pass through the cemetery in order to get to our eternal home on the other side. There are no detours, shortcuts or alternative routes. We must all pass through the cemetery. Rich. Poor. Tall. Vertically challenged. Young. Old. In the prime of life. Sick. Healthy. Happy. Sad. Cheerful and mad. Full life lived. Empty life regretted. It don't rightly matter, Elmer G. All of our life paths travel down the same dirt road at the end of our days........through the cemetery."

"When it's time for me to go," said Elmer G., "will God send a comfortable comet for me to ride?"

"No Elmer G. God will not send a comet for you to ride."

"I know," said Elmer G. "I know. I need to have more faith in this Man I ain't never met, nor seen. Go on, Barley, tell me more about Hog Heaven. What's it like?"

"Hog Heaven is a beautiful place up beyond the clouds," said Barley. "Hog Heaven is whatever place you love the most in life."

"I don't know no place but this here pig pen," said Elmer G., in a small voice. "This is my home. I ain't never been no where else."

"Then your version of Hog Heaven will be just like home, which is this pig pen right here," said Barley, with a satisfied smack of his lips. "Hog Heaven is such a fine place. They say the streets are paved with giant loaves of French bread. The sidewalks are made out of humongous, garlic twist rolls sopped in real butter. There's so much extra butter dripping offa' those garlic twists that it just splashes up around your hoofs every time you take a step."

"Come on Barley," said Elmer G. "You for real?!"

"Yep!" said Barley. "Real as a tick bite. I'm telling the truth just like it's been told to me. 'Shore as I'm sitting here. And the size of the slop troughs. Elmer G......my boy......they say that in Hog Heaven, the slop troughs are big as backyard swimming holes. With slop just ah' splashing every which-a-way over the sides. They got so much food up there...it's just ridiculous. Blazing red apples the size of basketballs. Cinnamon rolls big as Volkswagen Beetles with ankle deep white icing slapped all over the top.

Freshly cooked potatoes big as NFL regulation-sized footballs. Cornstalks as tall as pine trees and the corncobs are as yaller as a country school bus."

"They got any mud pits up there, Barley?!"

"Shut yore' mouth!" said Barley. "Just hush right on up Elmer G.! Do they have mud pits?! Boy! They got mud pits in Hog Heaven like you ain't never seen. They say the mud pits are as big as Lake Michigan. They got folks to trim your hoofs all nice and even, while you relax under a fan. They got cantaloupes big as regulation sized volleyballs. Hot butter rolls the size of a pickup truck."

"Well….Barley, it sounds to me that Hog Heaven is a high quality type a place."

"That it is," agreed Barley. "Why…everybody is wantin' to go to Hog Heaven."

"If I understand all this," said Elmer G., "the only way to get there is to die."

"That's right," said Barley.

"One thing I don't quite understand," said Elmer G.

"What's that?" asked Barley.

"Since Hog Heaven is such a great place," said Elmer G., "I'm down right amazed that you're not volunteering to get yourself slaughtered, so you can get on up there. Don't you wanna' eat French bread and chow down on those giant yaller corn cobs? Seems like you and everybody else ought to be scrambling to line up to get yourselves killed as quick as possible. That way you can hurry up and get to Hog Heaven. By my estimations, you oughta' be dying to go there as soon as possible. Don't you think?"

"Well…ahmm….well…errr" stuttered Barley, as he tried to pull his thoughts together. "You see, Elmer G., we are all supposed to live as long as we can. You wanna' go to Hog Heaven when it's your turn to die. Not before then. You don't want to go to Hog Heaven out of turn. If you go volunteering to die before it's your turn, you would be messing up the order of the waiting lines. I'd be cheating somebody else out of their turn to go to gory....I mean......glory. Why....it'd be like breaking into the front of the line at slop time. That would be rude. Impolite."

"That may be all good and well," said Elmer G. "Then again....it may all be a lie. But I can't figure that far ahead. I'm still stuck on trying to figure out why I need a spiritual center. Religion sounds like a whole heap-a-work."

"It does, don't it?" said Barley, nodding his massive head in agreement. "But you gotta' do what I'm telling you, Elmer G, if you wanna' get God to roll up his shirt sleeves and commence to working to change Farmer Brown's heart about sending you to the slaughter house. The Bible says God works through heart-power."

"You sure it says heart-power in the Bible?" asked Elmer G., in a suspicious tone of voice. "I ain't never heard of no heart-power before."

"Well, it don't exactly say heart-power in the Bible," said Barley. "But that's what those parallels means."

"Parallels?" repeated Elmer G. "What are you talking about?"

"Don't you know nothing, Elmer G.?" said Barley, sighing in frustration. "All I got to say is that it's a good thing one of us has read the Bible and learned something from the experience. The Bible says that Jesus used parallels to teach His Disciplines spiritual lessons so they could go out among the other peoples and spread the gossip about what they had learned."

"Barley, we got pigs 'round here that can spread gossip right now without no spiritual teaching from Jesus. They do it now. For free."

"This is true," said Barley. "Let me think a minute. This don't sound exactly right. Maybe I got things mixed up somewheres. Maybe Jesus used parasols to teach His Disciplines how to spread the gossip. Wait! I got it!! Jesus used parables to teach His....uhhh....Disciples how to spread the....Gospel!"

"What in the world does that mean?" asked a frustrated Elmer G. "And what is a parable? I never heard of no Jesus, no parables or no Gospel. Are you sure that's what the Bible says?"

"Am I sure that's what it says?!" shouted Barley. "I *know* what the Bible says! I'm the one that read it. You ain't read no Bible. You *just* learned what it is. And now you carrying on all high and mighty like you know more'n me?! Boy….you better check yourself."

"Come on Barley, I'm not saying I know more'n you. I'm just saying…"

"Hush up!" said Barley, glaring at Elmer G. "Just hold your horses and let me finish. A parable is a short story you tell somebody to teach them a lesson about something you want them to understand. You understand?"

"Yeah. I understand," said Elmer G. "But I wouldn't complain if you throwed an example my way."

"Alright then," said Barley. "Remember the story I told you about the young pig who had to walk through the cemetery?"

"Yeah," said Elmer G.

"Did you learn anything from the story?" asked Barley.

"Yeah," said Elmer G. "I learned something."

"I know you did," said Barley. " 'Cause that was a parable."

"I guess it was," said Elmer G.

"Yep," said Barley. "And remember the story about Portabus? When we talked about his contribution to the farmer's breakfast?"

"Yeah," said Elmer G.

"That was a parable too," explained Barley.

"What about the Gospel?" said Elmer G. "What is that all about?"

"The religious lessons taught by the Disciples are called the "Gospel," said Barley. "It's like talking to pigs about what the Bible says so they don't have to read it. Verbal Cliff notes, you might say."

"Come again?" said Elmer G. "Verbal Cliff notes?"

"Never mind," said Barley.

"Sounds to me like the pigs that are in charge of spreading the Gospel can decide what to pass on to everybody else," said Elmer G. "It sorta' sounds like it could be gossip."

"I guess to a non-believer, the Gospel is sorta' like unsubstantiated gossip," said Barley. "But if the Disciples are true believers in God, they will spread the real messages from the Bible and not mix in too much gossip."

"What is a Disciple?" asked Elmer G.

"A Disciple is someone who quits the commercial fishing trade and starts fishing for God," explained Barley. "Disciples try to catch non-believers in their nets and persuade them to become believers. God teaches them spiritual lessons and they spend the rest of their lives teaching other pigs and men these same lessons about religion.

"And Jesus?" said Elmer G. "What's the skinny on Him?"

"Jesus is God's Son," said Barley. "God sent Him down to earth to try and help us all to believe in God faster by showing us His Holy powers."

"Was He successful?" asked Elmer G.

"Somewhat," said Barley. "Up until they killed Him."

"They killed Jesus?!" said Elmer G. in a shocked tone of voice.

"Yeahhhh!" said Barley. "They nailed Him to a cross on Mount Calvary. And here you are wondering how humans can slaughter pigs. Humans have a track record as far as killing goes. They even killed the Son of God. Wasn't no big deal though. Jesus had powers over death. On the third day He rose up and cake-walked up into Heaven to be with His Father. See Elmer G.....even Jesus had to pass through the cemetery to get home."

"Tell me again why I need God's help," pleaded Elmer G.

"That ain't hard," answered Barley. "If you wanna' get yourself snatched out of line when they march ya'll into the trailer truck to go to the slaughter house.....you're gonna' need God's help and every other piece of help you can muster up. By strengthening your spiritual faith, you will hold your fears back behind a dam of faith. Without spiritual faith, we are no better off than a snake or a rat that lives anxiously from moment to moment. Elmer G., spiritual faith gives us significance in an insignificant world."

"But what if everything is going pretty good in my life...which it ain't," said Elmer G. "Do I need to bother with having faith during the good times?"

"That's a good question, Elmer G. If you have a strong religious faith when everything is going well, then that's not the same as 'having faith'."

"Why not?" asked Elmer G.

"Because that's like holding four aces or a full house in your hand during a card game," said Barley. "That's not having faith. That's called 'having confidence'. The real test is whether we can keep our spiritual faith under extreme pressures. Having faith in somebody you can't see, like God, during times of difficulties is faith of the highest order. The greater the difficulties, then the greater our faith needs to be. This is why you hear pigs using the phrase 'grace under pressure'."

"Does that mean I have to learn to have grace under pressure?" asked Elmer G.

"Elmer G., I'm gonna' just flat-out tell you the truth. If you don't learn to have 'grace under pressure', then one day a human family will be mumbling 'grace over you' before they go to pouring gravy over your pork chops. You've got to work on strengthening your religious faith, boy. I'm just trying to help you save yourself."

"But Barley," said Elmer G., "to be honest with you, I still don't understand what faith is."

"Faith," answered Barley, "is just like you said yourself a minute ago. Faith is believing in something even though you ain't got no proof that it's true. Faith means stepping out into what looks like a deep and dangerous river. And even as you wade out into the swirling waters, you must believe with absolute certainty that there will be a shallow river bottom for you to stand on and keep your head above water. Faith does not mean you are not afraid. Faith means going forward in spite of your fears."

"So, what you're saying is that faith is the same thing as being brave?" said Elmer G.

"No, it's not, Elmer G. Hogs that are smarter than me have been saying for ages and ages that faith is the breeding ground where the seeds of bravery and courage sprout their first blooms."

"What is courage?" asked Elmer G.

"Courage is a feeling you get inside you when times get tough," explained Barley. "Courage means that even when you are scared....you still step bravely forward into the storms of life."

"So, you're saying that courage is going forward to do something when you know you will win," said Elmer G.

"Not exactly," said Barley. "Courage does not mean going forward when you know you will win. That is ambition. Courage means going forward when you know you may fail. Courage means having the willingness and fortitude to go forward when there is a chance you may fail. You can be afraid of something and still deal with it in a courageous manner. Elmer G., you must be fortified by a strong faith before you can cultivate courage. Let's take a run at this from another angle. Let me ask you a question. What is the first thing you'd do if you wanted to build a pig pen from scratch?"

"I guess I would clean the building site up pretty good, first," said Elmer G.

"And what would you do next?" asked Barley.

"I'd lay a foundation made outta' cinder block wood beam posts," said Elmer G.

"That's exactly right," said Barley. "And believe it or not, faith works the same way. Faith is the first building block we use to build a monument to demonstrate our relationship with God. What will happen to your pig pen if you put up the fence without the foundation beams?"

"It'll probably fall down in no time flat," said Elmer G. quickly. He was glad Barley finally asked him a question he knew the answer to.

"It shore' will," agreed Barley. "And your religious faith works the same way. If you start with a weak foundation, then your courage will falter as soon as you face tough challenges. The reason your courage will falter is because your faith is too weak to give your courage a proper foundation to support it. On the flip side, a strong faith makes your enemies seem shorter than Shetland ponies. The Bible says that with a faith the size of a mustard seed, we can move mountains. If we believe they can be moved."

"Well, you've certainly said a mouth full," said Elmer G. "Although I ain't terribly optimistic about this prayer and faith thing working in my favor, I'll give it a shot. I'm gonna' go ahead and pray to try and find my spiritual center. It ain't like I got a lot of options. Now Barley….I don't mean to be rude….but as powerful as God is supposed to be….you'd think he'd speak to us or something. If nothing else, just to at least acknowledge that He hears our prayers."

"When you think that God doesn't hear you, Elmer G., it's your faith that keeps you believing in God."

"Barley, I feel kinda' bad about this, but as hard as you've worked to explain to me what 'faith' is and how it works….I still don't get it," said Elmer G.

"Don't feel bad, Elmer G. Faith is not an easy thing to understand. It's hard to understand faith when you don't have physical evidence to see and touch to base your faith on. Let me explain it another way. Faith is a belief inside you that calms you during troubled times. It is the absolute belief that God's will is being done, no matter what the outcome. Faith is a whisper in your ear that tells you to stay strong because God has built a solid wall around you every day to protect you from harm. If you have faith, Elmer G., you will be comforted no matter what happens on the day you march up the ramp into the truck that will take you to the slaughter house."

"But I don't wanna' go to the slaughter house, Barley. I wanna' live. Why can't it be God's will to let me not get picked by Farmer Brown to go to the slaughter house?"

"No matter what happens to you Elmer G., it is God's will. If you survive the slaughter house, it is God's will. On the other hand, if you go there and they clamp your little feet down with those silver metal clamps and shoot you in the head with a stun gun and slit your throat and then scrape your hair off and start chopping your shoulders up…"

"Barley! Spare me the details! Pu…lease!" said Elmer G. "I get your point."

"I'm sorry," said Barley. "But like I was saying, even if you die, that is also God's will. If you don't have no faith, then your fears are gonna' be so heavy they'll feel like you're lugging around a suitcase crammed full of bricks. Faith in God is what gives you the courage to face the slaughter house with grace and courage. Instead of being scared to death."

"But, what if I am scared on that day? I'm pretty scared now," said Elmer G.

"Elmer G.," said Barley, softly. "Son, there ain't nothing wrong with being scared. We're all scared of something. Only a fool is never scared. But, when you build a relationship with God, you trust in Him to help you carry your burdens when you got more'n you can carry by yourself."

"So what you're saying is that God is like a hotel valet," said Elmer G.

"What?" asked Barley, with a puzzled look crossing his face.

"Never mind," said Elmer G. "Finish your explaining."

"What I was saying," said Barley, "is that when you have a whole bunch of spiritual faith, you send fear scurrying over to the nearest corner, shaking and trembling. And when you have a lot of spiritual faith, you know God is with you every step of the way, no matter what kinda' situation you're walking into. But before you can have this kind of faith, you *must* develop a relationship with God."

"How do I do that?" asked Elmer G.

"You develop a relationship with God the same way you would if you wanted to get to know another pig," said Barley. "You talk to God. Conversate with Him. Tell Him about your hopes, your fears and your dreams. If you're like most pigs, you'll end up spending a large chunk of your prayer time telling him about your problems. Then you'll go to identifying stuff you want Him to give you. Now, don't get me wrong here. I'm not saying there's anything wrong with that. I'm not saying that at all. All I'm saying is that you have to also remember to ask God to walk with you every day. God can help you make good decisions about things you do. Ask God how He wants to use you to do His will."

"But, God doesn't talk back," said Elmer G., in a perplexed tone of voice.

"God does talk back, Elmer G. He answers our prayers."

"How does He do that?" asked Elmer G. "He doesn't talk to us."

"Well, He answers us though His actions," said Barley. "Sometimes He gives us strength and wisdom. But He does it in a round-about sorta' way, so that we don't even know it was Him that helped us out."

"Well Barley," said Elmer G., "it seems to me He does a great job of being discreet. If I get a fantastic idea, or if I spark up on a burst of courage, then I might think it's just Elmer G. being so brave. If I don't know for sure that it is God working in my life, then I may just gobble up the credit for myself. How can I tell when God is at work and when it's me doing the heavy lifting? I mean...I don't wanna' be hogging all the credit if it oughta' really be going on God's account."

"You know Elmer G., that's one problem with religion that nobody has figured out yet. Most pigs rush to take credit for everything good that happens to them. Then they turn right around and blame God for all the troubles in their lives. But personally, I believe the hand of God is being waved over everything we do. There are prime examples of His works all around us, blinking like neon lights."

"I don't see no examples," said Elmer G.

"That's 'cause you ain't looking in the right places," said Barley. "Look around you. What you see?"

"A pig pen," announced Elmer G., glad to get another question he could safely answer.

"This is gonna' be harder than I thought," said Barley, in an exasperated tone of voice. "Elmer G....son...look-a-here. Work with me now. You can take this next statement to the tank."

"To the tank?" asked Elmer G.

"To the bank or what...ever!" said Barley. "The point I wanna' make is that the greatest miracles in the world are things we can't see and can't explain."

"Such as?" said Elmer G.

"Such as?" repeated Barley. "You trying to be funny, boy?"

"Nawww, Barley. I really don't understand about all the miracles God is supposed to be sponsoring."

"Well, I can't rehash the whole list of God's previous accomplishments, but let's look at a few," said Barley. "Look at the sky, for example. God created the sky and everything hanging around up in it. I mean really look at the sky. Elmer G., have you *really* looked at the moon and the sun. Take the stars, for example. Look how perfectly positioned they are, as they twinkle and wink at us. The stars are hung in the sky as beautifully as any van Gogh or

Rembrandt painting hanging on the wall in the New York Metropolitan Museum. The museum paintings are carted off to different museums around the world as showcase pieces for folks to ooooh and ahhh over. They are stolen, lost and damaged over the passage of the years."

"What does that have to do with the stars shining?" asked Elmer G.

"The stars tiptoe out in their white nightshirts and shine up a storm," said Barley. "Been doing it every night since the beginning of time right up until tonight. Look at how perfectly positioned they are, as they shine like it was their first time hanging out this late. What we don't see is God performing maintenance on the stars and slapping on a new coat of blue and white paint every couple of months to keep it fresh."

"Come on Barley," said Elmer G. "You can't be serious."

"Yes I am serious too," said Barley. "Just stay with me now. Stay with me. Let me ride this trotter down the home-stretch and flog it on across the finish line. After God does maintenance on the stars and the sky, He sits back in His rocker and commences to rotate the planets. Notice how the sun rises and sets every day exactly when it's supposed to. The moon is shining just right, every night. The stars are on-stage every night, all in the exact right place. This incomprehensible organization of the solar system could only be created by God. The solar system works as well today as it did sixty zillion gazillion years ago. There is no 1-800 number to call for solar system repairs. Except for man, God's creations don't break down, or get out of sync. For the most part....God's works are perfection personified."

"Barley, God may have made the sky, the moon and stars," said Elmer G., "but if someone sings a song or writes a great book, maybe it was just *their* talent that allowed them to do it. Maybe God doesn't get involved in day-to-day stuff like that. Maybe He just busies Himself with big miracles."

"Elmer G., you are darn dense! But I'm gonna' help you see the light, even if it kills you. First of all....God is everywhere. There is no problem so tall that God won't stand on His tiptoes and extend a helping hand. And there is no problem so small that He won't stoop down and pick us up when we are feeling down. What we see as a big problem ain't no harder for God to solve than plucking a splinter of wood outta' your shoulder."

"But how do you *know* that Barley?"

Barley was silent for a few seconds. Then he said, "Elmer G., you see that junk pile over behind the corn shed?"

"Yeah," said Elmer G. "That's where the humans toss a bunch of their old trash, like newspapers, books, magazines and appliances."

"That's right," said Barley, "We found an old radio out there that we've been listening to. We also found a small, portable television set that some of us older pigs have been watching for years. We've learned a lot about humans by reading their discarded books, different versions of the Bible and old newspapers. On top of all that, we've got a warehouse of knowledge that past generations of pigs have passed down to us. As you can see, we've learned quite a bit about history, people and current events."

"What sorts of things you been learning about?" asked Elmer G.

"One thing we've learned is that humans get along just fine until they run into a shortage of love or money," said Barley. "They fight when they don't get enough of either one. Then, they turn around and fight even more when they get too much of either one. But the thing that really gets them to slaying each other without remorse is a principle that is built on love and tolerance as its foundation."

"What principle is that?" asked Elmer G.

"The same principle I am trying to get you to understand," Elmer G. "It's called religion."

"Religion?" repeated Elmer G.

"Yep," said Barley. "Humans fight like crazy when it comes to religion. Religious principles are supposed to be about universal love and raising the standard of living for the poor and downtrodden. In a sensible world, religion would seem to focus its energies on seeking the general betterment of every living creature and universal non-violence. Ideally, religion is based on flimsy mission statements like turning the other cheek, loving your fellow man, being nice to your neighbors and being faithful to your wife, or wives if you live in some place called Utah. Religion is about doling out forgiveness like you're handing out Halloween candy. But people have historically fought and killed more folks in the name of religion than for any other reason. Evidently, religion brings out the best and worst in its worshippers."

"But what does that have to do with God getting involved in small events in our lives?" asked Elmer G. "Where is God in our everyday life? I don't see Him."

"Where is God in our everyday life?" echoed Barley. "Is that what you said? Huh? Is that what you said just now? You saying you don't see God? So what? Just because you don't see Him doesn't mean He don't exist. It just means you're not looking through eyes of faith and understanding."

"Barley, I'm sorry, but I don't understand."

"See what I mean?" said Barley. "Look Elmer G. God is everywhere. Every....where. He's on the job around the clock. From sunup to sundown and every second in-between. He prowls around twenty-four seven, tossing out miracles, inspiration, hope and deliverance every which-a-way. Listen to Tchaikovsky's Waltz from the "*Sleeping Beauty*" and tell me that the hand of God was not at work. Listen to Dvorak's "*Adagio*" and Grieg's "*Piano Concerto No.1*". If you need further proof that God's fingerprints are on our works, see if you can listen to Grounod's "*Ave Maria*" without weeping at its beauty. Could just a man create such beautiful music without the hand of God being involved? Do you really think that Mendelssohn could have created the *Dance of the Clowns* from "A Midsummer Night's Dream", if God was not present at his writing desk with a bucket of inspiration splashing around all every which-a-way?"

"Barley, you are giving me goose bumps," said Elmer G. "Go ahead now. Please finish."

Barley smiled slightly and continued his explanation about God's presence in the world around us. "When men refer to the genius of Beethoven's *Symphony No. 5*" and Rossini's brilliant "*Overture: William Tell*"…the loudest applause is heaped upon the heads of the composers because they are men we can see with our eyes. But the real credit should go to God, who although He is not seen….is the One who inspired these composers. God is always guiding our hands whenever we create anything beautiful that has a shelf-life of popularity longer than three weeks."

"Okay, let's say I agree that God can write some really classy music," said Elmer G. "What about things other than music? I still don't see how we can tell when God is working in our lives."

"God is at work in all areas of our lives," said Barley. "Both men and pigs. Surely God smiled on Albert Einstein, Walden, Thoreau and Gandhi. God was shuttling back-and-forth between America and England, as He stood by Theodore Roosevelt and Winston Churchill during the chilling, pitched battles of World War II. God was there holding His own golden quill pen along side Benjamin Franklin, Thomas Jefferson and the other drafters during the creation of America's "Declaration of Independence", which became a living document that facilitated the Founding of a great Nation. At the time, America wasn't nothing but a runt of a nation that was just starting to take her first wobbly baby steps. I'm not sure why, but God likes to select underdogs, like young America, to work His miracles through."

"Underdogs? What does that mean?" asked Elmer G.

"He picks folks and nations, like Israel, that are small in statue——to work his miracles on. God works through people and pigs that don't have the normal strengths and physical attributes you expect in great leaders. In a way...you might say this is God's way of showing off a little bit. The less He has to work with....sometimes it seems like the more He's able to do with us. Obviously, the Man likes to play long odds."

"You got an example of that? I'm kinda' lost."

"Well...let's look at Moses."

"Who is Moses?"

"Didn't I just say let's *look* at Moses? I'm about to tell you who he is if you give me a chance. Doggone young folks! Making me lose my place. Where was I at? Oh yeah. According to the Bible, Moses was a reluctant Prophet. God chose Moses to lead the Israelites out of bondage in a far-away land called Egypt. Down in Egypt this old king named Pharaoh was a whipping the Israelites up a storm. He was just a bearing down on 'em with chunks and chunks of hard times."

"How come?" asked Elmer G.

"Because the Israelites were God's chosen people. And old Pharaoh didn't believe in the real God. He and his peoples worshipped idol gods made outta' gold and bronze and what-not. Like I was saying, the Israelites were having a tough time of it."

"What happened?" asked Elmer G. "Were they being slaughtered?"

"Worse," announced Barley. "They were slaves laboring in the worst kind of misery under the heel of Pharaoh."

"Doing what?" asked Elmer G.

"Pharaoh had 'em working like yard dogs," said Barley.

"Really?" said Elmer G.

"Oh yeahhh!" said Barley. "Now, bear in mind I ain't got this information first-hand 'cause this stuff happened a long time ago. But according to the Bible, Pharaoh had the Israelites hauling giant blocks of granite and straw in the hot sun, plus doing all kinds of odd jobs the Egyptians didn't hardly wanna' be doing themselves. Down in Egypt the Israelites sweated and labored in misery, under the merciless whip of Pharaoh. God gazed down on this sad situation and got a little hot under His collar. So He decided to do something about it. That's when He chose Moses to lead the Israelites out of bondage. God appeared to Moses in the form of a burning trough one day and told him about His plans for Moses."

"What was the big plan?" asked Elmer G.

"God told Moses He wanted him to go tell Pharaoh to let His people go free. Now Moses was no fool. He had some reservations about standing up to Pharaoh like God was asking him to do. Moses had a stutter when he talked, yet God chose him to be His communicator to tell Pharaoh to let God's people go free out of Egypt. God was with Moses when he held up his wooden staff, parted the Red Sea with his faith and ushered the children of Israel across the sea bottom unharmed."

"Wow!" said Elmer G. "That's some powerful stuff God was laying on Pharaoh. God must be strong. But one set of miracles don't prove your case Barley."

"Elmer G., you ain't got enough time in your little hourglass of life to hear about all the miracles God has performed. Evidently, God likes sports too."

"Why you say that?" asked Elmer G.

"Take Michael Jordan, for example," said Barley.

"Who is that?" asked Elmer G.

"I'ma' tell you!" yelled Barley. "I'ma' tell you! Just hold your horses, boy. Michael Jordan wasn't much of nobody until God went to work on him. Michael was cut from his High School basketball team. Yet, he became one of the greatest Basketball Balladeers to ever perform a pirouette above the rim of a basketball goal. God rubbed some jump-juice on his legs. Squeezed almost all the body fat outta' the boy. Thumped his head and plopped in a set of eagle eyes so he could see the basket from the parking lot of the stadium. Strapped some extra long fingers onto the ends of his wrists, so he could grip a basketball like it wasn't nothing more'n a orange. And snapped on some extra long feet, so he could have a smooth landing when he did finally fly back down to earth."

"Barley," interjected Elmer G., "is all this true?"

"Yeah!" said Barley. "And that ain't all. With all his new equipment from God's Footlocker Store. Michael Jordan became the greatest basketball player in the world. One morning when God was working on Michael, he accidentally dropped him into a bucket of Baptism water and Michael sloshed around in there 'til he almost drowned. God snatched him out just in the nick of time. Scared Michael Jordan so bad, the boy has a lifelong fear of water."

"Good gracious of life!" said Elmer G. "God shore' is a piece of work, ain't He?"

"That's what I been trying to tell you all along," said Barley. "God don't make no mess and God don't mess around. If He's gonna' do something......He do it right. He ain't no half-stepper. Look what he did for Larry Bird. Larry Bird couldn't jump but six inches off the ground and he darn near led the Boston Celtics to that many NBA championships. God sprinkled magic powder over Magic Johnson's head when he was a baby and he became a magician on the basketball court. You know why?"

"Nope," said Elmer G.

" 'Cause God gave Larry Bird and Magic Johnson a sixth sense, so they could see things on the basketball court that nobody else could see. Plus, He gave both of 'em an extra pair of eyes...in the back of their heads so they could see behind them when they played. And check out Wayne Gretsky, the greatest hockey player of all time. God gave him a special talent."

"What was that?" asked Elmer G.

"While all the other hockey players skated to where the puck was......Gretsky said he was able to skate to where the puck was going to be. He had a built-in advantage. God is culturated too. He's into artwork and what-not."

"He is?" said Elmer G.

"Oh yeahhh," said Barley. "God's tastes jump all over the place. He pretty much likes most things, once He's properly introduced to the materials. His tastes varies across all kinds of autistic endeavors. Basically, God likes to knock about the house and paint peoples, pigs and landscapes to calm His nerves. After listening to billions of people and animals all over the world praying to Him about all their personal dramas, it just wears Him down to a gristle. So He whips out his canvas and brushes and paints watercolors to relax and knock the edge off."

"Is that right?" whispered Elmer G.

"No doubt about it," said Barley. "And He helps other folks paint too. Some of the folks God tries to help don't pan out, like Alvin Tucker."

"Who is Alvin Tucker?" asked Elmer G.

"Alvin Tucker was a regular house painter over in Alabama. Boy was horrible when it came to painting. He could throw a bucket of paint at the side of a barn and miss everything. God watched all of Alvin's troubles as he went around messing up people's houses, trying to paint. God jumped in and blessed Alvin with some extra talent so he could paint better."

"Did it work?" asked Elmer G.

"Nawww," said Barley. "It didn't work. Boy seemed to paint worse after God blessed him. Now, you are in bad shape if you don't get no better after God has gone outta' His way to throw a blessing your way. On the other hand, you got some peoples that are just born with a lot of ability to paint. Like van Gogh. As I said earlier, God was an excellent painter. But the artist, Vincent van

Gogh was not a shabby act neither. He only sold one painting while he was alive."

"Who bought God's painting?" asked Elmer G.

"What?" said Barley.

"I was just asking who bought God's painting that He sold," said Elmer G. "You just said He sold one painting while He was alive."

"God ain't sold no painting, boy!" said Barley. "I was talking about Vincent van Gogh. Elmer G.....I'm gonna' have to be patient and grow you, son. Vincent van Gogh sold only one painting while *he* was alive. But after he died and folks discovered he was a genius, his paintings sold for tens of millions of dollars......each. You know why?"

"No idea why," said Elmer G.

"Because God rubbed His hands across van Gogh's soul," explained Barley. "Then He spit on van Gogh's hands and rubbed His own spirit into them, so that he could paint pictures that were infused with the spirit of God Himself. But God accidentally dropped baby Vincent while He was working on his hands and Vincent landed on his ear. All his life he had ear aches until one day he cut one of 'em off trying to get rid of the pain. Now, what do you think about that?"

"Barley.....come on now. Tell the truth. God did all that?" asked Elmer G.

"Yeah!," said Barley. "You might not know this, but van Gogh used to sit up and eat his paints. Some folks tried to claim he ate 'em 'cause that's how he got his inspiration. Truth is, the boy was eating his paints 'cause he was hongry'. And the reason he was hongry' was because he couldn't sell no pictures. 'Course, this was before God got to growing him. God did all that for van Gogh and a lot more," said Barley.

"Like what?" asked Elmer G.

"Wait a minute, boy! I'm gonna' give you some more examples, if you just let me catch my breath a minute. That's the problem with you young pigs today. Ya'll in too much of a hurry. And you don't have a clue about where you're going. I lost my train of thought. What am I supposed to be giving you an example of?"

"How God works in our everyday lives," said Elmer G.

"Oh yeah…now I remember," said Barley. "Another good example is Johnnie Lee Gray."

"Who is that?" asked Elmer G.

"A painter from Spartanburg, South Carolina who had no formal training. Yet, he painted some of the most enduring and moving paintings of the Jim Crow era and the civil rights struggle. That man loved painting so much that sometimes he painted on the back of stray pieces of plywood. See now, having Johnnie Lee paint on the back of plywood was another case of God just showing off. His work is beyond beautiful. If you see his painting called *"A Cloud of Witnesses"*, you know that God swept His hand across Johnnie Lee Gray's soul. In his painting called the *"Backbone of the South"*, the great panorama of slaves picking cotton in the sweeping cotton fields is no less a masterpiece than any Rembrandt, van Gogh or Matisse. The cotton looks so real that when I saw the picture, I tried to pick some off and stuff it into my cotton gathering sack hanging by my side."

"Wow, Barley. It all sounds so beautiful."

Another example of God at work is what he did with David," said Barley.

"David?" said Elmer G. "Was he another painter?"

"Naww," said Barley. "David was a Shepard boy they wrote about in the Bible. Mostly, he watched over his daddy's sheep and played with his Gameboy when he got bored. David wore a white cotton skirt and leather sandals, but don't let that skirt fool you. David was the kinda' fella' you wanna' have by your side if you get into a brawl at the slop troughs."

"So, you're saying David liked to fight," said Elmer G.

"No," said Barley. "David *loved* a good fight. That curly-haired boy would hike all the way over to another country if he heard a fist-fry was brewing. David could throw down, baby! God sent His Angels to walk with little David out across the expanse of rolling green battlefields to meet the Philistines' greatest warrior——a bow-legged, big bodied, gap toothed giant named Goliath. They slapped up giant advertisement posters all over town. They plastered 'em on the walls in the malls, on the street signs and on the sides of the buses. It was just such a big old to-do. Even King Saul took time out from his busy schedule to come down and see the fight. It was the 'Fight of the Century'."

"What's the big deal about Goliath?" asked Elmer G.

"What's the big deal?" said Barley, in a mocking tone of voice. "Goliath was the big deal. Goliath was over nine feet tall!! The man had never been defeated on the battlefield. And poor David wasn't much taller than you! Goliath was so big, so thick and so tall they had to use a Hummer just to carry his shield and armor."

"A Hummer?" repeated Elmer G.

"That's right," said Barley. "God sent a mess of His Angels down to the battlefield to help David fight Goliath. They pulled up on the scene rolling in a canary yellow military truck called a Hummer. God's Angels told David not to worry because they were gonna' help him defeat Goliath."

"What I wanna' know is, how does the story about David help me in my life?" said Elmer G.

"Because it gives you an example of what having faith in God can do for you," explained Barley. "The Bible is a big old book. It's God's instructional manual on "How To Get Religion". Sorta' like a "Driving Manual". You read it to learn how to drive your way down the winding roads of life to the House of Faith. Course, there are a lot of pigs that are driving and teaching other folks to drive and they ain't even read the "Driver's Manual" yet. Now you take David. He read his Driver's Manual. Because even though Goliath was over nine feet tall.....little David *ran quickly towards* the battle line to meet Goliath."

"Why did he run towards the giant?" asked Elmer G.

"Because David's faith was so sincere and strong," said Barley. "David, you see, was favored by God…"

"What flavor did God make David?" asked Elmer G., innocently. "Now, you take me, I'm partial to strawberry flavor. But I can eat apple flavor too. It's just those raspberries that I can't stomach because they have those tiny seeds that get stuck between my teeth. Now…there was this one time I tried some caramel flavor and liked it pretty good too. I'm making myself hongry' thinking about it. But you wanna' see some eating action! All you gotta' do is sit me down in front of a tub of fudge. I love myself some chocolate fudge topped off with some…."

"Stop it, Elmer G.!" yelled Barley. "Hold it right there! What in the world are you blabbering about?"

"Flavors," said Elmer G.

"Flavors?" said Barley. "What are you talking about boy?"

"You just said that God flavored David and I asked what flavor he made him. That's all."

"What flavor God made David?! Elmer G., you are about as dense a pig as I ever met. God didn't *flavor* David!"

"But you're the one that said God flavored David. All I did was ask what flavor He made him. You ain't got to huff all up at me! I ain't meant no harm."

"I know Elmer G. It's just that sometimes….I mean…the questions you come up with….Look a here. I said God *favored* David. This means that God *liked* David and He did some special things for David to make him the greatest warrior of his times. David knew God liked him and that he was God's *favorite* warrior."

"Ohhh," said Elmer G. in a small voice. "My bad. How did David know he was God's favorite?"

"'Cause God had already helped him kill a lion and a bear that were trying to sneak off with his sheep for their supper. David believed that God would help him fight Goliath. Goliath was a-bad mouthing God and calling Him a fake and all. You can imagine how proud God was of David when he told Goliath to stop low-rating and bad-mouthing the one true God. You know how you feel when somebody's bad-mouthing you and one of your friends steps up to the plate and says "Shut up! Elmer G. is the bestest buddy a pig could have. Say something good about Elmer G....or just shut up!" It makes you proud and protected and warm all over. Well, God musta' felt the same kind of pride when David went to battle to defend God's good name. David told Goliath he'd better stop dragging God's name through the mud."

""Did Goliath stop?" asked Elmer G.

"Nawww!" said Barley. "Goliath ain't even paid David no mind. Goliath told David to pack a sack lunch to eat on his way to h....."

"Barley!! Shut your mouth!" said Elmer G.

"But I'm talkin' 'bout Shaft!" said Barley, in a remorseful tone of voice. "I mean...I'm talking 'bout David. I've gotta' cut back on those TNT late night movies."

"It don't matter who you're talking about, you need to be careful what you say," advised Elmer G., feeling kind of good being in the role of the teacher.

"I'm sorry," mumbled Barley, hanging his head slightly in mock shame.

"Now go on with your story," said Elmer G.

"Well anyway," said Barley. "Goliath told David to step on down and pick up his prize. Goliath said he was about to beat David into next week."

"What did David do?" asked Elmer G. "You still didn't finish explaining why David ran towards the battle line."

"He ran towards the battle line because he felt sure God would deliver a victory to him," explained Barley. "David's faith caused him to run towards his problem, instead of away from it. David knew that God would deliver the victory, especially against over-whelming odds. We can learn from David's adventure."

"Learn what?" said Elmer G.

"Never bet against the house," said Barley. "At least not when it's God's House."

"Exactly how did God deliver a victory to David?" asked Elmer G.

"He sent a slew of His Angels down to help David beat Goliath," said Barley. "God has some folks with superpowers called Angels. They do contract work for Him, as the need arises. His Angels used their frequent flyer mileage and came down to throw their weight behind David's plough. They helped David select one of the five smooth stones from the pocket of his flow-ing Shepard's robes. Then the Angels helped David load it into his slingshot. David flung his slingshot around his head three times and let the smooth stone fly. POWYA! Bling! Bling! God's Angels helped guide the stone to the perfect spot in Goliath's forehead to kill him."

"So David hit Goliath in the head with the stone?" asked Elmer G.

"Cracked Goliath right smack between the eyes," said Barley. "After he got smacked in the head he crashed to the ground....dead."

"That a great story, Barley. So God sends His Angels to protect people..."

"And pigs..." added Barley.

"And pigs," repeated Elmer G.

"That's right," said Barley. "The Bible is stocked full of stories where God helped people that believed in Him. God sent His Angels to protect Daniel when the King's soldiers tossed Daniel into the lion's den to be eaten alive. Daniel was allergic to house cats. So, he didn't stand a chance against a rowdy mess of hongry' lions. If it wasn't for God's Angels showing up....Daniel would have been ripped to pieces in no time a'tall."

"So God was there with Daniel?" asked Elmer G.

"Not only was God was there *with* Daniel," said Barley. "He was there *for* Daniel."

"What did God do to the lions?" asked Elmer G.

"God's Angels used the force of God's Holy Spirit and made those old lions back up into a corner," said Barley. "Then the Angels locked the lions mouths shut. Those old lions stayed away from Daniel. The next morning, when the King came to retrieve what they thought would be Daniel's bones, he was shocked and happy Daniel's God had saved him."

"Why was he happy Daniel was alive?" asked Elmer G. "I thought the King was the one who had him thrown into the lion's den."

"That's sorta' right," said Barley. "People around the King tricked him into throwing Daniel into the lion's den. But, truth is he really loved Daniel and didn't wanna' kill him. Because they were friends, you see. Being a King and all…he ain't had that many friends to start off with. So he 'shore wasn't fancying losing another one in no lion's den. Like I was saying, the King was thrilled when his friend Daniel came strutting out of the lion's den that morning. Daniel yawned, gapped, stretched and scratched himself. Then he asked the King's cook to run scare up some whole-wheat bagels, cream cheese and a mess of scrambled eggs, so he could eat a little something to tide him over a spell. Daniel said he was so hongry' he could near 'bout eat a lion."

"Sounds like God is pretty strong," observed Elmer G. "But how can He be everywhere at the same time?"

"God is strong," said Barley. "He is everywhere He needs to be. God was sitting by Abraham Lincoln on the train, as they penned the Gettysburg Address, which began with those stirring words, "Fourscore and Seven years ago…" God jogged down through the Ages. His powers were heard flying from the Beatles's guitar strings as they urged us to "*Let It Be*". God's powers surged through Jimi

Hendrix's fingers as he performed a ballet on the thin strings of his guitar, twirling, whirling, dipping and diving, as he took the world on a tour through his private musical maze in the throbbing, pleading notes of his masterful *"Purple Haze"* and graced us with the simple beauty of *"Little Wings"*.

"Barley, I just love the way you describe God. It all sounds so wonderful."

"I ain't even finished," said Barley. "Now, gimme ten more compliments like that———-and shet' up. God hurled fastballs with Nolan Ryan. God did the Ali shuffle with Muhammad Ali when he crushed Sonny Liston to the mat with a jab so quick, no one saw the punch. He threw football passes with Johnny Unitas. God blew a strong wind at Jesse Owens' back as he ran and jumped during the Olympics. He swung Joe DiMaggio's bat with the beauty of a bunch of lilies in the field bending gracefully under the onslaught of a fall breeze. And God graced Ted Williams with so much ability to hit a baseball that he made it look 'bout as easy as swinging at houseflies with a commercial-sized fishing net."

"So you're saying God is involved in everything we do?" said Elmer G.

"Yep," said Barley. "God is a part of everything we do. From Elvis' swinging hips....to the melancholy lyrics dripping from Frank Sinatra's lips. God was there with Reverend Martin Luther King when he penned his "Letter from a Birmingham Jail." He was there when Martin Luther King gave his prophetic and haunting *"I Have A Dream"* speech on the steps of the Washington Monument."

"What's the big deal about a little old speech?" asked Elmer G.

"This wasn't no ordinary speech, Elmer G. This speech was so powerful, it rang doorbells around the world, inviting Everyman's Conscience and Humanity to come outside to play in the streets of Birmingham, Alabama. This single speech announced the arrival of a new day in the nonviolent campaign against man's inhumanity to his fellow man. God could turn a phrase too. He likes to write."

""He does?" said Elmer G.

"Oh yeah," said Barley. "When Mark Twain wrote "*Huckleberry Finn*", God was there. God was guiding Mark Twain's fountain pen, as he dipped it into God's personal inkwell that contained memories from Twain's boyhood. God's inkwell contained the gritty, gripping boyhood memories that Mark Twain said he summoned from his past. Listen here to a few words that Mark Twain wrote. He said, *"The fountains of my great deep are broken up and I have rained reminiscences for four and twenty hours. The old life has swept before me like a panorama. The old days have trooped by in their glory, again. The old faces have looked out of the mist of the past. Old footsteps have sounded in my listening ears. Old hands have clasped mine. Old voices have greeted me. And the songs that I loved ages and ages ago have come wailing down the centuries."* Elmer G., who can listen to the beauty and cadence of these words and deny the existence of God? Great literature is evidence that God speaks across the centuries. This is why Mark Twain was able to write "*Huckleberry Finn*".

"Was *Huckleberry Finn* that good of a book?" asked Elmer G.

"It is one of the bestest books ever written. *Huckleberry Finn* was the beginning of all truly American writing in the sense that it celebrated America's different dialects and superstitions. It also exposed the institution of slavery as a blight against man and God. Mark Twain, bless his dear heart, lifted Nigger Jim up from slavery row by having Huck acknowledge that Jim was a human being who had feelings for his beloved family the same as white folks."

"Nobody had ever done that?" asked Elmer G.

"Nope," said Barley. "They did it with white characters, but never with black characters. This was the first time an author had done such a feat with a black character. 'Huckleberry Finn' was the first truly American novel because it was the first time an

American author had written a great book without trying to sound like a dang-blasted Englishman. Rather than sound like an Englishman, Mark Twain wallowed in the raw freshness and uniqueness of various American regional dialects. He exposed us to our different dialects, superstitions and attitudes in ways the world had never seen. According to Mark Twain, he used the "Missouri Negro dialect, the backwoods South-Western dialect the ordinary Pike-County dialect and four modified varieties of the Pike-County dialect."

"Sounds like Mark Twain was some kind of writer, Barley."

"You ain't never lied," said Barley. "Mark Twain wallowed in his mastery of "shadings" when it came to words and dialects. He said "The difference between the almost right word and the right word is really a large matter——'tis the difference between the light-ning-bug and the lightning," or something to that effect. He loved to use the gross exaggeration to blow an idea up like a cheap bal-loon——then prick conventional wisdom with a safety pin."

"Mark Twain must've been a wizard with words," said Elmer G.

"That he was," agreed Barley. "Mark Twain understood the rules of grammar, but tossed them out the window in order to write for the readers' ears, instead of their eyes. He was a Homerific figure who blasted into our mist around the same time as Haley's Comet and left right along side Haley's Comet seventy-five years later. Mark Twain said that God sent him in and out with Haley's Comet because they were both freaks of Nature. But what a funny and insightful freak he proved to be. A masterful sto-ryteller who conjured up the sounds, scents, noises, dialects and people from years and places that have long ceased to exist. That man did about as much good with Huck's raft as Noah did with an Ark full of animals. And not nearly as much of a mess to clean up."

"Barley, I don't know how you know about all this stuff...but it's holding my attention. I'll tell you that."

"But I'm just warming up," said Barley. "Let's talk about William Shakespeare. In his play *"Julius Caesar"*, the character Cassius was a big-time Hater. He was hating on his own friend, Caesar, because Caesar was the Emperor of Rome and Cassius couldn't even run his own house. A little case of Envy-Ti-Tus going on here. Listen to this passage from Shakespeare's character, Cassius, in the play "Julius Caesar". Cassius is talking to Brutus about Caesar."

> *"Why, man, he doth bestride the narrow world*
> *like a Colossus, and we petty men*
> *Walk under his huge legs and peep about*
> *To find ourselves dishonorable graves.*
> *Men at some time are masters of their fates:*
> *The fault, dear Brutus, is not in our stars,*
> *But in ourselves, that we are underlings."*

"I'm darn near sprouting tears now, reciting Shake-a-spear," said Barley.

"Shake-a-spear?" said Elmer G.

"Whatever," said Barley. "Shake-a-knive. Shake-a-gun. I 'shore love myself some Shakespeare. Listen to this scene from Hamlet. This is old Hamlet speaking to the *Ghost*."

> *"Angels and ministers of grace defend us!*
> *Be thou a spirit of health or goblin damn'd,*
> *Bring with thee airs from heaven or blasts from hell,*
> *Be thy intents wicked or charitable,*
> *Thou comest in such a questionable shape*
> *That I will speak to thee: I'll call thee Hamlet,*
> *King, father, royal Dane: O, answer me!"*

"Wow, Barley," said Elmer G. "That is so moving. So beautiful. I'm speechless."

"It is something special, ain't it?" said Barley. "I guess you can tell I read a lot. I know quite a few passages from Shakespeare. This is one of my favorites. This is Hamlet again. Check this out. Hamlet is one bad boy."

> *"To be or not to be: that is the question:*
> *Whether 'tis nobler in the mind to suffer*
> *The slings and arrows of outrageous fortune,*
> *Or to take arms against a sea of troubles,*
> *And by opposing end them? To die: to sleep:*
> *No more: and by sleep to say we end*
> *The heartache and the thousand natural shocks*
> *That flesh is heir to, 'tis a consummation*
> *Devoutly to be wish'd. To die, to sleep:*
> *To sleep: perchance to dream: ay, there's the rub:*
> *For in that......"*

"Barley!" said Elmer G. "That's enough Shakespeare for a few lifetimes. Shakespeare is like super-glue. A little bit of it goes a long way."

"I see your point," agreed Barley. "But all I'm trying to show you is that the beauty and wisdom of his words is lyrical proof that this was the voice of God speaking through Shakespeare. God was also speaking through Steinbeck and Cervantes. He ran with the bulls right next to Ernest Hemingway. God sat in the smoky Harlem bars late at night alongside Langston Hughes, as He showed Hughes how to craft his immortal Jessie B. Simple stories."

"Sounds like God is everywhere," observed Elmer G.

"That's what I've been trying to tell you, Elmer G.," said Barley. "God huddled in the cold, damp attic with Anne Frank. He held her small, trembling hand steady to the task, as she wrote in her little diary about her fears and hopes for a better, more humane and compassionate world. And she did this while she was listening to the German storm troopers stomping around downstairs from where she was hiding, searching for Jews like her to haul them off to the concentration camps to be executed."

"Barley, I never heard any of this stuff before. This is unbelievable," said Elmer G.

"God is something, ain't he?" said Barley. "God tossed a lasso with the immortal Will Rogers, as he entertained millions of people around the world with his country boy observations about politics, manners and society doings. As Will Rogers used to say, "All I know is what I read in the newspapers." Remember earlier when I said God liked to paint? Well, when you look at a Picasso painting, do you really believe that Pablo Picasso could create something reeking with more reality than reality itself? Not without God by his side handing him his paint brushes and plastering numbers on each section of the canvas to show Picasso what color tones and what type of painting strokes to use. Without God to inspire him, Picasso wouldn't have even been a decent housepainter, little less a world-renown artist."

"God did all that for Picasso?" asked Elmer G.

"He shore' did," said Barley. "I know somebody who knew somebody who saw a house one time that Picasso painted when he was a lowly housepainter."

"Did he do a good job on it?" asked Elmer G. "How did it look? It must have looked magnificent."

"You would think that, wouldn't you," said Barley. "But actually, it wasn't nothing to write home about."

"Really?" said Elmer G. "I'm surprised he didn't throw himself into it and do a bang up job painting the house."

"The peoples that owned that house were surprised too," said Barley. "They got back home after he had finished and did a double-take."

"How come?" asked Elmer G.

"Picasso messed them peoples' house up so bad with that sixteen color abstract design," said Barley, "that the people who hired him——refused to even pay the boy. I'm telling you the straight-up truth, Elmer G. Pablo Picasso wasn't hitting on nothing until God blew the breath of creative genius into his lungs. Picasso was struggling trying to make a living as a housepainter before God got a-holt of him."

"Barley, are you sure about that?"

"Yeah!" said Barley. "Nobody wanted to pay Picasso their hard earned money to slap those strange abstract designs on their house. Before God commenced to growing him, Picasso couldn't paint but two or three houses in the same town. Once folks got a gander at some of those weird designs——Picasso had to ride his raggedy old bicycle over to a different town every two or three weeks to pick up another house painting job, so he could buy food and paint."

"So, you're saying that there was a time when nobody would hire Picasso to paint their house?" said Elmer G.

"That's right," said Barley. "Nobody in their right mind wanted to hire Picasso to slap those strange designs on their house they paid good money for. And back then——a dollar was a dollar. People worked hard for their money. They ain't had no stock options like these corporate folks getting today. They were forking over real money. So they wanted full value for it, even a paint job on a house. But after God got through inspiring Picasso, he painted with such brilliance that he and God were about the only folks who understood what his paintings represented."

"Barley…how do you know all this stuff?" asked Elmer G.

"I told you I read a lot," said Barley. "I also listen to the radio and watch a little television, mostly PBS. I'm dissing those sitcoms because they are really out the box these days."

"Out the box?" repeated Elmer G., obviously not understanding what Barley meant.

"Must've been watching more MTV and BET than I realized," said Barley. "I'm illing out on you here. But sometimes….in life....you just gotta' drop old habits and pick up new ones. As for your old beliefs...you gotta' drop 'em like they're hot. If you're ready for some more info....I'll wind up and give you the 411."

"411?" repeated a puzzled Elmer G. "Drop 'em like they're hot?"

"Whack! Ain't it?" said Barley. "What I mean is that you have to drop your old beliefs like they're something hot you're holding. It's just an expression. But back to my point about God working in our lives. Do you believe that Michelangelo could lay on his back and paint such colorful and wondrous religious scenes on the ceiling of the Sistine Chapel with just his human talents? Not hardly. Without God's help, Michelangelo couldn't even lay bricks straight while laying on his back. I have a friend who knew a sow whose second cousin was shipped over to America from Rome. One time her cousin saw some bricks that Michelangelo laid. It was a right pitiful job of brick laying. Her cousin said the bricks were so crooked and chipped that they couldn't even use 'em for nothing except as an example of how *not* to lay bricks. But that was before God started growing him. The point I'm getting at, Elmer G., is that all of these artistic creations are examples of God's spirit inspiring mortal men to step into a space where they are greater than other men, but still less than God."

"Why did God inspire Michelangelo to paint pictures while laying on his back?" asked Elmer G.

"Like I said earlier, sometimes, in situations like what happened with Michelangelo....God may be kinda' showing off a little bit. God is showing us that He is so good that He can create master-pieces by inspiring Michelangelo to paint like a genius while lay-ing on his back. I agree with you on this one. I mean......who paints masterpieces while lying on their back? As you can see Elmer G., God is always standing nearby taking part in all the great and small achievements of men and pigs. We just have to know where to look."

"Barley, you have shore' said a mouthful," said Elmer G. in humbled tone of voice. "I hadn't really thought about God being present in all of the day-to-day things we do. Most of the folks you mentioned, I ain't never heard of, but they sound awful smart and important. I feel like I've got a glow in my belly. That means I'm plumb full of either inspiration or indigestion right now. I don't believe I know nearly as much as I thought I did before we commenced to talking. I'm appreciative to you Barley, for pulling my coattail and trying to help me get my head on straight. I am mighty thankful to have a friend such as yourself. Mighty thankful."

And with these words, Elmer G. slowly walked away with conflicting thoughts, slumped shoulders and a heavy heart.

"God 'shore is one complicated fellow", he thought to himself. "Complicated as all git' out."

CHAPTER 6

Searching For Salvation

"Finding your spiritual center is more than a notion. It's flat-out hard work. Praying to God for help is 'shore a sight easier than hitching your britches up and living right in the first place."

E lmer G. was confused by all the new information he was receiving. He felt fine when he was talking with Barley. This was because Barley was so supremely confident about what Elmer G. needed to do to save himself. 'Course, Barley could afford to be confident when he was gambling with Elmer G.'s chances for survival. Especially since Barley was too old himself to worry about being sent to the slaughter house. Although Elmer G. gained strength from Barley's confidence, when he was alone with his own thoughts, Elmer G. was paralyzed by his fears and anxieties. Sometimes he found himself wishing he had ignored what he'd found out about the slaughtering, like Cliché and the other pigs. That way he could at least enjoy his life up until the time they marched him into the Cornmasher's pens.

Early the next morning, Elmer G. woke up and remembered his conversation with Barley. Before he said his prayers, Elmer G. scrawled another message on the pig pen fence.

"Sometimes the truth is so terrible that the smart pig may be the one who flops down, buries his head in the mud and remains happily ignorant."

Then Elmer G. bowed his head and prayed, "Good morning God. It is cold out here. I hope you're having a better time of it than I am. I'm feeling poorly these days. I've been miserable ever since I found out they're gonna slaughter me one day. I'm having nightmares about my hams hanging in the rafters of the smoke-house, right along side slabs of bacon, banging into each other as they swing from side-to-side. You know...God. There is this one other little thing I was wondering about. What I want to know is......why did you have to make me a pig in the first place? I mean.....all I can do is grow up and be slaughtered. Why couldn't you make me something else so that I could live to a ripe old age?"

Elmer G. went quiet for awhile, as he gathered himself up and collected his thoughts. Then he plowed on through with an additional prayer. "God....what I'm trying to say is that if you'd really had your 'A-Game' the day you made me, then you wouldn't have made me a pig. I know that sounds like I'm being critical of your work....and truth be told...I guess I sorta' am. But let me put it another way. If you are as smart as Barley says, then you should have made me something else like........a turkey. If you had been thinking this thing through.....see....you could have made me a pretty, plump Heritage Turkey with those big red, yellow and white tail feathers sprouting out all over the place. Lord....I'd give anything to be a turkey instead of a pig. Amen. Ohh! I almost forgot. Please remember those who are less fortunate than me. Although I don't know who that is, since I can't think of nobody who is worse off than a pig. Amen."

"That wasn't too bad," Elmer G. thought to himself. "Getting my spiritual focus is gonna' be easier than I thought. It's like a pri-

vate gripe session with God. And it didn't hardly take no time a'tall. I didn't even break a sweat. If I'd known that praying was this easy…why I might've started sooner."

Elmer G. had started his day by bowing his head, clasping his hands together, raising his face skyward and asking God for guidance. He felt like he had built up some goodwill with God, so he spent the rest of the morning raising cain. He threw mud at some of the other pigs. Elmer G. pushed two smaller pigs out of his way at the feeding trough. A good friend of Elmer G.'s, named Hattie, dropped a piece of bread on the ground. Elmer G. stepped on it and laughed. Hattie started crying, as she raced away.

Next, Elmer G. hooked up with Scruff Daddy and his gang. He joined them as they crawled under a loose board in the fence and escaped. Elmer G., Scruff Daddy, Freddy, So-So, Ben, Glen, Theodore and the rest of the gang roamed around the woods for several hours before Farmer Brown caught them and dragged them back home kicking and screaming. After Farmer Brown unceremoniously threw them back into the hog pens, Elmer G. leisurely wallowed in the cool mud until suppertime. Pleased as pie with himself….he was.

After supper, an excited and filthy Elmer G. raced over and told Barley how easy it was for him to find his spiritual center. "Why I jumped up this morning and prayed up a storm for all of five minutes," bragged Elmer G.

"What did you do the rest of the day?" asked Barley, amused at Elmer G.'s new found enthusiasm for prayer.

"I gave God the heads-up," said Elmer G. "I told Him that if He was really smart, He would have made me a turkey instead of a pig. That way I could live until a ripe old age without worrying about being slaughtered," said Elmer G., beaming at his own intelligence. "Looks to me like I may be smarter than God. You may wanna' send your next platter of prayers to me instead of God."

"Maybe so, Elmer G. Then again, maybe not," said Barley.

"What you talking about, Barley?" asked Elmer G.

"Elmer G...........you ever heard of Thanksgiving?"

"Nope," said Elmer G.

"In late November each year," said Barley, "every family in America roasts a turkey for supper. That's the day they celebrate all the blessings they've received from God during the year. The suicide rate in October and November and December among turkeys is higher than that of any animal."

"I 'shore wish God had made me something else so I could live forever," said Elmer G., in a wishful tone of voice.

"Well," said Barley, "there are only three things that can live forever. A lie, a section of the United States Tax Code and a federal program."

Elmer G. chewed on this information a while, then said, "Well, neither one of them would work. Maybe God should have made me a chicken."

"Ever heard of Kentucky General Fried Chicken?" asked Barley. "Pluto's Chicken Shack? Filet-a-la-Chicken Shacks? Roscoe's Chicken Shacks? These are restaurants where humans sell fried chickens as their main menu item. Course...they sell vegetable side dishes too. But it's mainly fried chicken that folks pop in to pick up. First, they light a blazing fire up under a metal deep fryer basket, pour two yards of grease into the fryer and bring it to a boil. They cut the chickens up into individual pieces. You've got your legs, thighs, wings, breasts and your necks. Then they sprinkle twelve different herbs and spices on the meat to season it and add flavor. Next, they drop the seasoned chicken pieces into the boiling, bubbling hot grease, which splatters all over the walls and the floor 'cause it's hot————and then..."

"Alright! I get the picture!" screamed Elmer G.

"Course, if you were a chicken on a small homestead," said Barley, "they wouldn't do all that stuff to kill and eat you."

"They wouldn't?" said Elmer G.

"Nope," said Barley. "They would just snatch you up by your scrawny neck and whip you around in the air over their head a couple of times to generate some decent spin action and snap your head off. Your headless body would be still running around the yard flopping around every which-a-way trying to find its head and..."

"Okay Barley!!" said Elmer G. "Forget about me being a chicken. Maybe I could be a sheep. Then I could live on a quiet farm. Keep myself warm with my white fuzzy wool overcoat."

"Ever heard of a dish called grilled lamb chops?" asked Barley. "They serve 'em in all the finer restaurants, especially at Easter."

"Then God should've made me a lobster," said Elmer G. "I'd have me some sharp claws. And a hard shell for a body. Be a pretty hot pink color and swim around all day in the ocean."

"Well Elmer G., you would be hot and swim around all day, but probably not the way you think."

"What you talking about, Barley?"

"Ever heard of the Orange Lobster Restaurant chain?" asked Barley. "They put a number on each lobsters' backs. Then you sit in a tank of water until one of the customers picks you out."

"To take me home for a pet?" said Elmer G.

"Not exactly," said Barley. "While you're still alive, they drop you into a pot of boiling water until you're nice and tender. Then they serve you up to paying customers on a white, porcelain dinner plate with a small side cup of hot melted butter. They even have a little tiny lobster fork they use to dig your meat out of your shell after they boil you."

"Forgitdaboutit then," said Elmer G. "I don't wanna' be a lobster. How about God making me a horse?"

"Elmer G., humans slaughter horses to make dog food. They'd grind your meat up and stuff you inside these tin cans and stamp 'Nibbles and Vits' on the outside on a paper label. Sell 'em at the local supermarkets for what——-thirty-seven cents a can."

"Could I be a shrimp?" asked Elmer G. "Would that save me?"

"Small chance," said Barley. "Ever heard of Short Juan Silverton's South American Seafood Restaurants? They'll plop you into a pan of cornmeal batter mix. Next, they'll toss you into a boiling basket of popping hot grease. Fry you up to a nice crisp, golden brown texture. Then they serve you up to their customers nice and hot on a platter with a side order of cole slaw so fresh it'll make a pass at you. And don't forget those crispy French fries."

"I didn't want to go this low, but maybe God should have made me a snake," said Elmer G., with a bit more confidence in his voice. "Surely nobody eats snakes, since they're poisonous."

"Look at Bobby Lee's cowboy boots the next time he's down this way," said Barley.

"They're made out of snakeskins...aren't they?" said Elmer G.

"Yep," said Barley, with a slight nod of his head.

"How about if I was an alligator?" said Elmer G. "My teeth would be twelve inches long. Surely nobody would carry me around in their lunch bags."

"You're right," said Barley.

"It's about time I found something safe I can be," said Elmer G. "See there. I told you I'm smarter than God."

"Nobody would carry you around in their lunch bags," said Barley. "But a whole lot of women would be carrying you around on their shoulders as 'shoulder bags'. Elmer G., they would use your hide to make ladies' handbags and wallets. Either that, or they'll make you into a pair of alligator shoes. Or a nice belt. Unless you'd prefer to be a watchband. You know something, Elmer G......you'd make a pretty impressive alligator briefcase."

"Forget being an alligator," said Elmer G. "I could be Elmer G. the Elephant. I could be a gigantic elephant with huge ivory tusks. I'd kill any human that came near me."

"If you were an elephant, you wouldn't have to worry about humans coming near you," said Barley.

"That's more like it," said Elmer G., as he puffed his chest out at having found an animal he could be that was safe from humans. "That's what I'm talking about. I finally found an animal that humans will stay away from. You sure I don't have to worry about humans coming close to me if God made me an elephant?"

"I'm sure," said Barley. "You don't have to worry about them getting close to you if you were an elephant. At least not any closer than a thousand yards."

"Why a thousand yards?" asked Elmer G.

"That's about how close poachers would need to get to blast a giant bullet hole in your head," said Barley. "From one thousand yards away. Poacher. Rifle. Scope on top of rifle. Poacher pulls trigger on rifle. Bam! Elmer G. the elephant has big old hole in the middle of his head. Elmer G. the elephant is dead."

"Why Barley? Why would somebody shoot a harmless elephant?"

"To carve off your tusks with giant, stainless-steel knives to make ivory jewelry," said Barley. "It's illegal, but the poachers somehow manage to get over their guilty conscience and blast you in the head with a 50 caliber rifle anyway."

"How about Elmer G. the Gorilla?" said Elmer G., in a hopeful voice. "I'd be fierce. Strong. Scary looking."

"Locked in the zoo," said Barley. "No freedom. So few left in the jungles that they're almost extinct."

"Lion," said Elmer G. "King of the jungle. The whole jungle will be my palace."

"They've moved the Lion King's Palace to a new location," answered Barley.

"Moved it to where?" asked Elmer G.

"The Lion King's Palace is now located at the Municipal City Zoo," said Barley. "His Majesty now resides two doors down from the Almost Extinct Gorillas. Elmer G., the Lion King, will be lying on a rock...sunning himself....looking bored as all git' out."

"So......being a pig may be the best thing that could've happened to me," said Elmer G., resigning himself to his fate. "I'm better off than a turkey, but not as lucky as a lion. It seems like how I feel about my life depends on how much better off or worse off I think somebody else is."

"Maybe so, Elmer G. Maybe so. But look. Don't go to making yourself depressed. You need your strength. What else did you do today?"

"Well," said Elmer G., "I threw mud at some of the smaller pigs. Just to keep them on the up-and-up. It was good exercise for them."

"Why was that good exercise for them?"

"I made them run from me while dodging those mud clods I was throwing at them. Sorta' like forced jogging, you might say."

"What else did you do?" asked Barley, prodding him on.

"I stepped on Hattie's bread and smashed it into the mud. Next, I hung out with Scruff Daddy's gang. We rooted through a hole in the south portion of the fence and ran away. Talk about a rippin' good time! I mean we laid one on! We had us a fine time roaming 'round the woods. We scooted off and ran like crazy when Farmer Brown tried to catch us. Whoooo boy!! I'm still tired! I had a blast of a good time. I even kicked at Farmer Brown when he caught me."

"Well Elmer G.," said Barley, "finding your spiritual center is a mite larger task than saying an insincere prayer when you wake up in the morning, then spending the rest of the day being bad. What you want to shoot for are sincere prayers in which you ask God for wisdom to help you make good decisions all day long. Your actions each day should match your prayers for guidance. If you don't find your spiritual center through prayer, you'll find yourself posing as a ham on a dinner plate with a family of humans saying grace over you right before they eat you for dinner. Think on these things and come see me again."

Reluctantly, Elmer G. left. He trudged over to his sleeping area in the corner of the pig pen and scooted way back inside the dark recesses of his hog-head barrel, with his head balanced on the edge of the front end of the barrel. He wasn't sure if he was cut out of the right stuff to master the survival lessons Barley was sharing with him. But he knew in his heart that if he did not try harder, he would be marching up onto that dreaded trailer truck for an ill-fated trip to the slaughter house.

CHAPTER 7

Doing The Right Thing

"It's easy praying and asking God to make someone else do the right thing, rather than trying to do the right thing yourself."

The next morning Elmer G. bowed his head and prayed for wisdom. He also prayed for spiritual guidance. Elmer G. asked God to help him make the right choices. Next, he prayed for the strength to avoid making bad choices."

He finished his prayers so quickly that he didn't think God would be satisfied with such a sparse offering. So he wandered around as he said his prayers from this point forward. Initially, he started out praying for worthwhile things like world peace and a cure for ticks and flies. As the sun beat down on him he commenced to gravitate towards slightly more selfish prayers. He prayed for chunky slop portions. In particular, he asked God to drop him off three whole cooked potatoes, four slivers of peach pie, two thick wedges of cornbread, four French rolls, six cinnamon buns and a gaggle of cooked broccoli stumps. Not wanting to appear selfish in God's eyes, he ordered the broccoli stumps to give away to his friends. Next, he prayed for God to provide him with some tall shady trees, sticky mud pits and a bunch of other what-nots, mostly additional foodstuff he liked to snack on. Finally, he got tuckered out and just quit praying. Since he'd spent so much time praying for slop, he felt guilty tramping off and getting into trouble.

So, on this particular morning, Elmer G. didn't throw mud at the smaller pigs playing in the mud. Instead, he sauntered over and wallowed in the cool mud himself. He thought to himself, "if I get myself dirty enough, maybe Farmer Brown won't send me to the slaughter house, since they may not wanna' eat a dirty ham. Being good all day makes for a very long day. Being good all day seems darn near impossible. Time sure drips by slowly when you're acting good."

Although Elmer G. managed to be good for most of the day, he discovered he could resist 'most everything....except temptation. Scruff Daddy and his gang dropped by and told Elmer G. they were breaking out again through a hole in the north fence. Elmer G. reflected briefly on his new-found religion, then he raced over to the hole in the fence. He was the first one scampering away in a cloud of red dust, as he romped through the leafy woods, head-ed for Bull Creek, where he could wallow in the mud pits and fin-ish enjoying his short spell of freedom.

Later, he got tired of playing in the cool, bubbling, dirty brown waters of Bull Creek, so he wandered on back home, wet, tired and sticky. As he lazed under an oak tree, he was not sure what to do next. He spent a good part of the day thinking about his situation, but he didn't come up with any worthwhile solutions.

He scrunched up his face in frustration, as he thought briefly about giving up on Barley's self-improvement ideas.

"I can go back to my old life," he thought to himself. "It 'shore was a lot easier than this scavenger hunt I'm on. Even though I'm searching for salvation from the slaughter house, I feel like I'm lost. All these dang blasted rules Barley's got me living under are making me feel plumb hemmed in. Right now, I'm 'bout as nervous as a cat selling stale biscuits at a Dog Show. I guess I could quit Barley's self-improvement program. But, there's just one problem. Now that Barley done gone and stretched my mind with these new fangled ideas, it's kinda' hard to ignore all these facts sitting across the table, relaxing on their platters of knowledge, winking at me."

He thought to himself, "I know in my heart that I have to either change my ways, or I'm definitely going to be carted off to the slaughter house."

Elmer G. decided to visit Barley and see if he could help him sort things out.

"Hi Barley," said Elmer G., as he walked up.

"How you doing?" said Barley, barely glancing up.

"I'm maintaining," said Elmer G. "Everything's copathetic. Barley, I've got an idea I wanna' run by you."

"Shoot," said Barley. "What's on your mind?"

"I've been giving a lot of thought to figuring out a way to avoid the slaughter house without working myself to death. I wanna' become a Disciple and work with Jesus, like the other twelve Disciples. If I became a full-fledged, official Disciple, then I could spend my time convincing some of these other no-account pigs to get religion. That way, I'd have more free time to play. I could spend part of the day harassing everybody else into finding *their* spiritual centers and play the rest of the day. If I was a Disciple, maybe God would give me some extra credit for all the lost souls I helped save. This way, God would still have a reason to usher me into a front row seat in Hog Heaven. If I became a Disciple, it would be easier than living proper and finding my own spiritual center."

"I don't think you're gonna' be able to become a Disciple, Elmer G.," said Barley.

"How come?" asked Elmer G.

"Well," said Barley, looking thoughtful. "You know I've been studying the Bible. It's a pretty hefty book, so I'm not claiming I read all of it, but I b'lieve I can fill in the blank places for you. According to the Bible, Jesus reached His limit after recruiting the twelve original Disciples. He had such a time of it trying to teach those twelve how to heal the sick and administer to the poor that He decided not to take on any new Disciples for a few million years. Matthew, Luke, Mark, John, Judas, Peter, James and the rest of 'em plumb wore Jesus' patience down to the size of a piece of corn silk."

"Why?" asked Elmer G. "What did they do?"

"They forgot to bring the wine for the wedding," said Barley. "And Jesus had to pull their marshmallows outta' the fire by performing a miracle and turning water into wine. Then, when Jesus preached His Sermon on the Mount over in Decapolis, bordering the east side of the Sea of Galilee, somebody forgot to bring the fish and bread. It was hot out there and things got all confused. The people attending the Sermon got hongry' and started complaining. Jesus had to whip up some fried fish and French loaves on the spot for over five thousand people without no proper advance notice a-tall."

"Who forgot the fish and bread?" asked Elmer G.

"From what I read," said Barley, "Jesus took Judas over on the back side of the hill after He finished feeding the multitudes and had a heart-to-heart talk with him."

"Was Jesus mad?" asked Elmer G.

"Nawww," said Barley. "You know Jesus don't get mad at nobody. According to one of the other Disciples, Jesus' told Judas, "Judas, you know we are a team. Everybody on the team has responsibilities. Those responsibilities are clearly defined. When you didn't perform *your* responsibilities, you disappointed these five thousand people, you let Me down, you let the team down and most importantly, you let yourself down. Now, Matthew and James were responsible for our transportation. I brought the balmy weather. And what were you supposed to do?" Judas mumbled "I was supposed to bring the fish and bread." "That's right," said Jesus. "And did you do that?" "No," said Judas softly. "Jesus, I forgot." Jesus said, "Hahhmm," as he exhaled and let His breath escape with a frustrated sound. Then Jesus said, "that's okay, Judas. It's alright. I'm not blaming you. And I'm certainly not angry with you. Matter of fact....if you want to see angry....you should see the fists-to-cuffs session My Daddy had with Job, but I'll leave that for another day. I still love you, Judas. And you have my complete confidence. The reason we are having this talk is because I want you to grow from this experience. As you know, My people....being My Disciples...are My most important assets. You have a lot of potential...inside. I am like a coach. I want to help you unleash that potential and become the person you are *capable* of being. If you take this talk the right way you can turn this into a win-win situation and leave here all the better for it. Now, come over her and give me a hug." After they embraced, Jesus said, "let's get back and join the others."

"What happened then?" asked Elmer G.

"The other eleven Disciples were gathered around the water well getting a drink when Judas finally wandered off," said Barley. "They said he looked down-right pitiful, trudging across the field carrying his little brown leather sandals by their straps in his left hand, dragging his bare feet through the dirt. The Disciples said Judas was never quite the same after that."

Barley went on to explain that one of the Disciples forgot to pick up Lazarus' medicine at the pharmacist. Of course, later that day, Lazarus expired. Then Jesus had to hitch up the arms of His robe one more time and go fetch Lazarus back from the dead. By the time the poor man got finished performing various miracles He had planned as part of His own show, then doing all these stray miracles He *hadn't* planned on.....why....He was plumb worn down to nothing more'n a frazzle."

After taking a sip of water, Barley continued. "Now....I heard the first twelve Disciples were poor learners," whispered Barley in a low, conspiratorial tone of voice. "The word I got is that they rubbed Jesus' nerves raw to the point that He just plumb lost His taste for training any more new Disciples. According to the story I got, there may have been fourteen original Disciples. But......a couple of 'em may have drowned trying to master the walk on the water miracle."

"Seems to me," said Elmer G., "all the prime jobs, like being an official Disciple, are always snatched up by somebody else."

"When it comes to the Disciple business," said Barley. "You're right."

"Barley," said Elmer G., "I'm curious about something else."

"What's that?" asked Barley.

"Surely some other pigs around here besides you have avoided going to the slaughter house. Somebody must've figured out how to skip the slaughter house without getting religion. There's got to be an easier way to avoid the slaughter house besides praying. Being good all the time can't be the only way outta' this mess."

"Now that you mention it," said Barley, "I do seem to remember some pigs that did just what you said. There were some pigs that took a shortcut to avoid the slaughter house. They tried some different schemes besides getting religion in order to by-pass the slaughter house."

"That's what I'm talking about," said Elmer G., as his breathing quickened in anticipation. "Now we're rolling in the right mud pit. We're cooking in grease now, Barley! What are some of the ways they used to try and escape going to the slaughter house...besides being good all the time and getting religion?"

"Well, let me think a minute now," said Barley. "There was this friend of mine named Tiny Muffins. Tiny decided to eat his way out of the slaughter house line."

"Eat his way out? Barley...what you talking about? How can you eat your way out of going to the slaughter house?"

"If I'm lying, Elmer G....... I'm flying. I swear to you on a stack of hot buttermilk biscuits that Tiny Muffins was one of the smallest pigs in the pig pens...when he started out. He was smaller than you used to be before you started porking up. Tiny tried to eat his way outta' going to the slaughter house. I know it's true 'cause I was there. Sure as I'm sittin' here."

"Let me repeat myself here," said Elmer G. "How in the world can a hog eat his way out of going to the slaughter house? It don't make no sense. No sense a tall."

"Well," said Barley, leaning forward and dropping his voice a shade, as he warmed up to telling his story. "Tiny came up with a theory that some humans could get so rich that they were too rich to be killed by other humans. So he applied that same theory to pigs."

"I give up," announced Elmer G. "I'm lost."

"Just stick with me for just a little longer, Elmer G. I'm gonna' break it down for you. Basically, you see.....Tiny decided that he would eat like a hog, pork up and get too fat to be killed. Tiny's theory was that if he weighed in at over one thousand pounds, then Farmer Brown couldn't send him to the slaughter house."

"Why not?" asked Elmer G.

"Why not?" echoed Barley. "Elmer G....don't you know nuthin'? Let me run this by you one more time. Tiny was figuring that if he got too fat, then Farmer Brown couldn't send him to the slaughter house because he wouldn't fetch a top price. Everybody knows that."

"Well I didn't know it," said Elmer G., in a defensive voice. "It just seems like Tiny would be worth more at the slaughter house if he weighted more."

"It does seem that way," said Barley. "But that's not how it works. The peoples at the slaughter house don't wanna' pay cold cash for flabby fat."

"Finish telling me about Tiny," said Elmer G.

"The peoples that own the slaughter house don't wanna' buy hogs that are too fat," explained Barley. "They want lean meat to sell. In other words, a medium-sized, lean pig is worth more than a fat hog. When humans barbeque a rack of pork ribs and commence to frying a stack of pork chops, they don't wanna' be messing with too much fat. They wanna' clamp their dentures into some lean pork chops. Tiny thought that if he gained a ton of weight, then his hams, ribs and pork chops would be soaked in too much fatty tissue. And if he was too fat, then he wouldn't to be worth much money on a per pound basis at the slaughter house."

"Did Tiny gain the extra weight?" asked Elmer G.

"You betcha' he did," said Barley. "That boy started gobbling up everything in sight. He was tying on the feedbag like you wouldn't believe."

"Was Tiny's theory right?" asked Elmer G.

"Yep," said Barley, pursing his lips in a thoughtful manner like he was deep in thought. "His theory was right on the money. 'Shore was. Farmer Brown weighed Tiny three times before he decided he wasn't gonna' be able to truck him down to the slaughter house."

"Okay then," said Elmer G. "Go on with your story."

"Farmer Brown decided to keep Tiny at home because he was too fat to truck off to the slaughter house," explained Barley. "Then he stood there by the north gate stirring around in half-circles with his hands shoved deep down in his pants pockets, looking depressed and down-in-the-mouth. After a long, uncomfortable silence, Farmer Brown announced to Bobby Lee that Tiny was too fat to fetch much money at the slaughter house. Farmer Brown told Bobby Lee, "I 'spect we gonna' have to let Tiny live. It's not like we got much of a choice." And that's just what he did. You can say what you wanna' about him, but Farmer Brown is a man of his word. If he says he's gonna' slaughter you, then you can bet the bank he's gonna' respect his word and kill you. Yep! He 'shore will. But on the flip side, if he says he's gonna' spare your life, then you can bet he's gonna' do just that. Pigs can say what they want about him, but for my money Old Farmer Brown is an honorable man."

"Well," announced Elmer G. "That's proof enough for me. I'm gonna' to gain a thousand pounds like Tiny. 'Cause Tiny was smart!"

"That he was," echoed Barley. "Tiny 'shore was smart. I kinda' miss old Tiny."

"What do you mean, you kinda' miss old Tiny?" said Elmer G. Where Tiny at now?"

"Where Tiny at now?" repeated Barley softly, as though he did not understand the question.

"Yes Barley," said Elmer G. "You heard me. You're just stalling for time. Where is Tiny at now?"

"Dead," said Barley in a small, solemn tone of voice, as he quickly looked away from Elmer G. and focused his gaze upwards towards the sky like he was suddenly absorbed in counting clouds.

"What?" asked Elmer G. "Speak up please. I can't hear a word you said. Where is Tiny now?"

"Tiny's uhhhh.....sorta' dead," said Barley, still gazing skyward and counting the clouds.

"Sorta' dead!?" said Elmer G. "What in tarnation does that mean!? He's either dead or he ain't dead. Which is it?"

"Drop the "sorta'", advised Barley.

"So you're saying Tiny is dead?" asked Elmer G.

"Yep," said Barley. "He's dead."

"Dead?!!" repeated Elmer G., like a parrot in training.

"Yesirree," said Barley, relieved to finally get this revelation off of his chest. Now he could open up all the throttles and finish plowing this field. "Tiny's pushing up four leaf clovers out back in that field on the west side of the pig pens."

"What?!" said Elmer G. "You said yourself how smart Tiny was. How can he be dead?"

"Oh!" said Barley, huffing up with an attitude. "So what you're saying is that smart pigs can't die?"

"I'm not saying smart pigs can't die," said Elmer G. "But I thought you said Farmer Brown didn't sell Tiny to the slaughter house."

"That's true," said Barley. "He didn't sell Tiny to the slaughter house."

"Then what happened to him?" asked Elmer G.

"He died a few days after he got a reprieve from going to the slaughter house," said Barley.

"Died?! From what?!!" asked Elmer G.

"Calm down Elmer G. You gonna' stress yourself out, son. You know they got studies by medical experts that say stress can kill you."

"You're right," said Elmer G. "I need to calm down and relax. I wouldn't wanna' risk dying from stress——when I can wait awhile and get my throat slit at the local slaughter house!!! Okay. Breathe deeply. Okay now. Now I'm ready. Finish telling me about Tiny."

"Tiny was so fat that he slumped down in a heap one afternoon, as he was waddling over to the slop trough," said Barley. "It was a sad sight. So sad. Poor Tiny. Makes my heart heavy even now thinking about it. The boy weighed twelve hundred and forty-six pounds. Or was it twelve hundred and forty-seven pounds? I think he weighed twelve hundred and forty-six pounds because I remember forty-six used to be my mama's lucky number. But daddy's lucky number was forty-seven and sometimes I get them confused. Elmer G., my memory ain't nothing like it used to be when I was your age. Back then, I could remember everything. I remember a time when once I got a number in my head…..any number…you could ask me a week later and I could rattle it right off the tip of my tongue. Like it wasn't nothing. But now….I can't hardly remember my own birthday. I guess I'm having a senior moment. Elmer G.——do me a favor. Ask me what day my birthday is. Try me. I used to remember when I could…"

"Barley!! You are driving me crazy with these ramblings that don't have nothing to do with nothing! Pu…lease finish telling me about Tiny!" shouted Elmer G. in exasperation.

"If I was small minded…I'd make you find out about Tiny somewheres else," said Barley, glaring at Elmer G. "Even though I like you Elmer G., you need to be nicer to me. As I was a-saying….Tiny was a massive fella…he was. And that's why he had a heart attack. His poor heart was working too hard trying to pump blood through that massive body of his. He looked right pitiful lugging all that extra weight around. The poor fella' developed high blood pressure. Bottom line is that Tiny got so fat he just plumb wore his little heart out."

"So what you're saying is that Tiny gained weight to avoid going to the slaughter house," said Elmer G.

"Yep," said Barley.

"And the extra weight killed him," said Elmer G.

"Dead as a doornail," said Barley.

"Is there any other way to avoid the slaughter house besides eating yourself to death?" asked Elmer G., with just a hint of sarcasm in his voice. "Barley, you've *got* to tell me something that is gonna' advance the ball further down the field. I mean….help me out here."

"Well…there was another friend of mine named Plumper Willis," said Barley, as he got excited again. "Now….Plumper was smart. He was even smarter than Tiny. Yes he was. Plumper was nobody's fool. That boy could think things out to a logical conclusion. Plumber was nice too. He wasn't saddity acting a-tall."

"Finally……somebody with some sense," said Elmer G. "How did Plumper escape going to the slaughter house?"

"Plumper was already a hefty fella'," said Barley. "Born big….he was. And stayed that-a-way. His mama darn near died trying to push him outta' her womb. About twelve minutes after he was born, Plumper got up and wobbled over to snack on some slop. Yessiree. Plumper was born big. Everybody knew Plumper was gonna' fetch Farmer Brown a ton of money at the slaughter house. You see, Plumper was large, but not too fat. That boy was lean in all the right places. If you looked at Plumper, you could just picture his impressive ribs laid out in a fine fashion on a smoking hot barbecue grill. He was the perfect size to fetch a top price."

"So, what you're saying is that Plumper knew Farmer Brown had his number," said Elmer G.

"Oh yeah, baby," said Barley, practically bubbling over with excitement, as he strolled back through the dirt roads of his younger years. "Farmer Brown had Plumper at number one on his top ten hit list…riding with a bullet. Now that you brought that up….I'm gonna' tell you something I saw with my own eyes. Some days…Farmer Brown would come down here to these pig pens and just lean up against the top fence rails and stare."

"At what?" asked Elmer G.

"At Plumper," said Barley.

"What in the world for?" asked Elmer G.

"Farmer Brown was looking at Plumper like he was in a daze," explained Barley. "He had that far-away look in his eyes. Like a man absorbed in silently counting the mad money he was gonna' make off Plumper when he sold him to the slaughter house. Yep. He was measuring Plumper for a date with a roasting pan. The way he stared at that pig, I wouldn't have been surprised if Farmer Brown had whipped out a couple of slices of Colonial bread, a slab of cheese, a chunk of tomato and just made a sammich out of Plumper right then and there."

"Barley…that's awful," said Elmer G.

"Well, it's true," said Barley. "Sometimes, at dusk, Farmer Brown would be staring at Plumper and counting pork ribs and dollars bills. In his mind, he saw pork chops and dollar bills waltzing around on the top rails of the pig pen fences, dancing the night away. Farmer Brown had his money and his mind and his mind on Plumper's shoulder hams, pork chops and ribs. See....Farmer Brown was planning on making some mad money offa' Plumper when he sold him at the slaughter house."

"That's such a terrible picture you're describing," said Elmer G. "To tell you the truth, you're depressing me with this kinda' talk."

"I'm just telling it the way it happened," said Barley. "Besides, that's all just a part of the circle of life. But let me get back to telling you what happened to Plumper. Now Plumper was nobody's fool. No siree! He had a good head on top of his shoulders...and he wanted to keep it there. Plumper was such a fine hog, he knew his own self that he was a prime target for the slaughter house....'cause he was smart that way. Plumper was a thinker. Boy could figure stuff out. One day, he thought up the perfect plan for escaping the trip to the slaughter house."

"What was Plumper's plan?" asked Elmer G. anxiously.

"Plumper's plan?" mumbled Barley, as he barely avoided dozing off to sleep.

"Barley! Wake up!!"

"Oh yeah," said Barley. "Plumper did come up with a plan to avoid the slaughter house. He decided to starve himself as a foolproof way to avoid going to the slaughter house."

"Starve himself?!" asked Elmer G. in amazement. "Why in the world would he do that?"

"So he could get skinny," said Barley. "That way, Farmer Brown couldn't sell him for much money on a per pound basis, least not enough to make it worthwhile. I mean.....by the time you deduct Farmer Brown's sunk capital costs for slop, water, fence repairs and corn mash to raise Plumper, plus the trucking expenses to haul him to the slaughter house and what-not...he'd be lucky if he made more'n a nickel in profits for his efforts."

"Well then," said Elmer G., "I'll starve myself down to a skinny size like Plumper. Finally, somebody has an idea that works."

"Ahhhummm!" Barley cleared his throat to get Elmer G.'s attention.

"Plumper died anyway," said Barley reluctantly, in a soft stage whisper.

"What?! What do you mean, "Plumper died anyway?" Come on Barley! Don't tell me that!! How did Plumper die? Old age?" asked Elmer G., in a wishful tone of voice.

"Nope," said Barley.

"Then, what'd he die from?" asked Elmer G.

"Starvation," answered Barley.

"Starvation?!" shouted Elmer G. "How could Plumper die from starvation in a hog pen fulla' slop? Look at all these giant slop troughs 'round here. How is a hog gonna' die from starvation up in here? You can almost gain weight around here by sniffing the air."

"Plumper had a unique situation. The boy got so skinny from not eating that he wasn't nothing but a bag of bones. He staggered every time a light breeze whacked him in the sides. One day a pig named Wallace Jones tried to fly Plumper like he was a kite. He got him quite a ways up in the air before an old boar named Cyrus made him pull Plumper down."

"Barley, I still don't understand how Plumper starved to death with all this slop 'round here."

"After Plumper lost as much weight as he wanted and Farmer Brown spared his life by not sending him to the slaughter house, he tried to start eating right again so he could gain some of the weight back. But he was too weak to walk over to the feeding troughs in time to eat. All the best slop was always gone by the time he staggered over to the feeding troughs. You know how these pigs push and shove to be first in line. Plumper was too weak to fight his way up to a good spot to eat. So he starved to death.

Right smack dab in smelling distance of all that sumptuous slop. Don't that just beat all? What a way to check out. He was so close to the feeding troughs when he died that slop actually splashed onto his legs, as he scarfed up his last few breaths of air. It's kinda' sad that Plumper died of starvation a few measly inches from slop and salvation."

"Barley....I can't believe Plumper starved to death. And you just said yourself how smart he was and all."

"Don't go hatin' on me!" exclaimed Barley. "I'm just plowing through the facts the way they happened. When Farmer Brown walked up to Plumper laying sprawled out dead....in front of the feeding troughs, he gently reached inside the front pocket of his overalls and whipped out a teaspoon. Then he carried him out back over there and commenced to digging Plumper's little grave with that bent teaspoon. There wasn't but a handful of meat left on poor Plumper. About enough for one or two ham sammiches. That is....if you use one piece a ham for each sammich and don't go to stacking the ham slices to the rafters because..."

"Barley!" yelled a frustrated Elmer G.

"All I'm saying is that one slice of ham is plenty for a sammich. Especially if you add a thick slab of cheddar cheese and a leaf or two of green lettuce and a chunk of ruby red tomato......"

"Barley!!" screamed Elmer G. "You quit that rambling on about ham sammiches and finish your story! I mean it!"

"Hold your horses!" said Barley. "I'm just telling the story the best way I know how!"

"But the details you're giving," said Elmer G. "You 'bout to scare me to death."

"I just wanna' make sure you get the flavor of the story," said Barley. "That way....you'll have a taste for what *really* happened."

"Well, get on with it, why don't you?" said Elmer G.

"Don't be getting mad at me," said Barley, drawing himself up. "Anyway, like I was saying, Plumper was so little that Farmer

Brown wrapped him in a sweaty handkerchief he dug outta' the pocket of his overalls. Since Plumper was so skinny and all from his starvation diet, Farmer Brown didn't feel he deserved a full prayer. So he just mumbled the shortest prayer in the Bible, which is "Jesus wept." And then he plopped Plumper into a shallow grave right next to Tiny."

"In spite of what happened to Plumper," said Elmer G. "I still can't believe nobody has figured out how to avoid the slaughter house. Surely somebody has figured out a foolproof way to get around going to the slaughter house without going to the trouble of getting religion and all this other foolishness."

"Well, there was another pig named Scooter Simmons," said Barley. "Scooter tried to beat the system another way. Scooter was smarter than Tiny and Plumper put together."

"Now you're talking my language," said Elmer G. "What did Scooter do to beat the system?"

"He acted like he was sick all the time," said Barley, as he started getting excited again about telling another story.

"Why?" asked Elmer G.

"Why what?" said Barley.

"Why would acting like he was sick keep Scooter from going to the slaughter house?" asked Elmer G.

"Don't you know nothing, Elmer G.? Farmer Brown can't sell sick hogs to the slaughter house."

"How come?" asked Elmer G.

"How come? Elmer G., you are right pitiful. Farmer Brown can't sell sick hogs to the slaughter house because infected meat from a sick hog would make humans sick if they ate it."

"Like I said," said Elmer G., "what's wrong with that? They're killing us pigs left and right."

"What's wrong with that?!" said Barley. "Are you just scatter-brained or what? I can't believe you formed your lips to ask me that. Boy...humans have health code regulations they have to meet. Let me break it down to you. If Farmer Brown sold tainted meat from sick hogs to the slaughter house and people started dying right and left because of that, then that would be the end of Farmer Brown's hog selling business."

"But wouldn't that be good for us pigs?" said Elmer G. "I mean…if he didn't have any meat business, then we wouldn't have to be herded off to the slaughter house."

"Ohhh," said Barley. "So you wanna' beat the system. I tell you what. If you wanna' know how to beat the system, then let me finish telling you about Scooter."

"Did Scooter beat the system?" asked Elmer G. "Did he survive?"

"Almost," said Barley. "The boy was doing fine, but he got carried away with his acting abilities. He started getting praise and applause from the other pigs about his slick strategy. Naturally, all that fame swelled his head, which was considerably large to begin with. Scooter got carried away…..literally. He overdid the acting sick role."

"What happened to him?" asked Elmer G.

"Scooter was limping around at first," said Barley. "Like most Hollywood wannabes, he got too deep into his role. He started looking all sad and down in the mouth. Then the boy commenced to coughing and swaying from side-to-side every time Farmer Brown came around the hog pens. The closer Farmer Brown came to Scooter, the harder Scooter coughed, wheezed, fell out on the ground twitching and jerking his body around. Scooter even rubbed mud in his eyes."

"Why did he do that?" asked Elmer G.

"So he could make 'em look red and irritated," said Barley. But, like I was saying, all of his play acting was working too. Everybody felt bad for him. Farmer Brown excused Scooter from the next slaughter house group. But, like I said, the boy got carried away with his acting abilities. One day Scooter fell out at the pig pens in a fake faint as Farmer Brown was approaching him."

"What did Farmer Brown do?"

"Well," said Barley, "when Scooter fainted under that scorching sun, Farmer Brown evidently felt sorry for poor Scooter. He got sick of Scooter being so sick all the time. Farmer Brown had tears in his eyes, as he stared at poor, sick Scooter lying there on the ground in a helpless heap."

"So Farmer Brown set Scooter free?" said Elmer G.

"Sort of," said Barley. "I guess you could say Farmer Brown set Scooter free......sort of."

"What do you mean...sort of set him free?" asked Elmer G.

"Farmer Brown whipped out his pistol," said Barley, with the excitement rising in his voice. "Then he cocked it.....and blasted a single bullet right smack in-between Scooter's eyes. Put him outta' his misery. Farmer Brown felt sorry for Scooter, watching him suffering like that every day. So he thought he was doing him a favor by blasting a hole in his head. There was one piece of good news in all this though."

"Good news!? What good news?" asked a puzzled Elmer G.

"Scooter was doing such a good job play-acting," said Barley, "that he had his eyes closed like he had really fainted. So the good news is that he never saw the bullet whizzing his way. After he shot him, Farmer Brown carried Scooter away and tossed him in a deep grave out back, next to Plumper. As you can see, Tiny, Plumber and Scooter didn't fare that well in their efforts to escape the slaughter house."

"No," said Elmer G., "they didn't fare well at all. But yet and still...Barley, somebody must've figured out a way to escape the slaughter house. I just need to find out how they did it."

"Well now," said Barley, "a long, long time ago, there were these two pigs that were brothers."

"You mean they were Black?" asked Elmer G. "They were African-American pigs?"

"No!" said Barley, in exasperation. "You nit-wit! They were blood brothers born in the same litter. One was named Oraville and the other brother was named Willobur. Their last name was 'Right'. The Right Brothers were fascinated with science and technological mumbo jumbo. They were always puttering around in their little make-shift workshop building mechanical things and what-nots."

"Like what?" asked Elmer G.

"At first they built a printing press," said Barley. "They printed little newsletters. But they found out most pigs at that time didn't care much about reading. So next, they built a mechanical wheelbarrow that worked fine, except they forgot to add brakes. They quit that venture after they crashed into Bull Creek and almost drowned. Later, when Oraville and Willobur found out that Farmer Brown was sending us pigs to the slaughter house, they decided to use their scientific knowledge to escape from the pig pens forever."

"Now we're talking," said Elmer G. "Finally we've got some smart pigs that decided to make a break for the border. What was their escape plan?"

"The Right Brothers decided they would build some flying machines and fly far, far away from these pig pens," said Barley. "Then they planned to find a new home where they could live in peace and remain in one piece. They hammered away in their workshop for weeks. Their goal was to build some flying wings, which they did, using glue, bird feathers and plywood boards. Finally the big day arrived."

"This shore' is exciting!" exclaimed Elmer G. What happened then?"

"It *is* exciting, ain't it?" said Barley. "I remember it like it was yesterday. Sows, boars and piglets streamed in from all over the county to watch the Right Brothers fly away to freedom. Pigs brought picnic buckets filled to the brim with sumptuous slop. Hogs exchanged gossip, as they laid out on their straw mats to enjoy the goings-ons. It was such a festive occasion. Everybody had a big old time sprawled across the grounds, basking in the warm, soothing sunshine. Finally, Oraville and Willobur climbed up on top of that barn roof right over there. See that spot right at the top, on the front ledge? That's the spot where the Right Brothers launched their historic flight."

"Don't tell me they jumped from way up there," said Elmer G.

"They 'shore did," said Barley.

"That barn roof is pretty high up off the ground, Barley."

"I know," said Barley. "A couple of us mentioned that to Oraville and Willobur, but they laughed and shrugged it off. They said they needed to start their flight at a high altitude so's they could build up some flight speed. According to Oraville, this initial glide would tide them over until their homemade wings got to flapping properly and caught a solid breeze for the extended flight-time. They promised everybody they would soon be soaring over the pig pens like eagles. Willobur said they were taking a short flight for the local pigs and a giant flight for Pigkind. Not a dry eye in the place after he spit out those brave words. Although none of us had a clue what the boy was jabbering about, it sounded so....noble. Oraville said they intended to go where no pig had gone before...and truer words were never spoken."

"Did they fly away?" asked Elmer G.

"Indeed they did," said Barley, in a voice busting with pride, as he gazed off into the distance, lost in his remembrances. "Oraville and Willobur strapped on their wings made out of plywood boards and bird feathers. They each gave a short, inspiring speech about the future of air travel for pigs. After blowing kisses at the crowd, they both jumped high in the air off the barn roof and commenced to flapping their wings for all they were worth. If I close my eyes, I can still see Oraville and Willobur flapping their wings like crazy."

"What I wanna' know is, did the Right Brothers escape from the pig pens?" said Elmer G.

"Well…yes….and….no." said Barley.

"What do you mean by 'yes' and 'no'?" said Elmer G.

"Well…*technically*…Oraville and Willobur did escape from the pig pens," said Barley. "But the problem was that you had several hundred pounds of hams, ribs and pork chops being supported by some slender pieces of plywood lathered up with bird feathers. Obviously, this is not the best use of the laws of physics. Those flying pork chops and hams started spiraling towards the ground like they'd been hit by a Tomahawk Cruise Missile. Oraville splattered over there about ten yards outside the pig pen fence. It took Farmer Brown and his sandy-haired farmhands three days to scape up enough leftovers body parts from Oraville to give him a decent burial."

"How awful!" said Elmer G.

"It was awful," agreed Barley. "The only solid piece of Oraville that they found intact was an extra pork rib."

"An extra rib?" repeated Elmer G.

"Yep," said Barley. "Farmer Brown and his men found one spare rib that belonged to Oraville. Farmer Brown packed it in ice and barbequed it the following Sunday after church services. It was so good that all the humans started barbequing spare ribs from pigs. It started a whole new trend in barbequing."

"Well," said an amazed Elmer G.," "now don't that beat all. Did Willobur escape?"

"Willobur didn't escape," said Barley, "but he did a spell better on his flying distance than Oraville did."

"He did?" asked Elmer G.

"Yep," said Barley. "But unfortunately, Willobur suffered an even worse fate on his landing."

"What happened to Willobur when he landed?" asked Elmer G.

"Poor fella' caught a downdraft of wind," said Barley.

"And then what?" asked Elmer G.

"Well," said Barley, "he introduced himself to a pine sapling."

"How can you introduce yourself to a pine sapling?" asked Elmer G.

"Head-first————is one way," said Barley. "He darn near took down that pine tree when he hit it head-on. He hit the pine tree just as he was waving hello to his Mama, Willamina Right, standing down in the crowd. I guess you could day that Willobur waved 'hello' and 'goodbye' to Miss Willamina at the same time. Willobur bounced off the pine tree and crashed into that barbed wire fence over there."

"Surely you're exaggerating," said Elmer G. in stunned disbelief.

"I kid you not," said Barley. "That barbed wire fence cut Willobur up into a million bits and pieces."

"Barley!" said Elmer G. "Come on now. Stop making stuff up."

"I ain't making nothing up!" protested Barley. "I'm telling the truth. For real! That boy's body pieces were diced and spliced into a neat batch of bite-sized pieces. Farmer Brown used a paper plate to scrape them up into a plastic bowl. He laid a paper towel over the top of the bowl to keep the flies off and hand-carried it to Mrs. Brown."

"What did she do with Willobur's remains?" asked Elmer G.

"She scooted back up to the house carrying what was left of poor Willobur in that big old plastic bowl. Then she plopped in a serving spoon full of mayonnaise, tossed in a cup of freshly chopped green peppers, threw in a dash of salt and pepper, added a cup of crushed onions, topped it all off with some Louisiana Creole seasoning and viola!"

"Viola!" repeated Elmer G. "Viola what?"

Barley glanced thoughtfully at Elmer G., then he continued with his story. "Viola, as in they made a ham salad out of Willobur's remains and served him for lunch. Mrs. Brown cooled him all afternoon in the refrigerator before she added the other ingredients. Willobur always said he wanted to be 'cool'.

Said he was tired of being a nerd. Well, he was served cool that day after Mrs. Brown chilled him in the refrigerator. The Browns and their neighbors dined on ham salad and potato chips at a spur of the moment luncheon they held out on the back porch. If I remember correctly, they washed Willobur down with a pitcher of raspberry flavored iced tea. So I guess you could say some good came out of this whole episode. If you're partial to ham salad.......that is."

"Barley! That's a terrible story!!" said Elmer G.

"I know," agreed Barley. "A right pitiful set of events, to tell you the truth. And the Right Brothers came so close to making it out safely. On a less breezy day, it might've been a completely different outcome."

"So the Right Brothers almost made it outta' here," said Elmer G.

"Yep," said Barley. "The Right Brothers almost made it out. And they would have made it out...if..."

"If what?" asked Elmer G.

"If only pigs could fly," said Barley.

"I've heard that saying before," said Elmer G. "Some of the pigs say that from time-to-time."

"Course you've heard it before," said Barley. "And now.......you know......the rest of the story. The next time you hear a pig saying 'if only pigs could fly', you'll know where that saying came from. Yep. I guess Oraville and Willobur would've flown on outta' here if they'd been the Wright Brothers, instead of the Right Brothers, but that's another story."

"Barley, let's try this one more time," announced Elmer G. "You got any more examples of pigs that tried to escape from the slaughter house without going to the bother of getting religion?"

"Well," said Barley, "there was once a group of pigs that formed a support group called 'Slop Eaters Anonymous'."

"How come?" asked Elmer G.

"They decided to take a shot at escaping from the slaughter house without going the religious route," explained Barley. "So they formed a support group."

"What kind of group is that?" asked Elmer G.

"Basically," said Barley, "a group of twelve pigs got together and formed a support group."

"To do what?" asked Elmer G.

"To encourage each other to lose so much weight that Farmer Brown wouldn't be able to fetch much money for 'em at the slaughter house," said Barley. "They decided that Tiny Muffins had the right idea about getting so skinny, he wouldn't be worth nothing at the slaughter house. The members of Slop Eaters Anonymous decided that the reason Tiny failed was because he was working alone and didn't know when to ease up on losing weight. According to Slop Eaters Anonymous, Tiny didn't execute his plan properly. So they decided to meet twice a week to encourage each other to cut back on their slop consumption."

"So Slop Eaters Anonymous was stealing Tiny Muffins' idea," said Elmer G.

"That's exactly what they were doing," said Barley. "They were stealing Tiny Muffins' idea and expanding it to a group level. Each of the twelve pigs had to stand up at their meetings and confess publicly to being a Slop Addict. After each confession, the other members of the support group cheered and applauded the courage of the confessing pig for standing up and admitting he or she was tragically addicted to eating slop. Then each pig shared stories about how many times they could've eaten more slop the past few days, but had exercised extraordinary discipline by refusing to gorge themselves. Naturally, this brought on another deafening round of enthusiastic applause, catcalls and ear shattering whistles."

"Did the Slop Eaters Anonymous' strategy work?" asked Elmer G. "Did they lose weight and escape the slaughter house?"

"Yes," said Barley. "Their strategy worked…..at first."

"What do you mean, 'at first'?" asked Elmer G.

"Now, hold your horses," said Barley. "You see, what happened is that at first, they all lost weight and none of them was sent to the slaughter house because they were too thin."

"And?" asked Elmer G., since he was now suspicious of Barley's stories.

"Well," said Barley, "you sure you're up to this?"

"Go ahead Barley," said Elmer G. "I'm up for it. Whatever *it* is."

"I think the Slop Eaters Anonymous might have succeeded on a long-term basis, if they had not taken to having longer support meetings," said Barley.

"I'm not following you," said Elmer G. "What does the length of their support meetings have to do with them losing weight?"

"When they first started getting together," said Barley, "the meetings were short and to the point. The twelve members wrapped things up in a timely manner, went home and rolled into bed. And everybody was losing a lot of weight. But one day a pig named Tater Jones found an old, tattered copy of the Robert's Rules of Parliamentary Procedures. Naturally, they started using some of those rules. Their meetings took on a new flavor."

"What happened?" asked Elmer G.

"The first thing they did," said Barley, "was to draft some By-Laws. From now on, they declared in their new By-Laws, there were to be four Project Activity Teams. For each meeting a Project Activity Team was assigned the responsibility of preparing a Meeting Agenda identifying what items would be discussed and how much time each item was to be discussed. In addition, each Project Activity Team, or "PAT", as they were called, had to develop at least three new business plans for continuous improvement of the Slop Eaters Anonymous Club. Then, the PAT that was in charge that week had to also develop an action plan to implement each of the three Continuous Improvement Ideas, or "CIIs", as they were called. Members of the Slop Support Group had to hold their right trotter up in the air and be recognized by the floor before they could even speak at the meetings."

"Really?" said Elmer G.

"Oh yeah," said Barley. "One time they spent a whole month of meetings developing a Mission Statement for Slop Eaters Anonymous."

"A Mission Statement?" asked Elmer G.

"Yep," said Barley. "That's a statement telling other pigs what your group is supposed to be doing. It's called 'sharing your goals' with the general public."

"What did their Mission Statement say?" asked Elmer G.

Barley cleared his throat and answered, "Their Mission Statement said "Pigs get fed and hogs get slaughtered, so don't be a hog by over-eating." After they came up with their Mission Statement, they'd get mad if you called any of 'em hogs. They would only answer if you called them pigs."

"But what does this have to do with them avoiding the slaughter house?"

"I'm going to get to that," said Barley. "Just let me finish telling the story. Now, like I was saying, in the beginning the meetings started out lasting twenty minutes tops. After the rule-making and procedural protocols kicked in, the meetings stretched out to seven hours and some change. Course, the pigs started feeling cramped up, grumpy and right hongry' around the third hour. So, they decided to start bringing potluck salads to snack on and tide them over until these marathon meetings ended. But they struggled with eating just a light salad."

"How come the salads didn't fill 'em up?" asked Elmer G.

"Because they were already on a diet," explained Barley. "Remember, in order to lose weight, they had already quit eating slop at feeding time. Salads was mostly what they were chomping down on during regular feeding times. They sat there during the meetings getting grumpier and hongrier', as the speakers droned on and on. Morale was losing weight right alongside the pigs. One night a pig named Sarah Green brought a small, insignificant bucket of slop for them to snack on. That was all she wrote."

"What happened after she bought a small bucket of slop to the meeting?" asked Elmer G.

"The charter members of Slop Eaters Anonymous experienced a breakdown in their group's resolve," said Barley, "as they commenced to fighting over that little tin of slop. At their next meeting, twelve giant slop buckets were sitting in the middle of their discussion circle. Each one of them had shown up with their personal bucket of snack slop."

"What's so bad about that?" asked Elmer G., as he noticed he was feeling kinda' hongry' himself. His stomach was growling like a GTO in need of a tune-up.

"From that point forward," said Barley, "they ate so much slop at their Slop Eaters Anonymous meetings that all twelve of them grew into hefty hogs in no time flat."

"Why did they gain so much weight so fast?" asked Elmer G.

"For one thing, they revised their By-Laws," said Barley. "They made it an official requirement that all members of Slop Eaters Anonymous must eat a full load of slop at feeding time and a slop snack at their support group meetings. As a result, they were eating slop twice a day."

"I still don't see the harm in any of this," confessed Elmer G., feeling hongrier' by the minute.

"What happened," explained Barley, "is that the members of Slop Eaters Anonymous got so fat, so fast, that Farmer Brown ended up hauling all twelve of those hefties directly down to the slaughter house. And the funny thing is that he took them down there sooner than they would have gone if they had gained weight on a more regular schedule. Naturally, Farmer Brown was thrilled at this chain of events."

"Slow your roll now, Barley," said Elmer G., "and let me make sure I've got this straight. So what you're saying is that the members of Slop Eaters Anonymous ended up eating slop snacks at their support meetings, gained weight faster and were shipped to the slaughter house sooner than they were originally scheduled to go?"

"You've got it," said Barley. "And after all this happened, the membership in Slop Eaters Anonymous dwindled down to nothing. Ain't that something? Yep. The more dinner rolls they ate....the faster their membership rolls pretty much died off."

"That's about the most amazing story I ever heard," said Elmer G. "I'm still hard-pressed to believe that not a single pig has figured out a way to beat the system and skip going to the slaughter house."

"Part of the problem," said Barley, "is that our destinies as pigs may have been set in the past and we can't change it."

"What are you talking about now?" asked Elmer G.

"A long, long time ago," said Barley, "even before I was born, there was a pig named Andy Warthog. Andy put a curse on all future pigs to pay them back for making fun of him."

"Why did the other pigs make fun of Andy Warthog?" asked Elmer G.

"Andy liked to draw pictures all the time," said Barley. "But he only drew pictures of over-sized slop barrels and had the nerve to call it 'art'. But in reality, they were just plain old pictures of slop barrels. Not art. The other pigs laughed at him and poked fun at his paintings. So he put a curse on all future generations of pigs by declaring that from that moment on, every pig in the world would at some point in their lives experience 'fifteen minutes of flame'."

"Fifteen minutes of flame," repeated Elmer G., softly.

"Yep," said Barley, "according to Andy Warthog, every pig in the world will experience fifteen minutes of flame. As the story goes, every pig born since this curse was announced by Andy

Warthog has been hard-pressed to avoid his fifteen minutes of flame."

"What is fifteen minutes of flame?" asked Elmer G.

"When humans plop sausage patties into a skillet to fry for fifteen minutes," said Barley, "you have your fifteen minutes of flame. When they lay bacon strips carved from your side-sections in neat, horizontal rows in a piping hot skillet for fifteen minutes, you have your fifteen minutes of flame. But if they barbeque you, it'll take a couple of hours to cook your ribs through to the bone and seal in the flavor and moisture, so you might call that two hours of flame because...."

"Barley!!" screamed Elmer G. "Please show some respect for the dead!!"

"Hold on now!" exclaimed Barley, in protest. "Don't go getting twisted off with me, Elmer G. I didn't mean to scare you, but I'm just telling you the stories passed down to us by our elders over the years."

"It's just that all of your stories have such terrible endings," said Elmer G. "Don't you know any stories that have a happy ending. Like some pigs that actually escaped the slaughter house?"

"Now, let me think," said Barley. "There was a sow named Gabriella Guchi. Gabriella 'shore was smart. Deep thinker, she was. Sharp as a tack. Gabriella decided to hide and slip out of the pig pens under the cover of darkness."

"Did it work?" asked Elmer G.

"Almost," said Barley. "The only problem was that she hid under the trailer truck that drives the pigs to the slaughter house."

"That's okay, said Elmer G. "As long as she didn't get in the truck. What happened next?"

"Gabriella had eaten a big, outlandish slop supper that night," said Barley. "You know how heavy and sleepy a good load of slop makes you feel. All warm and drozy. Eyes starting drooping until....."

"Barley! Wake up!!" screamed Elmer G.

"I'm sorry," said Barley. "Where was I? Oh yeah. Gabriella ate a heavy supper and got sleepy while she was hiding under the trailer truck until Farmer Brown and his men cleared out. While she was waiting for the coast to clear, she fell asleep and didn't wake up in time to move to a safer place."

"And?" asked Elmer G.

"Unfortunately, the truck ran right over her early the next morning. Squashed her flat as internet stock prices. You could flip her like she was a pancake."

"What?!" said Elmer G.

"I'll explain about the internet later," said Barley. "Anyway, the only piece of Gabriella that Farmer Brown found the next day was her right ear. He gave it to Mrs. Brown and she spent a whole week trying to sew it into a silk purse. But she wasn't able to do it."

"Why not?" asked Elmer G.

"Because," said Barley, "after a whole week of sewing and not making any progress, Mrs. Brown finally realized she couldn't make a sow's ear into a silk purse. So she settled for a pig skin change purse instead. She's still carrying it around now. The next time she's down here take a peek at her change purse and ...."

"Barley!" said Elmer G. "I get your point. You don't have to go on and on with all the details."

"But I like to give you the trimmings that go along with the stories," said Barley. "That's what adds the seasoning and flavor."

"This is still not the example I'm looking for," said Elmer G.

"Now there was another pig named Pooter Potter," said Barley. "Pooter was brilliant! Pooter tried to slip outta' the pig pens to avoid the slaughter house. His method was certainly unusual."

"What did Pooter do?" asked Elmer G., as his hopes started rising again.

"Pooter had this old ratty blanket that he loved to wrap up in at night when he went to bed. Pooter decided he would hide under his blanket and walk out the main pig pen gate right along with the farm hands at quitting time."

"Wouldn't the men spot him and yank him out of line?" asked Elmer G.

"That's what we tried to tell him," said Barley. "But Pooter had a mind all his own. He hatched a plan to hide under his blanket as he walked out the gate. You know, a homemade disguise. I tried to tell Pooter not to be messing with those peoples like that. But he acted like he ain't heard a word I said."

"Did Pooter's plan work?" asked Elmer G. "Did he walk out the front gate?"

"Oh yeah," said Barley. "Pooter made it outside the gate wrapped up in his little green blanket. But right before he got far enough away to break out in a dash for freedom, the edge of his blanket got caught on a low hanging tree branch. The tree limb pulled Pooter's blanket offa' him. Poor Pooter was still a-creeping and a-tip-toeing along like he was still hid under his blanket, grinning from ear-to-ear. Farmer Brown and his farm hands were standing there watching Pooter tip-toe towards the edge of the clearing, acting like he was invisible. Pooter didn't have a clue that he'd lost his blanket."

"What happened then?" asked Elmer G.

"Finally, a sow named Cheryl McGruder, yelled out to Pooter and told him to check his blanket. Pooter turned around, saw that his blanket was flapping in the wind, as it swung from that tree branch. Pooter near 'bout fainted."

"What did the farm hands do to Pooter?" asked Elmer G.

"They killed him," said Barley. "They cooked Pooter and ate him. But there was some good that come of it."

"What was that?" asked Elmer G.

"They named a dish after Pooter," said Barley. "Ever heard of 'pig in the blanket?' This is when they wrap a hot dog wiener or sausage link in a dough shell and bake it until the dough browns on the outside and the juices from the meat inside the dough ...."

"Stop it Barley!!" said Elmer G. "Why you got to go into such graphic details? Don't you have any stories where the pigs get away alive?"

"I don't know of any pigs that got away," said Barley, "but the cows shore' had a fantastic idea. They came up with a different plan about how to avoid going to the slaughter house. The cows were smarter than Tiny, Plumper, Scooter, the Right Brothers, Gabriella and Pooter."

"They were?" said Elmer G., as his hopes started swimming towards the surface again.

"Yep," said Barley. "They sure were. Actually, now that I think about it, the idea the cows came up was a pretty innovative scheme to avoid being slaughtered."

"Are you gonna' tell me about it?" said Elmer G. "I mean like, sometime today, maybe?" He was getting impatient with his search for to find a way to avoid being trucked off to the slaughter house.

"Well, the cows held a big ole' meeting and agreed on a plan," said Barley.

"They wanted to make sure everybody was operating off the same play-sheet, you know. Ohhh, it was a grand idea. The sort of plan that gives me the shivers just thinking about it. It was so bold....you just get excited when you hear about it. So....outrageous. It was just....different. The cows were definitely thinking outside the box when they came up with this idea. I'd even go so far as to say...it was brilliant."

"Barley.....I ain't got all day to hear this story," said Elmer G. "You're shore' milking this for all it's worth."

"Alright! Take a chill pill, Elmer G. You young pigs are always in such a hurry. Ya'll don't know how to slow down and...and...and...let...life marinade around you a little bit. The big plan was this. The cows all got together and decided to start acting crazy."

"Is that all?" said a frustrated Elmer G. "They decided to start acting crazy? That was their brilliant plan? What's the big deal about that? We've got crazy pigs around here that still get sent to the slaughter house."

"This is true," agreed Barley. "You've got a point, there. But wait until you hear the rest......of the story," he said, with a knowing glance and an up-and-down nodding of his large head.

"What did the cows do that was so brilliant?" asked Elmer G.

"I mean to tell you those cows *really* started acting crazy," said Barley. "The cows started walking around in circles. Just a walking round and round and round in endless circles...going nowhere. Strangest thing I ever seen. They scared me...and I knew they were play-acting. Some of the cows drank Milk of MacAneisha to make it look like they were forming at the mouth. They were rolling their eyes around in their eyeball sockets. Some of 'em commenced to laying out in the pasture..... on their backs....legs sticking straight up in the air.....for no reason. And refused to get up."

"Barley...are you serious?" asked Elmer G.

"Serious as a heart attack," said Barley. "And that ain't all. The cows stopped giving milk. Humans were sitting on their little stools pulling on the cows' teats and not one drop of milk came splashing into the milk pails. And you know humans get mad when little Johnny don't have no milk to wet his breakfast cereal. I mean peoples were starting to pay attention to the cows' strange behavior. Some of the cows were just standing still....staring blankly into space, like they had lost their minds. The cows wouldn't come over to the humans any more when they called their names."

"Wow, Barley! Sounds like they were doing a good job of play-acting," said Elmer G.

"Who you telling?" said Barley. "Actually, they did such a great job at acting crazy that it scared the humans to no end. The humans gave the cows' behavior a name. They said the cows had some kinda' new disease."

"They did?" said Elmer G.

"Yep," said Barley. "Called it the 'Mad Cow Disease'. Elmer G. Let me ask you something. You ever had a disease named after you?"

"Nope," said Elmer G. "Can't say I have."

"Me neither," said Barley, with a hint of regret in his voice. "Do you have any idea how hard it is to get a disease named after you? I was so proud of those cows, doing such a stand-up acting job. Scaring those humans to death. Made my chest poke out...just...just...watching 'em throwing down. A little payback from the animals further down the food chain for all the misery they've caused us. For a hot minute...I thought about acting crazy my own self. I shore' did consider it. I thought about joining my cow brethrens in a kind of 'sympathy protest' against slaughtering, but it was near slop time....so I had to run grab a bite to eat instead. I was so hongry'."

"So, you didn't' help the cows with a 'sympathy protest' because you were hungry," said Elmer G.

"This wasn't no regular 'hungry'," said Barley. "Elmer G., you just don't know how'hongry I was. I near 'bout fainted from honger' pains. You ever get so hongry' your stomach starts to twitching and growling like a Doberman on pep pills? That's an awful tough decision choosing between joining a sympathy protest and scarfing down some fresh, chunky slop."

"Barley...pu....lease tell me what happened next," pleaded Elmer G. "We may be on to something here."

"That's what I've been trying to tell you!" said Barley, excited that Elmer G. was finally seeing the light. "Now you see where I'm coming from. Hush up now and let me finish telling you what happened. The humans were terrified that they might get sick and go insane if they ate the meat from these here Mad Cows. So get this. They stopped sending cows to the slaughter house."

"I guess the humans started starving to death, since they were scared to eat beef?" asked Elmer G., all excited and in a lather.

"Not exactly," said Barley.

"What do you mean?" asked Elmer G.

"Well," said Barley, "once they stopped eating beef, the humans started eating more pork.....which is us."

"See what I mean!" said Elmer G. "Your stories always have the worst endings for pigs."

"But I'm not through telling it yet!" said Barley. "Calm down and hear me out. Please. Just bear with me a while longer here, Elmer G. Like I was saying, the humans stopped eating beef. MicDenerds and Burger MooQueen were suffering badly because nobody was gobbling down hamburgers no more. I mean to tell you they put the brakes on burgers. There were so many humans switching to become vegetarians that I thought the sixties had returned."

"We can do something like that for pigs!" said Elmer G., busting at the seams with excitement. "We'll get all the pigs together and start acting crazy. That way, the humans will stop slaughtering us, because they'll think we have the Mad Pig's Disease. And then we'll...... "

"Not so fast, Elmer G. It won't work," said Barley, with a hint of sadness and resignation in his voice.

"Why not?" said Elmer G. "Didn't you just say that they stopped sending the cows to the slaughter house because the humans thought they had Mad Cow Disease?"

"They did stop sending the cows to the slaughter house," said Barley. "But…"

"But what?" asked Elmer G., in a solemn tone of voice. His shoulder muscles involuntarily tensed up a taste, as he waited for the other proverbial shoe to clank down onto the ground.

"Well," said Barley, "the cows weren't the only animals that went mad."

"What is that supposed to mean?" said Elmer G.

"The humans got mad too," explained Barley.

"You mean the humans started acting crazy like the cows were doing?" said Elmer G. "I don't understand. Why would they do such a foolish thing?"

"Elmer G....now don't get mad now, but the humans got mad....at..."

"Mad at who?" asked Elmer G.

"The cows," said Barley.

"They got mad at the cows?" said Elmer G. "For what?"

"For acting crazy," said Barley

"So?" said Elmer G.

"When humans get mad," said Barley, "the other animals further down the food chain better watch out. The reason is because when humans get angry, they've got the ability and weapons to do something about it. Which is why they marched down to the pastures and..."

"And what?" said Elmer G.

"And they shot all the Mad Cows," said Barley.

"Shot them?!!" said Elmer G.

"Yep," said Barley. "And that ain't all."

"It's not?" said Elmer G.

"Naw," said Barley.

"You mean there's more?" said Elmer G.

"Yeah," said Barley. "After they shot all the cows in the head, the humans dumped the dead cows into these deep ditches they'd dug with those bright yaller bulldozers. Elmer G, let me axe you something. Do you know how much noise a bulldozer makes when it gets to really roaring?"

"What!?" said Elmer G. "What are you talking about?"

"The amount of noise those bulldozers make. They keep up a lot of racket with all that URRRRHHH!!!! RRRPPPFT!!! Shore' woke me right up. I'm getting the cold shivers right now just talking about it. I'll be doggone if that racket didn't rattle my cage something fierce-like. They were making enough noise to wake the dead. Which was a considerable job....under the circumstances. I tell you...they need to put some mufflers on those bulldozers to cut some of that-there racket. I can't even imagine the gas mileage those things get. Probably two miles to the gallon and with these high gas prices we got today......"

"Barley! Barley!" yelled Elmer G. "Get back to the cows, please."

"Oh yeah," said Barley. "After the humans dumped the dead cows into those deep ditches, they poured gasoline all over 'em. Now this part is innneresting'. Several men walked up and down on each side of the ditches and sloshed gasoline on the cows' dead bodies. They poured the gasoline from these pretty red cans with long nozzles at the top, or were the nozzles on the sides? Naww. I'm pretty sure the nozzles were sticking out the tops of the cans....I b'lieve. But then again....I seem to recollect them nozzles hanging out the side....of the cans. Maybe I'm wrong.....let me think now. Elmer G., I can't recall if the nozzles were on top of the gas cans or if they were on the sides...."

"Barley!! It don't matter!!" yelled a frustrated Elmer G. "I'm telling you! It don't matter!! Get on with your story."

"I'm sorry," said a remorseful and chastised Barley. "My bad. Although I can't remember off-hand the particulars about those nozzles, one thing I can tell you for sure. The gas cans were red. I'll never forget 'em if I live to be a hundred. Pretty, shiny red color, like a prime apple. But those nozzles are throwing me for a loop. You know what I'm saying? I guess I'm having a senior moment on those nozzles. Let me think now....you know Elmer G., humans don't really care nothing about wasting gasoline, do they?"

"What makes you think that?" said Elmer G.

"First of all," said Barley, "they come tearing up in here racing around in those low mileage, bright yaller bulldozers. Then they just sloshed gasoline all over the cows. If they had slowed down a hot minute to think about it, they could have accomplished the same thing by doing some strategic sprinkling of gasoline in a few places at each end of the ditch. They would'va still gotten a fairly decent blaze going.....”

“BARLEY!!” screamed Elmer G. “I can't take no more of this. I'm going home.”

“Okayyyy,” hissed Barley. “Okay. Hold your horses, Elmer G. Where was I? Oh yeah. They sloshed gasoline over the cows’ dead bodies, struck a match and tossed it into the mix and POOF!! Set ‘em on fire. What's amazing is that they did it so casually, like it warn't nothing more’n lighting a friendly campfire. Why…if they were roasting marshmallows ‘stead of dead cows, then I guess it would've been more along the lines of a campfire…”

“Barley! Pu…lease! Stop it!!” said Elmer G.

“I'm telling it like it happened,” said Barley. “Don't get all agi-tated at me. It ain't my fault they set ‘em on fire. Don't shoot the messenger just because you don't like the message. Where was I anyway? Oh yeah. I was telling you how the humans set those cows on fire. It smelled like a toe-jam convention. The smell was enough to knock you out for the count. It smelled bad enough to make you faint, unless….you like grilled steaks….well-done. In that case, you'd have done a back-flip for joy at the sight of all those sizzling steaks stacked up in piles that seemed to darn near reach the sky. Then they cranked those yaller bulldozers up again and commenced to pushing those gigantic mountains of dirt on top of the blackened cows’ bodies and then they……”

“That's enough ex….plaining!” screamed Elmer G. “I get the picture. Pretending like we're all crazy may not be the best idea in the world. Barley, I noticed you didn't mention religion when you were talking about the cows. Why don't the cows get religion to save themselves from the slaughter house?”

“Elmer G.,” don't you know nothing?” said Barley. “Cows can't get religion because of the ‘Separation of Powers.’”

"Separation of powers," said Elmer G. "What does that mean?"

"Obviously you ain't read the Constitution of the United States and the Bill of Rights," said Barley. "It's a good thing I've read 'em. Otherwise, you'd be up a creek without a paddle. The U.S. Constitution and the Bill of Rights are rules that the people who live in America have to live by. One of these rules says that there must always be a separation between the executive branch of government, which is the President of the United States and the other two branches of government, which is the Congress and the Supreme Court. Each one of these groups have a special job that only they can do and the other two groups can't be getting in the way."

"But what does this have to do with the cows and religion?" asked Elmer G.

"If you hold onto your britches a minute, I'ma tell you!" said Barley. "Now, like I was saying, there are branches of government that have to operate by their lonesome when they are doing their job. There's one more rule laid down by the Constitution of the United States and it says that there must always........always....be a strict separation between the Church and the Steak. So there you have it. That's why cows can't get religion. You've got to have the Church on one side of your plate and the Steak on the other side of your plate. They cannot be mixed up together. The Church has certain powers to do its job. And the Steak has been granted certain powers to do its job. And the two of them can't be mixing up together, influencing each other and socializing."

"But what does the Steak have to do with the cows?" asked Elmer G.

"Elmer G., I can't believe some of the things that come outta' your mouth. You asking "what does the Steak have to do with the cows?" Let me answer that question with a question. You ever seen a Steak come from anywhere other than a cow?"

"No," said Elmer G.

"Then there you have it," said Barley. "The Constitution of the United States has declared that there should always be a strict separation between the Church and the Steak, which means...the cows. This means that cows can't get religion. You want some more proof that what I'm saying is the truth?"

"Yeah," said Elmer G.

"You ever met a cow, anywhere, anytime, on any occasion, for any reason...that believed in God?"

"Now that you mention it," said Elmer G. "I ain't never met a cow that believed in God, or even brought His name up in a conversation."

"Ever had a cow break off a conversation with you in order to drop down and pray?" asked Barley.

"Never!" said Elmer G.

"I rest my case," said Barley. "There is a real separation between the Church and the Steak."

"Now I see what you mean," said Elmer G. "Barley, you must be a genius or something. You just know everything under the sun."

"Stop it, Elmer G." said Barley, in a feeble attempt at being modest. "If you scour the earth and look hard enough, you pro'bly can find something I ain't up-to-date on...I 'spect."

"Well...Barley. Let me give it one more try here. Let's say I decided I wanna' be a camel. Last week, I snuck in one night and saw a show on the television set about camels. They said on the show that camels are prized by rich Arabs. I can work as a camel and make a lot of money. Then I'll pay Farmer Brown *not* to kill me."

"But you will still die one day," said Barley. "Don't you wanna' go to Hog Heaven, Elmer G.?"

"Can't I go as a rich camel?" asked Elmer G.

"The Bible says it's easier to get a camel through the eye of a needle than for a rich man to get into Heaven," said Barley. "I assume it'd be equally hard for a rich camel to get into Heaven too. Don't you think? And besides, if you were a camel, you'd have a big old hump on your back. Elmer G., listen to me carefully. I know you're looking for an easy shortcut to avoid the slaughter house, but there really aren't any shortcuts when you're trying to get yourself saved. You have to be seriously committed if you want to save yourself from the slaughter house."

What do you mean?" asked Elmer G.

"The more you look for shortcuts," said Barley, "the more likely you are to go thinking up immoral ways to avoid going to the slaughter house. Right now, for example, you're ready to trade in your rich heritage as a pig and sell your soul just to avoid the slaughter house."

"You calling me immoral?" asked Elmer G.

"Yes I am," said Barley.

"Why?" said Elmer G.

"Because you *are* immoral," said Barley. "Now that you brought it up, let's talk some more about morality and ethics. In order for somebody to have morality and ethics means that you must commit yourself to always follow the rules no matter what everybody else is doing."

"That fits me," said Elmer G. "I follows the rules."

"No you don't," said Barley. "Now, as you know, each day we all take turns handing out potatoes from the slop troughs to make sure that every pig gets his or her fair share of potatoes, which are a delicacy."

"That is correct," said Elmer G.

"And as you also know," said Barley. "The rule is that the pigs sorting the potatoes and handing them out are not supposed to cheat by keeping more than one potato for themselves."

"I know that," said Elmer G.

"And you're not supposed to hand out more than one potato to your friends and family neither," said Barley.

"That's what the rules say," said Elmer G.

"Elmer G., you break those rules every time you hand out potatoes. You keep six or seven potatoes for your midnight snack. Plus, you hand out extra potatoes to Scruff Daddy and his gang because they're your friends and you're afraid of them."

"What's wrong with that?!" protested Elmer G. "Everybody does it!"

"Well," said Barley, "morality and ethics require that you take a different road from what everybody else is doing. You have to follow the rules and do what's right. In this case, your moral conscience should demand that you keep only one potato. You have to also stand up to Scruff Daddy and his gang and give them only one potato each. Along this same line, you should always be proud of who you are. Even if you are just a pig."

"I am proud of who I am, Barley. This slaughter house thing just made me a little crazy. But I still like being a pig. As for stealing extra potatoes, don't nobody even know that I'm keeping a few for myself. How can it be wrong if nobody knows I'm doing it?"

"*You* know you're stealing 'em," said Barley. "So it's still wrong. That's the whole point of having a moral and ethical value system. You have to do the right thing all the time. It's not much of an accomplishment to do the right thing when you're standing in a crowded pig pen with everybody there eyeballing you. It's more important to do the right thing when you are by yourself making private decisions about what's right and what's wrong."

"So being moral and ethical means doing the right thing when you are alone and could get away with it," said Elmer G.

"That's right, Elmer G. Some young pigs will see you doing the right thing and they may decide to follow your example. Behavior is like a virus. It tends to spread itself around, whether it's good or bad. Doing the right thing is hard. Your moral and ethical compass must be personalized to the point that you are committed to the morally correct position at all times. Remember....Elmer G., there is never a wrong time to do the right thing."

"I do the right thing...sometimes," said Elmer G., in a small voice.

"You can't pick and choose when to do the right thing," said Barley. "Who do you think you are son....a stockbroker? You have to do the right thing every chance you get. This is how we establish our reputations and define ourselves. Remember this, Elmer G. We are embraced by our peers because of what we say, like when we use soaring oratory skills to make inspiring speeches. But we are immortalized by our peers and judged by God based on what we do every day. Pigs that know you should be astonished when they find out you did something wrong. Folks that know you should not be shocked.......when you do something right."

"I don't understand what you mean, Barley."

"The trick, my friend....is to live your life in such a way...that when you die...every pig in the whole world rubs their balled up fists in their eye sockets and bawls in anguish. A lot of pigs live such terrible lives and are so mean that when they die, a large crowd attends the funeral....shaking the casket.....to make sure they are really dead."

"Are you serious Barley?"

"Yes I am," said Barley. "You take Cecil McNally. Cecil was a mean hog."

"Who is Cecil McNally?" asked Elmer G.

"I grew up with Cecil," said Barley. "Now that was a mean pig. Cecil stole food from his friends. He didn't even pay no mind to his own mama. Cecil could steal sugar outta' gingerbread and never break the crust. Cecil's reputation was so bad, he couldn't even qualify for a car loan. And as you know, anybody breathing can get a car loan. That boy lied to pigs he hadn't even met. The most pleasant words he said to anybody was "I'm about to slap you silly!"

"Why was Cecil so bad?" asked Elmer G.

"Folks say Cecil was born under a bad sign," explained Barley. "He laughed at the Cornmashers, as they were being herded into the trailer truck to be hauled over to the slaughter house. Cecil laughed and made a slashing sign across the underside of his neck as they were being led away. One day, some of Farmer Brown's farm hands threw a giant log from the truck bed over the fence to use as a fence post. They weren't looking when they tossed it. The log smacked Cecil square in the forehead."

"Did Cecil get hurt?" asked Elmer G..

"Hurt?! Hurt?!!" said Barley. "You ever been cracked in the head with a full-sized log? The blow killed him on the spot. Best accident we ever witnessed. When they cut Cecil open, they plucked out his heart with a pair of tweezers. Cecil had a heart that was near 'bout as big as a mustard seed. Truth be told.....he may have had a small heart, but the boy had the biggest funeral you ever saw. Yessiree. I was there that day. Not a wet eye in the house....unless you count his mama. And later, his mama 'fessed up that she was crying and hollerin' because he owed her when he died. Everybody was so happy Cecil was finally dead that we cried.....tears of joy. Yeah buddy!! We shouted in jubilation. Somebody broke out a boom box and the party was on. The celebration started before the first spade full of dirt even smacked the top of Cecil's casket. But that's another story."

"I'm glad it is another story," said Elmer G. in a stage whisper. "I'm plump exhausted from listening to all these crazy stories bout pigs' dying and what-not."

"What's that you mumbling about, boy?" asked Barley.

"Nothing," said Elmer G. "I didn't say nothing."

Elmer G. decided to head home and mull over this latest conversation with Barley. He'd spent so much time thinking about all of this new information that he was whipped. Plain hog-tired. And hongry' too. Elmer G. ate supper and lit off to bed early. Tomorrow was a new day filled with promise.

"I will worry about all this tomorrow," thought Elmer G. to himself. "Facing reality is a tough row to hoe," he whispered to himself, as he drifted off to sleep. "A very tough row to hoe......indeed. And now only one potato in the row is mine," he mournfully thought to himself.

CHAPTER 8

Who Let The Pigs Out?

"Just because you see a hole in the fence, doesn't mean you oughta' squeeze through it. If you decide to run away, make sure you're running to a better place than the one you left. 'Course, you won't know that until you get there."

The next morning Elmer G. decided he wanted to remember the lessons he was learning from Barley. As he laid there soaking up the sunshine, his thoughts rolled around in his head. He decided to write down one thing he'd learned. So he scrawled another message on the inside of the wooden slats of the pig pen. He wrote:

"Praying by itself ain't good enough to get into Hog Heaven. You gotta' act good too. Being good day in and day out may be stimulating for the soul, but it 'shore ain't a whole heap a fun for the body."

After he finished writing, Elmer G. prayed for something besides his daily wish to find a whole apple core in the slop trough.

Like Solomon, he prayed for wisdom. And he added another new twist. Elmer G. was becoming somewhat unselfish, as he prayed feverously for God to have mercy on some of his friends. He asked God to help his friends that he identified by name.

"God, please bless Hattie, Freddy, So-So, Ben, Theodore, Glen, Mickey and Scruff Daddy. As for everybody else....." He didn't finish his sentence, but he thought to himself, "Lord....they on their own."

Elmer G. roamed restlessly around the pig pens in a listless fashion. He wallowed for two eternities in a fantastically cool, mushy mud pit. Whomp! Squish! Whap! Sweech! Thump!" He sounded like a strong woman washing clothes on an old fashioned tin washboard, as he rolled in the mud. He splashed it up under his armpits, onto his back and all underneath his belly, smiling with pure contentment the whole time. When he finished, he looked as satisfied as a cat arriving at the scene of a wreck between two eighteen-wheelers carrying cargoes of fresh salmon.

Later, he watched the sunset with a satisfied glow, then slept like a log. Elmer G. rose the next morning, said his prayers and strolled over to visit a spell with Barley. After he rehashed the events of the last three days, telling Barley how he'd prayed for some of his favorite friends, but not others, Barley smiled and seemed sorta' pleased.

"Elmer G., you are making progress in your quest to find your spiritual center. You are learning to pray for God to give you the wisdom to recognize the right course of action. You're also asking God to give you the strength to do the right thing. Sounds to me like you're becoming unselfish, as evidenced by the fact that you are praying for the salvation of others besides yourself. But now, there is one area you could stand some brushing up on. You really should pray for everybody to receive blessings and not just your friends. However, all and still, you *are* making prayer a habit in your life. All and all I am pleased with your progress."

"Thank you, Barley," said Elmer G., beaming from this verbal whack on the back.

"Now," said Barley. "Let's talk about the second lesson that will help you avoid the slaughter house. You need to start doing some other things that make you stand out in Farmer Brown's eyes in a positive way. In order for you to succeed in your quest to avoid the slaughter house, Farmer Brown must view you as a pig worth saving. You have to convince Farmer Brown that he needs to have you around all the time, sorta' like a pet."

"But how can I do that?", asked Elmer G.

"Well, for one thing," said Barley. "You can stop running away in the woods every chance you get. For example, just because Scruff Daddy and his gang root holes in the fence and invite you to join them don't mean you gotta' go. The grass is *not* always greener on the other side of the fence. Sometimes, although it seems dull, staying home can be a good thing."

"But Barley," pleaded Elmer G., "Do I have to drop every bad habit I like? I *like* running loose in the woods." Elmer G. started feeling kinda down in the mouth, as he realized the *new* sacrifices he was going to have to make to avoid being shipped to the slaughter house.

"Elmer G., let's get real. This is not about what you like. This is about staying alive. The goal is to get Farmer Brown to *like* you. If he likes you, you live. If he doesn't like you.....you die. All and still, one thing is for sure. Farmer Brown does not like chasing run-away pigs through the woods and dragging 'em back to the pig pens, kicking and squealing. That's hard work on a cool fall day and double hard duty under a scorching sun. You have a choice, Elmer G. Sometimes in life, you just have to pass up some of the fun things when you're positioning yourself to survive. But remember.....you always have a choice."

"You mean Farmer Brown will let me live if I stop running away?" said Elmer G.

"No Elmer G.....he won't let you live just because you stop running away. It's not that simple. As you continue finding your spiritual center, you are adding one positive weight on your side of the scale. When you stop running away, you will be adding a second positive weight to your side of the scale. Let me tell you something. Life is divided up into two categories. Things we need to do to survive. And there are things we just wanna' do because they're fun. The key to surviving is understanding the difference between "I needa'" and "I wanna'.""

"Barley," said Elmer G., "I'm not sure I understand what you're getting at. All I know is that I wanna' avoid trotting off to that there slaughter house. "

"Elmer G......if you *wanna'* avoid trotting off to that there slaughter house, then you *needa'* stop running away in them there woods. Think on these things and come see me on the third day."

CHAPTER 9

Busting Loose

"Sometimes, we run away to new places that turn out to be just like our old places.....in disguise."

Elmer G. got up the next morning and scrawled a new message on the fence. He wrote:

"Finding my spiritual center 'shore is hard work. No wonder there ain't many pigs marching in the army of Christian Soldiers. I never knew how much fun I was having without a spiritual center, until I started improving myself. I'm not sure how much more improving I can stand."

Then Elmer G. said his prayers. He thanked God in advance for all of the great things God was going to do for him in the future. He prayed for *all* of his fellow pigs, both friends and foes. He prayed for the birds, rats and even the snakes. Then he prayed for wisdom and strength of character. Finally, Elmer G. prayed that God would help him remain strong in his spiritual faith.

"I think I'm becoming a fairly decent prayer," thought Elmer G. to himself.

Around mid-morning, Scruff Daddy and his gang came sauntering up.

"Come on Elmer G.," said Scruff Daddy. "It's time to roll."

"We're breaking out again," said Ben.

"We've found a hole on the west side of the hog pens," said Theodore.

"I'm not feeling well today," said Elmer G., trying to sound sickly. "You guys go on without me," he mumbled. Elmer G. made a mental note to add "*Stop lying*" to his growing list of spiritual goals.

"Suit yourself, wimp!" said Scruff Daddy, in his most scornful tone of voice. "What you trying to do anyway? Show us up?"

"You wanna' be Farmer Brown's pet?" asked Glen in a harsh tone of voice.

"So.......I guess this means you not no regular pig no more?" said Freddy, who was one of Scruff Daddy's sidekicks. "Huh? Is that it? You think you're better than us now? Is that it what you think, Elmer G.? Good as we all been to you and this is the thanks we git'? You oughta' be ashamed of yourself. I'm ashamed for you. Treating us like you better than us."

"Noooo," pleaded Elmer G. "I don't think I'm better than nobody else."

"Ohhh!" said Glen. "so now we just a bunch a *nobodies*. You heard him boys! I oughta' wallop you upside your fat head right now!!"

"That's not what I meant," said Elmer G. quickly. "All I'm saying is that I just don't wanna' run away no more."

"That's your call, Elmer G.," said Scruff Daddy. "But one day you'll regret it! I've seen pigs like you before, Elmer G. You git' a leg up in the world and all of a sudden your old friends ain't *good* enough no more. We ain't *special* enough. We ain't *religious* enough for you? I heard about your little lessons you been getting from Barley. Well, it ain't gonna' help you none. Thinking you all that and some spare change. What are *we* now, Elmer G.? Chopped liver?! I won't stand here a minute longer 'cause the sight.....of you.....turns my stomach!"

"Scruff Daddy," said Glen, "I think those green plums we ate this morning is what's turning your stomach. I'm feeling poorly myself and....."

"Shet' up Glen!!" screamed Scruff Daddy. "Let me finish talking! Like I said before, I won't stand here a minute longer 'cause the sight of you turns my stomach! Come on boys! It's time to rock on up outta' here!!"

Scruff Daddy and his wrecking crew raced away, whooping and hollering up a storm, leaving a trail of brown and reddish-orange dust trailing in their wake. Elmer G. stayed home, painful as it was, wistfully hoping that he had done the right thing. So far, the only thing between him and the slaughter house was his daily prayers. He was still concerned about praying to a God that he wasn't sure even existed. Barley said his religious faith was supposed to save him.

"Yeah.....right," thought Elmer G. to himself. "And pigs can fly too. Now here I am giving up one of my favorite pastimes.....running free in the woods."

"Finding my spiritual center is a mighty big sacrifice," thought Elmer G. to himself. "It means having blind faith in somebody way up in the sky who is supposed to be listening to my prayers."

"Religious faith," Elmer G. decided, "is believing in stuff that any pig with an ounce of horse-sense wouldn't give a second thought. I don't see why I got to stop running away into the woods. I love running away. Why can't I find my spiritual center by giving up something I *don't* love, like cauliflower? Or cucumbers. To tell you the truth, I'm beginning to understand why the other pigs ain't working at avoiding the slaughter house. It's too much work and not enough fun. Nope. Not much fun a'tall."

CHAPTER 10

Backsliding

*"Sometimes, we are so busy worrying about dying.....
we forget to live."*

Since Elmer G. wasn't running away anymore with Scruff Daddy and his gang, he had more time to kill. So, he slowed down his pace and noticed the beautiful sunset, as the fading sunlight ricocheted off the green and orange leaves swaying through the tops of the oak trees. He inhaled deeply and realized that hogs 'shore stank up a place. Whew! The air was pungent with the medley of smells created by aging slop, mushy mud and rotting pine needles, as they all square-danced around the hog pens, mixing and mashing together to create an orchestra of symphonic odors.

Then Elmer G. caught a faint whiff of the scent from the wildflowers, as a gentle breeze brushed through the pig pens.

"I've been so busy worrying about *how* and *when* I'm gonna' die," thought Elmer G. to himself, "that I've pretty much forgotten how to appreciate living. I've been missing out on a zillion small pleasures all around me every day."

He sauntered over and joined a gang of the younger pigs in an exciting game of tag. Then they played hide and seek. Elmer G. was so busy having fun that he plum forgot he was supposed to be worrying about dying.

Elmer G. relaxed and enjoyed living in the present moment.

On the third day after his last visit with Barley, Elmer G. arose and walked over to holler at Barley.

"How you doing, Elmer G.?" asked Barley.

"I can't complain," said Elmer G. "Been praying pretty regular. I've been praying in a different sort of way lately. I've been thanking God for every-day miracles in my life."

"Like what?" asked Barley.

"Like allowing me to wake up each day in one piece, healthy and alive. I'm grateful that I can smell, eat, walk and feel things. I thanked God for these small miracles that I've been taking for granted," explained Elmer G.

"Have you thanked God for anything else," asked Barley.

"Actually I have," said Elmer G. "I've been thanking Him for saving me from being slaughtered."

"Why are you doing that?" asked Barley. "God hasn't even saved you from anything."

"I've decided to have absolute faith that God is on my side," said Elmer G. "I believe He will take care of me. I will keep my faith even when the time comes for me to go to the slaughter house. My faith is so strong that I no longer fear the future. Fear, I have decided, is a sign that we lack complete faith in God's ability to help us. I am certain God will come through in my hour of need. That's why I'm thanking Him in advance for the blessings He's going to give me in the future."

"Elmer G., you are gaining wisdom. But tell me this. Are you still running away with Scruff Daddy and his gang?"

"Nope," said Elmer G. "I stopped two days ago. They've been giving me a hard time about it, calling me names and such truck. But I don't care. I missed running loose something powerful at first. But the longer I keep to myself, I'm starting to see old things in new ways."

"What do you mean?" asked Barley.

"I've come alive," said Elmer G. "I'm noticing the beauty in a sunset. I hear an orchestra in every-day sounds around me like the birds chirping, hogs squealing and grunting. I hear the slop splashing, as it's poured into the feeding troughs. I look around and notice the flush look on my friends' glowing faces, as they lay stretched out after a fine supper. My ears perk up when I hear the distinct, "Burpppp!" of hogs breaking wind. It's sorta' like a compliment to the cook after a scrumptious meal of old beans."

"Didn't you notice any of these things before?" asked Barley.

"Not really," said Elmer G. "Did you?"

"Nawww," said Barley, in a tired voice. "I don't hardly notice nothing these days. I just get up and try to slip-slide through the day without getting stepped on."

"I know what you mean," agreed Elmer G. "Anyway, like I was saying, I've been so busy running away through holes in the fence that I never had time to appreciate the things that are around me. What I'm discovering is that I've been so busy worrying about dying, that I'd forgotten how to live. Barley, in some ways, I was already dead. In my quest to find my spiritual center, I've found a new life right here at home."

"Elmer G.," observed Barley, "it seems like you are starting to appreciate living, instead of fretting so much about dying."

"You're right, Barley. "My life is happening right now while I'm waiting to die. I know I'm....just a pig. And don't nobody give a hoot what happens to me. I mean......I feel like a flea.....hopping around in a super-sized Dog Pound and complaining that I'm being mistreated. Well, a Dog Pound is there to take care of dogs....not fleas. Along that line of thought, this world we live in......appears to be made to serve humans....not pigs. There ain't no special place in this old world......for pigs."

"What do you mean?" asked Barley.

"What I mean is.....my life ain't no big deal, compared to the human world around me. But it's all I've got. I want to enjoy my life. I know I'm gonna' die. I want to do some good things with my life. I'm gonna' appreciate every minute I got left. I'm gonna' live like I might die any minute. Which ain't far offa' the truth, with all this pig slaughtering going on 'round here."

"How are you going to do good things with your life and enjoy every minute?" asked Barley.

"Well.....I played tag and hide-and-seek with some of the younger pigs yesterday," said Elmer G. "I can't remember the last time I've laughed like that. I got caught up in the games, acting silly. I had plumb forgotten how to play and laugh. Barley......I'm too young to be this serious. After playing, we stretched out and wallowed in that black, cool mud. It's times like these....Barley....that make me glad to be a hog, even knowing all the downsides and what-not."

"It's interesting that you should mention wallowing in the mud, Elmer G.," said Barley. "Actually, the next principle I want you to work on concerns the mud pits. Elmer G., just because all the other pigs wallow in the mud doesn't mean you have to join them."

"But why not?" asked a puzzled Elmer G. "I *like* wallowing in the mud."

"Well, Elmer G., cleanliness is next to Godliness. A clean pig is a sight for sore eyes. If you want to stand out in Farmer Brown's eyes, you're going to have to be the closest thing to a pet that you can be. Humans don't like dirty, stinking pigs. You've gotta' have discipline when it comes to staying clean. For a pig, staying clean is as hard as keeping crumbs off of a kitchen floor. You've got to practice staying outta' the mud pits until it becomes a habit. Think on these things and return in three days."

CHAPTER 11

Sacrificing for Salvation

"Sometimes in life, you gotta' give up what you want to get what you need."

The next morning Elmer G. woke up and scrawled a message on the fence. He wrote:

"On top of everything else, now I gotta' stay clean in order to reach the Promised Land. No more wallowing in the mud. Seems to me I'm giving up all the heavenly things I love here on earth just to get into Hog Heaven."

He strolled over to where a group of pigs were wallowing in the nice, cool mud. Elmer G. was just itching to jump in. But he remembered what Barley said about staying clean. Reluctantly, he kept his distance.

"I sure hope Barley is right about keeping clean and praying," thought Elmer G. to himself. "'Cause I'm giving up a passel of small pleasures to avoid the slaughter house. If I'm gonna' die anyway, I shore' would like to go out muddy, with a full belly, after a nice, rip-roaring romp in the woods."

Later that day, when Farmer Brown came to slop the hogs, he stared at Elmer G. and flashed a tiny, snaggled-toothed grin. Before he left, he tossed Elmer G. a small, red apple. Farmer Brown flung his scraggly haired head back and laughed, as Elmer G. glared at him, then greedily gobbled it up. Elmer G. was mad at Farmer Brown for raising pigs to slaughter them for food. It didn't matter one bit to Elmer G. that for the first time in his life, Farmer Brown had tossed him a treat. As a matter of fact, he was sure Farmer Brown tossed him an apple because he was fattening him up for the kill.

Over the next two days, Elmer G. settled into his new routine. He prayed early in the morning and at night before he went to bed. Instead of running away into the woods, he was now playing games with the younger pigs. He was making new friends because he had time to get acquainted with the other pigs.

Elmer G. was also smelling better, since he was no longer wallowing in the mud. Although he was praying, logging more time at home and staying relatively clean, he felt down-right miserable inside.

"Being good," he thought to himself, "just ain't a whole lotta' fun. Believing in somebody you can't even see takes a huge rock pile of faith and discipline."

For example, strolling by an inviting mud pit without diving in was terribly hard on him. One day he found himself standing by a jet-black, slushy, ripe smelling mud pit mulling over having an accident. Elmer G. was thinking about tripping over his own feet and accidentally falling into the cool, inviting mud.

"I'm one desperate pig," mumbled Elmer G. to himself. "I'm losing my grip on reality. I need me some help. Quick."

As he looked frantically around, there was no one he could turn to....except the faint reflection staring back at him from the murky surface of the muddy water.

He started wondering if maybe the other pigs had the right

idea. "They're all pretending like they don't know about no slaughter houses. I can start pretending like I don't know about 'em neither. I can go back to enjoying my life....at least...what's left of it. If I did that, then I could wallow in this good old cool mud. I can smell as bad as I want. Never say another prayer to the Invisible, Silent One. Run off into the woods whenever the mood hits me. Why not? Who would know? Better yet, who cared? As far as I know, I'm the only pig in the pig pens trying to figure out how to avoid the slaughter house. Everybody else is just pretending like life is gonna' roll on forever, until they die from old age."

But there was one little problem with Elmer G.'s impending rebellion. Since Barley had opened up his mind by explaining the horrors of the slaughter house, Elmer G. was not able to ignore his new knowledge. Although he tried, he couldn't seem to shrink his mind back to its original size. He could never go back to his old way of thinking before he knew about the horrors of the slaughter house.

He was fired up by a spanking-brand new emotion......hope. Elmer G. was planning on changing the odds in his favor, so he could avoid the slaughter house blues.

On the third day after Elmer G.'s last visit with Barley, he went to see him.

"Hello Barley," said Elmer G.

"Hello yourself," answered Barley. "What's shaking? You're looking pretty clean. You stop running away in the woods?"

"I ain't been running away," said Elmer G. "But this spiritual journey ain't no picnic in the park. This is hard work. I shore' hope you're right about me increasing my chances of avoiding the slaughter house."

"Keep the faith," said Barley. "Now, tell me, how you like your new habits?"

"I'm liking 'em just fine," mumbled Elmer G. with a shrug. He didn't have a half a pint of enthusiasm in his voice.

"What's bothering you?" asked Barley.

"Well," said Elmer G., reluctantly, "these new fangled habits just ain't a whole heap of fun, if you get my drift. I mean....I'm praying to someone that I can't see.....to save me. I'll say this about God. If He does visit us, He can sure come and go without making much noise. He ain't hittin' on much when it comes to swapping small-talk."

"I know what you mean," chipped in Barley. "He ain't much of a talker."

"Nope," said Elmer G. "Talking ain't God's strongest suit. I mean....he don't even mutter a 'Hello Elmer G. How are you?' He's a quiet sorta' fellow. He ain't big on explaining Hisself neither. But anyway, I'm still praying to Him. Can't honestly say I've got all my marbles bet on him. I kinda' go back-and-forth in terms of the strength of my faith. My feelings on faith are sorta' like the weather."

"How's that?" asked Barley.

"The weather shows up every day," explained Elmer G. "It's just that some days are sunny and bright, while on other days it's bitter cold. It all just depends. But anyway, I'm all off track here."

"Yep," said Barley, "you're a little ways off the beaten path here. But I don't mind. Don't mind a'tall".

"You were asking me about running away in the woods," said Elmer G. "Like I was saying, I'm not running away in the woods anymore. And I'm not wallowing in the mud. I'm staying clean. Smelling better. Now....I'm all for personal hygiene. But Barley, I don't know if you've noticed....but we do live in a pig pen. It just don't make sense. I mean....here I am in a stinking pig pen....trying to stay clean."

"Elmer G.," said Barley, in a gentle tone of voice. "I don't blame you for questioning the things I'm asking you to do. None of them, when viewed alone, make a whole heap a sense. But when you put 'em all together...you're changing your outward perception. Has Farmer Brown done anything to show he's noticing you?"

"Naw," said Elmer G. "He ain't done nothing to show he sees me as anything other than a future glazed ham, or a mess of fried pork chops. Matter of fact, he tried to hit me in the head yesterday with an apple. If I hadn't ducked out the way, I'd be blind. That Farmer Brown is a mean man. I'm gonna' have to pray for him."

"Think carefully, Elmer G. Did he throw the apple *at* you or *to* you?"

"I guess he threw it *to* me," said Elmer G., reluctantly revising his story.

"Has he ever tossed you an apple or anything before yesterday?" asked Barley.

"No," said Elmer G. "Not that I can recollect off-hand."

"Elmer G., your new game plan is starting to work," said Barley. "Don't you see? You've just had your first communication with Farmer Brown. You have successfully introduced your new self to him and he has acknowledged you. Now it's time for your next lesson."

"My next lesson?" asked Elmer G. "What is my next lesson? How many lessons I got to learn anyway? All this self-improvement stuff is killing me quicker than if I hustled my own self down to the slaughter house and kicked open the front door."

"Elmer G., I want to tell you about a healthy, quality of life enhancing exercise that is going to change your life. I want to share something with you that's fun."

"Healthy?" said Elmer G. "Sharing something fun with me? What are you doing now? Selling Amway products?"

"No Elmer G., I'm not selling Amway products."

"Good," said Elmer G.

"But I do have something exciting and fun to share with you," said Barley.

"Well…bring it on, if it's fun!" said Elmer G. "I need something fun to do."

"Elmer G., I want you to go on a diet and start exercising. I want you to eat a good tossed salad of lettuce, tomatoes and cucumbers at least twice a week. This will be healthier than gorging yourself on slop every day. And I want you to set aside some time each day to take a brisk walk around the pig pens for exercise. When you see how much fun this stuff is, you'll be wondering why you weren't doing it before."

"And you must be crazy!" said Elmer G. in frustration. "What happened to sharing something fun? This don't sound like no fun to me. I'm a hog! How you gonna' ask a hog to skip his slop a couple of days a week? I can tell you right now it just ain't gonna happen."

"Elmer G., I wouldn't ask you to go power walking and eat salads unless there was a good reason."

"And what reason might that be?" asked Elmer G. "It would've been better if you were holding me hostage and giving me an Amway sales pitch with the pyramid pictures and all. I'm gonna' have one heck of a time giving up slop two days a week. I'm losing weight just thinking about it. I'll pro'bly shrivel up and float away like a kite."

"No, you won't shrivel up and float away," said Barley. "But, you do need to firm up your thighs and shoulder muscles a little bit. Farmer Brown wants his pigs to be nice and fat when he takes them to the slaughter house because they pay him by the pound. The weight of each pig determines the weight of the wad of dollars he gets paid. Pigs going to the slaughter house need to be rocked up and large, but not too fat."

"So that's why they do it," said Elmer G.

"Do what?" asked Barley.

"Feed us slop," said Elmer G.

"You just figuring that out?" said Barley. "Course that's why they feed us slop. Farmer Brown wants to fatten us up. But if you go on a diet and eat salads a couple of days a week, you'll lose some weight, but not too much. Especially if you exercise too. Walking is a great way to tone up your muscles. You'll be increasing odds that you will be spared the rib tips…..I mean….spared the trip to the slaughter house. Farmer Brown may cut you some slack when he sees your smaller, muscular body compared to all these big fat hogs. That-a-way, you won't look nearly as tempting a prospect for slaughtering. All the other hogs will look tasty, rumbling around overweight, looking for a stove to climb up on and get cooked."

"Didn't you tell me that your friend Plumper tried the starvation plan?" said Elmer G., more than a little concerned. "And he shriveled up to nothing."

"Plumper's situation was different," said Barley. "Plumper ended up dying 'cause he was too weak to fight for a spot at the feeding troughs."

"I'm not going out like that," said Elmer G. "No way."

"Relax," said Barley. "You're not going to diet to that extreme. We're just gonna' tone up your muscles a bit. There's a fine line between the right diet and too much of a diet. Trust me. I won't lead you wrong. Elmer G., I know what I'm doing. How do you think I got in the position I'm in today?"

"Barley…no offense, but you're a hog just like me. And we both live here in these hog pens."

"Don't be smart Mister!" said Barley. "You know what I mean! I'm still living, ain't I? I ain't been to no slaughter house."

"Barley, I'm gonna' have to think about this one. You may be going too far this time with this diet and exercise. But don't count me out. Just let me think about it. Maybe I'll give it a shot."

"Or get shot," added Barley, raising one of his eyebrows, as he looked off into the distance, never betraying any sign of emotion, as his last comment rolled off his lips. He looked as though he'd said something as innocent as "Good morning."

CHAPTER 12

Gory Days

"Talking about your religious beliefs is as easy as popping a frozen, store-bought apple pie into the oven for baking. But most of us lack the dedication to live our lives according to our religious beliefs. Weaving your religious beliefs into your everyday actions is a mighty hard thing to do. Especially when it requires you to give up stuff you love doing. Actually, it's easier and more entertaining to harass someone else into reforming their ways, rather than reforming ourselves."

Elmer G. stared in awe as he watched the sun rise majestically across the orange and blue sky. His spiritual faith was strong. He felt like God had wrapped a cloak of invincibility around his shoulders...pro'bly to protect his shoulder hams. According to Barley, mighty Angels stood ready to do God's bidding at the drop of a hat. Today, at least, he was not worried about being herded into the pens with the wooden floors and put on a diet of corn mash. He didn't feel miserable. Instead, he felt calm, and to a small degree, confident.

"I've got me a plan," he thought to himself. "I've got some good goals. This plan for my self-improvement ain't much in the way of *fun*...but they're still good goals."

When his mind started wandering a little, he thought about praying. Sometimes that helped push away the negativity. He might have survived the day in a good, positive mood if he'd gotten up and stirred around a bit to keep himself busy. But he didn't. Instead, he loitered in one spot too long, alone. His thoughts turned south, and things started looking down. As Elmer G. laid there basking in the morning sunrise, trying to hunker down and say his morning prayers, his mood whirled around and turned dark. The host of avenging Angels in his mind evaporated in size, speed and numbers, until Elmer G. saw only two short Angels protecting his perimeters. And they were engaged in playing a heated game of tic-tac-toe, instead of concentrating on standing guard over him.

Once he started down that negative pathway of thinking, he hitched on several additional eighteen-wheelers loaded with trunks full of negative thoughts. In no time at all, he was bouncing up and down, gripping the steering wheel of the first truck in the convoy stacked to the rafters with negative baggage.

Flat out of the blue, he remembered he could no longer run away into the woods. He. thought about how he was no longer free to wallow in his beloved mud. Soon, he was feeling right miserable. He remembered Barley wanted him to go on a diet and start walking for exercise. It was just too much for him. Elmer G.'s optimism put on a red, white and blue tear-away running suit and jogged away, as he rehashed all the fun stuff he could no longer do. Then he snapped out of his dream-like state and glanced around. Even those last two pint-sized Angels playing tic-tac-toe were gone now. He was by himself.

"Doggone if all these mind games and new habits are about to drive me crazy," he thought to himself.

Elmer G. got his first dose of exercise that morning by stomping defiantly over to Barley and angrily confronting him.

"Barley!" Elmer G. said. "I'm miserable! Just pure D. miserable!! I hate this being good stuff. I'm sick of staying clean. And another thing! I ain't praying no more. I ain't exercising. And I shore ain't going on no diet. I love slop more'n anything in the world. I can't give it up. It's like asking me to stop breathing. I need my slop! And running away? I'll run away when I feel like it. And I'll be back.....when I get back! I'll just take my chances. I'm gonna have my fun right now. If it kills me....then I'll just die. I'm gonna die like a hog should. I'll die with my head held high and my shoulders standing straight! My back may be up against the wall baby, but ole' Elmer G. will be standing tall! Siemper Fi! At least I would've had me some good times! I'm gonna use whatever time I have left on this earth doing the things I love!"

"I understand where you're coming from, Elmer G.," said Barley, without a trace of emotion in his voice. "And I'm gonna' respect your wishes."

"You are?", said Elmer G., in a thimble-sized voice. He had expected Barley to put up a furious fight to keep him from quitting his self-improvement program. He was caught off-guard and didn't know what else to say.

"We all have to live our own lives on our own terms," said Barley. "After listening to you....I'm kinda' inspired and fired up myself. At the end of the day, it's your life and your choices about how you choose to live it."

"You got that right," said Elmer G., as he marched away, obviously angry. He was still confused by Barley's calm acceptance of his quitting the self-improvement program. Angry frowns framed his face every time his feet made contact with the loose dirt he kicked up as he stomped off.

"Hey Elmer G.!" shouted Barley.

"What is it now?" asked Elmer G., as he stopped and whirled around to glare back towards Barley.

"Are you going to Olivia's birthing ceremony?" asked Barley.

"Yes I am, as a matter of fact," said Elmer G. "I heard she was expecting to give birth to a new litter of pigs some time this morning."

"Well then, why don't we just walk over there together," suggested Barley. "There ain't no sense in you stomping around here mad at me for giving you advice that *you* asked me for. But let's put that matter aside. Come on Elmer G. Buckle up boy! We'd better hurry. You know how crowded these birthing ceremonies get."

Elmer G. and Barley walked briskly over to the southwest corner of the pig pens where Olivia was stretched out on a make-shift mattress of soft hay, surrounded by about forty-three or so pigs milling around, chatting, as they waited for her to begin pushing out her new piglets. As Elmer G. and Barley chatted with the other pigs, some of the sows began setting out snacks they had brought to the ceremony. Suddenly, Olivia grunted in pain and whispered to one of the mid-sows that she was ready to start pushing. Olivia pushed out the first pink piglet accompanied by a soft "plop!" sound.

"It's a boar!" announced Madeline, the attending mid-sow, as she proudly announced the arrival of the newborn piglet she was holding high above her head for all to see. "Hey everybody! It's a boar!!"

"Excuse me, Miss Madeline," said Elmer G. to the attending mid-sow, who was still cradling the newborn piglet. "We all know these here birthing ceremonies are a bore. Everybody here has known for years that they are boring as all git-out. They've always been boring. And always will be boring, standing round here looking at pregnant sows squeezing piglets out onto the ground. Messy too. But you don't have to yell it out and embarrass Miss Olivia here. This is her first litter of piglets. And now you done gone and ruint' it. What's wrong with you, anyway? Screaming out loud "IT'S A BORE!!" Like we don't already know it. Now apologize to Miss Olivia and these other pigs. I mean it! Go ahead and apologize. I still can't believe you said that. Shame on you! Just shameful behavior! That's not a nice thing to say. Why you oughta' be ashamed of yourself saying….."

"Elmer G.!" screamed Madeline. "You are a complete idiot!! I said "It's a boar! The first piglet is a BOAR!! B…O….A….R. A male piglet! You numb-skull! I never said the birthing ceremony was a bore!"

The scene was so quiet you could hear a gnat breaking wind.

"Oh," said Elmer G., softly. "My bad."

"Alright!" announced Barley, as he jumped in to pick up the slack. "Let's everybody calm down and remember why we're here. Look out! Looks like another one's on the way out."

"We have another BOAR!!!" screamed the attending mid-sow, as she glared directly at Elmer G., silently daring him to utter a word.

The newborn boar piglet was a hot pink color and looked like he didn't have a wink of hair on his body. The piglet lay there with his eyes shut, looking for all practical purposes, like he was dead. He was covered in a slimy, clear, paper-thin sack of membrane. As each piglet was pushed out by Olivia, one of the mid-sows immediately nudged the new piglet off to the side and commenced to licking the thin birthing sack off, so the newborn could breathe and get comfortable. In no time at all, they were squirming around and greedily nursing.

As was the custom, the audience observed this birthing ceremony in absolute silence and wonder, as twelve new lives were dropped into their mist. After the last piglet was cleaned up, Barley joined two other elderly hogs, Old Man Riles and Old Man Jacob, in extending a heartfelt welcome to the new piglets on behalf of the pig's community. Next, the three elderly hogs rubbed an ancient incense on the forehead of each baby and presented each of them with a tiny gift bag containing little toys.

Finally, Barley invited everybody to partake in the refreshments.

"Before we eat," said Barley, "I wanna' say a few heartfelt words to commemorate…."

"Ohhh good gracious of life," groaned Elmer G. "Here we go with "Mister I only wanna' say a few words"…"

A ripple of muted giggles erupted and made a half-hearted effort to make their way around the crowd.

"What are you saying there, Elmer G." asked Barley, eyeing him suspiciously.

"Nuthin'. I ain't saying nuthin'," mumbled Elmer G.

"As you know, I am pig of few words," continued Barley. "And I wanna' share a few of those words with y'all. We are here to celebrate the birth of nine beautiful new piglets..."

"Twelve," said Elmer G., as he interrupted Barley.

"What?!" said Barley, glaring at Elmer G. in frustration. "What did you say?"

"I said there are twelve new piglets," said Elmer G. "You said there were nine..."

"What......ever!!!" shouted Barley, as he rustled around to face his audience again. "As I was saying, we are here to welcome these nine to twelve piglets, as they take their first breaths of life. May the winds of life always blow at your backs. May your joys be plentiful. Your sorrows small. And your life spans long as...."

"This speech," whispered Elmer G., as a spasm of giggles flashed through the crowd.

"Did somebody say something?" asked Barley. "Who said that? Was that you, Elmer G.?"

"No sir," said Elmer G.

"It'd better not be," said Barley. "Like I was saying, may these piglets' life spans be as long as a cold winter's night. And may they all find love in as many places as there are colors in the rainbow. We ask that meekness...you hear me, Elmer G.! We ask that meekness follow you all the days of your lives because it is written that the meek shall inherit the earth and all that is in it. And finally, we ask that your time upon this earth be filled with the pursuit of happiness and love for your fellow pigs. We hope that you do not spend your time worrying about what you will eat and wear. It is written that God feeds the birds that fly in the air. And He clothes the lilies of the fields in a colorful array of garments that are not matched by the finest raiments worn by Kings. And the lilies of the field do not toil to earn money to buy clothes, nor do the birds run out to shop for food at the supermarket. And yet God provides what they each need. Surely He will do no less for you."

The pigs burst into a long roaring round of applause at Barley's eloquence.

"Hey Barley!" shouted Ticker. "You've got it going on! I mean that was sweet! I've never heard you talk like that before.'"

"And I hope we never do again," said Elmer G. "He talks too long and I'm hongry'. I need to eat."

"Who said that?" said Barley, as he whipped his massive head around to find the culprit. "Was that you Elmer G.?"

"Nawww, Barley," said Elmer G., in his most convincing voice. "It wasn't me that said it. I'm not even standing next to the pig that said it. Matter of fact…I'm not even standing next to the pig that's standing next to the pig that said it. I'm not even standing next to the…"

"Elmer G.!" yelled Barley. "That's enough of your funny business now! Boy! Get a hold of yourself. What done got into you? Carrying on like you ain't got good sense. Now let's get back to these here festivities."

Although he tried, even Barley had to struggle to hold himself back from laughing at Elmer's G.'s wisecracks.

A spirit of joy and celebration engulfed the atmosphere of the pig pens. The pigs milled about and complimented Olivia on her beautiful brood and nudged the new piglets gently with their stouts. The pigs seemed to bask in the peaceful feeling brought on by witnessing the creation of life. God's grace hung so heavy in the air, you could cut it with the blunt edge of a fork.

Elmer G. walked over to where Barley was standing.

"Barley," said Elmer G., "I'm going to go back to my old life and have me some fun. I'm running away into the woods this morning and wallowing in the mud pits this afternoon. I ain't exercising no more neither. All that praying and dieting and keeping clean is too much work. It's bringing me down. I'm telling you like the farmer told the potato. I'll plant you now…and dig you later."

Having had his say, Elmer G. marched defiantly off into the morning mist, headed back to his old life. Elmer G. did a little jig step, as he thought about all the fun he was going to have. The anticipation was almost too much for him to bear.

He was primed to jump into the first mud pit he saw, when there was a great commotion. First there was the sound of engines screeching and whining in the distance. This was followed by the sight of giant dust clouds being kicked up by a convoy of trucks and cars rumbling down the dirt road......headed their way. This colorful parade of vehicles froze him and all the other pigs....dead in their tracks.

It seemed like six million humans were suddenly converging on the pig pens. They arrived in bunches by foot, car and truck. The humans started milling around rousting up all sorts of racket. The women unloaded cooking pots, skillets, serving platters and giant spoons. The men were talking and laughing. They started unloading equipment while they talked. The newcomers were sucking on unfiltered cigarettes, chewing tobacco and smacking on Juicy Fruit chewing gum, as they rocked back and forth on their heels, laughing and swapping stories.

"Ya'll listen up here now," said a short, pot-bellied man named Chug Williams. Chug had large, calm eyes and was balding on top. His hands and feet were extremely small, like a child's. He most always wore a beaten up, weathered leisure suit with a large, matching belt around the middle. The faded, dark brown leisure suit he was wearing today was straining to hold his stomach in, making him look like he was hiding a volleyball under it. Chug was also wearing a brown cap that snapped together in the middle so that the top wouldn't flap around.

"Chug's gonna' tell a story, ya'll," said Leggs Willis, a tall man who walked with a limp as result of a war injury. Everybody immediately shut up when Leggs spoke. They were scared of him and no one was sure why. Leggs was a reserved type of fella' who never talked much about his Vietnam experiences. But he watched everything with great interest. Some folks said he'd taken a bullet in the leg going back to rescue a friend during a night patrol that turned ugly. Leggs never confirmed this, nor denied it. He simply lived with it.

Leggs had one quality that was amazing. He was a world-class negotiator. When he was negotiating something with you, he would say "I want to sell this tool for one-hundred dollars." You might say, "I'll pay you seventy-five and not a penny more." Then, he would fix a stare on you and his eyes would slam down to thin slits like a snake-charmer and he'd repeat his original offer in an even tone. You'd find youself saying "One-hundred dollars is good. Let me toss in another five spot for a delivery charge." He had that kind of effect on you.

The man was a walking impression. There was this air of "Don't mess with me" about him. He was the type of man you stood across the street from before throwing him wolf tickets. Except for Chug. Leggs loved Chug because Chug made him laugh. He let Chug browbeat him to no end. Sometimes, Chug even threw fake Kung Fu kicks at him and Leggs would fall down like he was hurt. Solomon Brickman tried to throw a playful karate chop at Leggs one time. Leggs caught his foot in mid-swing and karate-chopped Solomon in his adams apple with the edge of his left hand. Solomon carried around a pen and a note pad from that day forward to write notes when he wanted to communicate. Even Chug stayed clear of Leggs for a few days after that episode.

"Thank you there, Leggs," said Chug. "Thank you for clearing the table for me so's I can get started. I'ma' tell ya'll a funny story I heard the other day. Be quiet over there, will ya!? Alright then.

Thank you there. Let me get started here. One time, there were these two...ahmmm....rats that lived on a ranch. And...and...and aahhmmm....then. Wait. I...I got it now. Let me...let...me start over. It'll only take me a second. Okay. Uhhhh......There once was a rat that owned a farm. Nawww....that can't be right. Hold it. Hold on now. I got it now for real. One time..uhmmm...one time there was a ranch. What was that I said the first time? A ranch....or a farm?"

"It don't sound exactly right, but you said a ranch," said Snag Bowden, blowing air out through his pursed lips and looking frustrated, as he waited on Chug to finish.

"You sure about that?" said Chug. "I...I...I know it wasn't a hotel," continued Chug in an upbeat tone of voice. "That's the other story that has the uhmmm.....motel in it. Snag....you sure it wasn't a farm?"

"I don't know what it is!" shouted Snag. "It ain't *my* story, you know. Though we might be better off if'n it was. You the one telling it, such as it is. But you said it was a ranch!"

"Well, I was wrong," announced Chug, pleased as pie that he was back on track with his story. "It was a farm. One time there was a farm. And these two rats were visiting....no...they lived there...I think. The two rats lived...no......these two *mouses* lived on the farm. One night the mouses...they both fell....naww...it was around noon, which is really day-time. Yeah, because midnight would be nighttime, wouldn't it? One day the two mouses....that's both mouses you see. They ummm...they tripped over...a log and bumped into a bucket of.....no...no....wait....I got it now. What happened is that they both fell into a can...no....it was a pail....a bucket. I'm sorry. I tripped....I mean....they tripped...the mouses tripped up on a mothball and fell into a bucket of old dishwater, you see."

"Chug," said Charlie Lee Bossier, "what kinda' story you trying to tell?"

"I'm almost through," said Chug, calm as a wig propped up on top of a dead woman's head, as he meandered through his story, oblivious to the effect he was having on his audience. All his attention was focused on making progress and keeping his meager facts straight. He wiped some beads of sweat off the front of his forehead with a grimy handkerchief he whipped out of his back pocket, blew his nose violently, stuck his plow back into the ground.....and continued breaking old ground.

"I'm gonna' finish now," announced Chug, pleased as punch with his own initiative. "The two mouses fell into a bucket of old dishwater and almost suffocated....I'm sorry....I meant to say drowned. They almost drowned in the bucket of dishwater. Okay now...this is my last change. For real. Last chance. I mean...my last change. They fell into a bucket of cream....."

"What's your point, Chug?" asked Charlie Lee.

"I'm getting there," said Chug. "Quit rushing me. Just stay with me here. Now, like I was saying, It wasn't dishwater. It was a bucket of cream. I got 'em confused because the dishwater and cream are both white and foamy-like, so you can see how a body can get mixed up and mistake a pail of dishwater for a bucket of cream. Nope, ain't no shame on my part for making that little mix up. None a-tall. Where was I? Oh yeah. I remember now. Like I was saying, the mouses fell into a bucket of cream. It was whole cream and not skim cream."

"It don't matter if it was whole cream, skim cream or even chocolate cream, Chug," said Charlie Lee. "Just move it along, will you. Why you telling us what kind of cream it was anyway?"

"You're right, Charlie Lee," said Chug. "It don't matter. That don't affect my story, but I thought you all might be curious about what kinda' cream we're talking about. I had a cousin named Hallie Jones. She was curious about the smallest detail and..."

"Chug!" yelled Charlie Lee. "Tell the story or sit down, please!"

"Anyway," said Chug, glaring at Charlie Lee, "the first mouse tried so hard to climb out by scrambling up over the edge of the bucket of cream. But naturally, he got tired and fell back into the bucket. He was plumb tuckered out from trying to climb out and when he fell back in, he drowned in the cream. The second mouse, who had just recently celebrated his.....uhmmmm....was it his second birthday or third birthday? I don't know why I'm asking about his birthday 'cause it don't really matter no way. But I seem to remember he did have a cake. Vanilla? No, chocolate. Definitely chocolate. Funny thing about it was that it wasn't really a birthday cake. Just a kinda' pound cake with candles on top. Anyway, like I was saying.....the...uhmmm.....the second rat started ...."

"Mouse," said Charlie Lee, in a weary voice. "It was a mouse, Chug."

"I *know* that, Charlie Lee!" said Chug, trembling with indignation at being interrupted. "*That's* exactly what I said earlier. Didn't you hear me? Pro'bly not, 'cause you ain't exactly paying attention. Is you? Who telling this story anyway? Me or you? Anyway, like I was a-saying...the first mouse started flailing his......"

"You're on the second mouse now," said Charlie Lee, in his weariest voice.

"Chug, let somebody else tell a story," suggested another bystander named Hollis Jones.

"No," said Chug. "Just let me finish. The second rat...I mean mouse. The second mouse started churning around in the bucket of cream and flailing his feet and kicking so hard that he turned the bucket of cream into a solid block of cheese....no wait...he churned the cream into a bucket of butter. And then...and then....ummm.."

"What happened to the second mouse after he churned the bucket of cream into butter?" asked Charlie Lee in that patient, but weary voice.

"Well," said Chug, "he uhmmm…I remember it now. He got his little feet stuck in the butter. And he couldn't get loose no matter how hard he tried. Matter of fact, he darn near pulled one of his legs off trying to get unstuck. He was trying so hard to get out that he left scratch marks all along the sides of the bucket. And then he died stuck to the butter 'cause he couldn't get no food or water. Unless you count butter as a member of the food group. But he couldn't live offa' butter long no way. I'm done."

After Chug finished telling his story he looked around the crowd of faces as if he were collecting laughter and applause, but nobody was doing either. They all looked puzzled and confused.

"And your point is?" asked Charlie Lee, the group's spokesman. He was as puzzled and confused as everybody else.

"The point of the story," said Chug, "is that if you keep working at something and you keep struggling, then you get to live longer."

"Chug, what kind of story is that?" asked Hollis. "It don't even make no sense."

"Well," said Chug, "the second mouse lived longer than the first mouse because he kept kicking his feet until he turned the cream into butter. So, if you are facing a tough situation, then you need to keep fighting and thrashing around trying to get out and you'll live longer."

"I think I'm beginning to see your point, Chug," said Morris Jackson, who was slow of speech and sorta' dim-witted since Charlie Lee's horse had accidentally kicked him in the right temple about three years earlier.

"You like my story, Morris?" asked Chug, pleased as pie at this unanticipated development. Normally his stories weren't so well received.

"Yeah," said Morris, nodding his head up and down in agreement. I like your story. It has a good moral and makes a lot of sense. But I do have one question."

"What's that?" said Chug, as he barely retrained himself from hugging Morris for liking his story.

"How much longer did the second rat live than the first rat?" asked Morris. "The reason I'm asking is because depending on how much longer the second rat lived, your story may have a good moral to it. And it's a pretty funny story too. I'll remember this story long as I live. Especially the part where the rabbit falls into the bucket of cheese. Aha! Aha ha!! Matter of fact, why don't you tell it again. Come on Chug. Tell it again."

"Really?" asked Chug, who tried to hide his surprise because this was the first time anybody had asked him to repeat one of his stories.

"Yeah," said Morris, in an encouraging tone of voice. "I ain't got nothing but time. It's a good story. Tell us again from the beginning."

"That's a good idea," said Chug, as his breath quickened with excitement at being invited to re-tell his story. He decided to hurry up and jump right in before this opportunity evaporated. Chug squared his shoulders and commenced to plowing through his story again for the benefit of his appreciative audience of one.

"Once upon a time, a long time ago," said Chug. "There were these two...ahmmm....rats that lived on a ranch. I added the "once upon a time part". That's new. It gives my story a fairy tale sorta' texture. Well now, like I was saying......these two rats...."

"Ohh nooo!" shouted several of the men in unison.

"We've heard enough," said Hollis.

"Well," said Chug, pleased with himself and expecting a reward. "Ain't somebody gonna' offer me a drank or something? My throat is mighty parched from all this talking I've been doing."

"I'ma offer you a seat!" said Hollis. "Come on over here out the way and sit your tired self down somewhere so somebody else can tell a *real* story. Talking about —- is 'anybody gonna' offer you a drank'. Why....I wouldn't dare waste my good whiskey on a low-life like you! I mean it, Chug! I need to stop hanging out with you and get myself a better class of friends. That's what *I* need to do. Sit yourself right over here on this stump by me and git' out the way. We got any *real* storytellers here?"

A tall, lanky man named Travis stood up, held his fist to his mouth and cleared his throat. He was wearing tattered old black blue jeans and a faded white cowboy hat. He strolled out to the center of the circle of men and spoke.

"I've got a story for ya'll," announced Travis in an even monotone. His voice stayed steady and did not bounce up or down. He was obviously a man comfortable spinning a story. "There was this farmer one time who had a pig that saved his life."

"How'd the pig do that?" asked one of the other men, as he took a neat swig from a bottle wrapped in a brown paper bag.

"Well," continued Travis in that same steady, assuring voice that hinted that he knew where his story was going. "The story about the life-saving pig was so incredible that the newspapers printed it on the front page. Everybody at the barbershop, diner and filling station was speculating about this famous pig. A news reporter was curious about the story, so he hopped in his car and drove out one day to the farmer's house to see if the story would hold water. You know how reporters are. He wanted to get all the details, you know."

"Did the farmer tell him what happened?" asked Ed Brewster, one of the other men in the audience.

"Oh yeah," said Travis. "They talked up a storm. Naturally, the old farmer was pleased as pudding over all this attention being thrown his way. The reporter asked the farmer how the pig saved his life. "Well, said the farmer, "I was in the farmhouse sleep one night and the house caught fire. I didn't know nothing about it the way I was a-snoring and all. You know how it is after you been out before dawn mending fences, slopping hogs, feeding chickens and what-not. Naturally, I was plumb tuckered out to no end. All of a sudden, I heard this loud grunting and snorting and heard something crashing into my furniture and all."

"What was it?" asked one of the men.

Travis continued his story. "Well," said the farmer, "I woke up and there was my good old faithful pig snorting, grunting and nudging me in the side to wake me up and save me from the fire. I jumped up and me and my pig raced outta' the house in no time flat. My pig saved my life. Bless his dear heart."

"That's an amazing story," said the reporter. "Where is this life-saving pig? Can I see him?"

"Sure thing," said the farmer. "Then he took the reporter over to a special pig pen. Inside, laying in a corner was a pig. The farmer took a pole and nudged the pig so he would get up and walk around. The reporter, being a sharp fellow, noticed the pig was missing one of his back legs."

"What happened to the pig's leg?" asked the reporter. "Did he lose it in the fire?"

"Shucks nawww," said the farmer, looking at the reporter like he couldn't believe he had the audacity to ask such a question. Then the farmer leaned over towards the reporter and said, "Why.....you cain't eat a good pig like this.......all at one time."

The audience howled with laughter. They hooted and screamed, as they slapped their knees and wiped the tears from their eyes.

"Travis!" shouted on of the men, "you know you can tell a story! Boy, that was a good 'un! I never could've told it that-a-way. Not in a million years! Come have a drank on me!"

Several of the other men offered the storyteller a cigarette and additional swigs from the pint bottles wrapped in brown paper bags as a reward for telling such a fine story.

Chug was silently simmering because it wasn't fair, in his mind the way they were all mistreating him when he'd told his story. He thought to himself, "...and it was such a fine story too. Plus, I told it so well—in such a grand fashion. I made my characters come to life. That's 'cause *I* practiced telling *my* story before spreading it out before the public. You could tell Travis just did a hit and miss number on his'n. Now, here they all are back-slapping Travis and offering him swigs of good whiskey that should've been coming my way. It ain't fair and I won't stand for it. All this commotion on account of that sorry pig story Travis told. Pig story wasn't even funny and didn't make no sense a-tall."

As he sat there glowering like charcoals that had burned down to a whitish ash after an hour or so in the barbeque pit, getting madder and madder as he listened to the men heap praise on Travis, Hollis walked by where Chug was sitting. Hollis was on his way to pick up a bucket of water and unfortunately, he accidentally stepped on Chug's right foot. This latest humiliation was the final straw for Chug.

He thought to himself, "First they make fun of my story. And now they gonna' step all over me too. And the man ain't even got the common courtesy to say excuse me dog!" As hard as he tried to show some self-restraint, he was 'bout to bust a gut holding his feelings inside. He spoke in his most dangerous and ominous voice.

"Holler......ris!" said Chug, slurring his words slightly. "You stepped on my foot. You ain't gonna' say excuse me or nothing?" Chug squinted his eyes at Hollis and continued. "You always been jealous of me. Ain't you Hollis? Go on and admit it! You never liked me, have you? Well, I got news for *you*, Mister! You ain't never been *my* cuppa' tea neither. I'm pretty much a coffee man myself. Hic! Hup! You know something, Hollis. I ain't never been too particular about *you* from the git' go! And you didn't like my story—did you? Did you?! Don't you stand there and deny it!! I heard you loud-talking me over there. What was that you said? "Chug, what kind of story is that? It don't even make no sense." Well, see if it make sense when I wallop you upside your lopsided...."

"Hush up, Chug!" said Charlie Lee. "Why you always got to act ignorant and start a ruckus every time a group of us get together socially? Just let it go."

"Not for pie, I won't!" said Chug. "A lesser man might let it go," he continued, "but I'm a bird of a different feather." As he spoke, he stood and hitched up the front of his belt, like a gunfighter from the Old West adjusting his six-shooter holsters. Then Chug spread his fingers out wide on each hand and stretched his arms out by his side with his palms facing the ground like he was about to draw his imaginary pistols any second.

Chug started slowly bouncing his eagle-spread hands up and down from the middle level of his chest down to right below his belt. Then he twisted his head to the left and right like he was cracking his own neck. Chug started to pacing to the left six feet and back to the right six feet in a straight line, hunched over in a boxer's crouch, head poked out and weaving it like somebody was swinging at him——eye-balling Hollis all the while. He kept twisting his neck form side to side as he walked and bouncing his flat palms up and down gently, as though he might whip out his six-shooters at any instance and start blasting away. Chug was pacing back and forth like a tiger that had been caged up too long at the zoo. He was filled with self-righteous indignation at all of the imagined insults the other men had supposedly heaped on him. Finally, he stopped pacing and squared off again in front of Hollis.

"Hollis!" shouted Chug. "Personally, I'm dead set against fighting you. That's just the kinda' man I am. But my daddy would turn over in his grave if I let you git' by with insulting me this-a-way! So, I'm honor-bound to step up to this nasty plate of insults you pushing over here in front of me. I wanna' walk away from this fight. But I can't rest if I do. Wouldn't be able to sleep no more. I ain't got no choice in the matter. It's outta' my hands. Looks like I'ma' have to teach you some manners, boy. If your mama had a done her job when you was little....why...it'd save me some trouble....and I wouldn't have to do it now."

Hollis stopped smiling, as his neck stiffened. Then, as a ball of fiery anger rolled up and percolated from the bottom of his feet to the tip-top of his hair, his eyes slammed down to become thin as razor blades, as he involuntarily clenched his fingers into fists.

"Chug," said Hollis. "Man...you done gone too far now. Nobody talks about my mama."

"I tole' you to hush up, Chug!" said Charlie Lee, jumping in and trying to starve off a fight. "Have you just completely lost your mind, or what?! Come on Hollis. Don't pay Chug no never mind. You know how ignorant he gits' when he's had a few drinks. Sit down and let bygones be bygones. And you Chug! I tole' you to just let it go."

"And I tole' *you* that a lesser man might let it go," said Chug. "But I ain't cut from the same cloth as most men. I was a mean baby 'cause I was raised on sour milk! I'm a mean man 'cause I eat raw onions. I ain't never backed down from no man alive. I'm a double-jointed terror from the backwoods of Georgia. And where I'm from...why...if a man disrespects you.....you gotta' call him out! Holler....ris! I'm a-calling you out. You just wanna' walk all over me 'cause I'm little. But I won't stand for it! No sireee! I'd rather dance on my daddy's grave first!"

"Chug," said Hollis, "what are you talking about? You sound like you done lost your mind."

"You mean to tell me you gonna' stand here——all up in my face——trying to stop *me* from telling the truth!" said Chug. "The truth makes you nervous, don't it Hollis? Conscience kinda' bothering you now? Huh? Can't sleep at night? I'ma' tell you what your problem is. See now, I know what the *real* problem is between me and you. Are you a hater, Hollis? I b'lieve you are. You hate me 'cause I'm short. You got it in for us folks that are vertically challenged, ain't you Hollis. I've seen you looking down on me."

"Chug," said Hollis, in a weary voice. "How I'm gonna' look *up* to you when you're shorter than me?"

"So you admit it!!" shouted Chug. "Now we're gettin' some-wheres. We're gonna' slap some lipstick on this pig if I have to stay here *alllll* day. It's the principle of the thing. A man that won't fight for his principles......ain't fit to live!"

"Ohhh boy," groaned Leggs. "Here we go again."

"Hush your mouth, Leggs," said Chug, glaring at Leggs in a menacing manner. "This ain't even about you—— but it can be, if you don't shift gears and back up. Now, back to Mr. Hollis. Hollis....I been noticing things have been headed this way for a longgggggg time. Yes! Me and you been headed for this head-knocking confirmation for a long time! Ever since that day I walked up into the County Courthouse and married your sister——Ella. Well, for your information...Mister High and Mighty....I never wanted to marry your sister no way. I did it 'cause she was so crazy about me and I hated to break her heart. According to her, the sight of me in a leisure suite———I mean—suit—- near 'bout drove her crazy. Nothing would suit her but to have old Chug all to herself. Out of respect for her feelings for me....I married Ella. And you've had it in for me ever since! And I have had enough...."

"Ahmm. Excuse me, Chug," interrupted Blookie Allen, in a stage whisper. "But that was *my* sister Ella you married. Don't you remember? It was September of 1976. Ella had just been crowned Miss Bicentennial Sausage Queen of Opelousas, Louisiana. Remember how grand she looked wearing that red, white and blue gown with the white lace. I was so proud of her. She had on that gorgeous, fiery-red sash draped across her mid-section. And don't forget those fabulous blue pumps she squeezed her size thirteens into and her red rhinestone tiara and white hose with the runs on the side and....."

"Whatever!!" shouted Chug, glaring at Blookie like he'd lost his mind. "It don't rightly matter no way! 'Cause this rascal standing here has still got rocks sticking in his craw when it comes to me!! And Blookie! You just remember one thing! Whatever is said here amongst us mens...stays here. You ain't got to go running off telling Ella about nothing I said. Not that I'm afraid of her. You know what I'm saying? Where was I at before Blookie took over my conversation? Oh yeah. Mr. Hollis over here is in denial. You don't care for me Hollis...and you know it's true!! Stand up like a man and admit it!"

"Chug," said Hollis. "Quit all this loud-talking you doing to me. Man...you know I ain't got no quarrels with you. None a'tall. But I will have some if you keep bad-mouthing me. I didn't start this fight Chug....but I'll 'shore finish it if I have to."

"So....Mr. Eloquent," said Chug, in a mocking tone of voice, as he commenced to pacing methodically back-and-forth again. "This is just more proof of what I've been saying all along. You starts off with an apology and ends up...threatening me. I ain't done nothing to deserve no threats from you. But that's okay. I know what's going on. This issue between us is about more'n you stepping on my foot. You feeling froggy, Hollis? Well....go ahead and jump!"

"Chug," said Hollis, "I ain't got nothing against you. I ain't got no beefs with you a'tall."

"Yes you do!" said Chug quickly, sensing his prey was trying to slip away out the back door by apologizing. "Don't you try to slouch away from me by denying you got it in for me! You've had bad feelings towards me brewing on the back of your stove for a longgggg time. I seen it coming. But! In order to keep our friend-ship on an even keel——I denied all the evidence sittin' on my plate right in front of me. For your sake, Hollis! I did it all for *your* sake! 'Cause *I* wanted to be a good friend to you! But, it's always the good ones like me, that get stabbed in the back."

"I ain't never stabbed you in your back," protested Hollis.

"Yes you did!" said Chug, slamming his right fist into the palm of his left hand with a loud "Smack!". You did it. And you know you did it! And you know that I know that you know you did it." Chug paused. "What was I saying?"

"You were saying that "You know that I know that you know you did it," said Blookie, in an attempt to be helpful.

"Shut up Blookie!" said Charlie Lee. "Chug...calm down and..."

"Don't be taking his side against me, Charlie Lee," said Chug. "Hollis! 'Cause of you, I got a knife sticking outta' my back just like that there salad boy. Yep. This is the exact same thing that happened to that Roman boy that got rich selling all them salads. Ya'll know who I'm talking about. Who was the boy that wore the skimpy, white skirt and the sandals that you have to lace the straps up all the way to your knees? Somebody help me out! What's his name? Iceberg? Ice Cube? Cobb? Nawww. Caesar. That's it!! Caesar. His friend stabbed him in the back too. What was Caesar's friend's name?"

"Et Tu!" shouted Blookie from the sideline, as the other onlookers gazed at him with an appreciative nod of their heads at his knowledge of classical literature.

"Yeah," said Chug. "Like I was saying, Caesar's friend, Et Tu, stabbed him in the back too. Now you done stabbed me in the back the same way. Just like Et Tu stabbed Caesar, the salad bar—
—I mean—-Caesar, the salad boy."

"Chug," said Blookie. "You comparing yourself to Caesar now?"

"That's right!" said Chug. "And why not? Ain't Caesar good enough to compare hisself' with me? I bet you didn't know how much edumacation I had, did cha'? Me and Caesar was both in our prime when we took a knife in our backs."

"Chug," said Blookie. "Man, what you talking about? Caesar was an emperor, or a king or something like that."

"I *know* that!" said Chug. "He was the King of the salads. And I am the King of the used tire retreads unit at Wally's Tire World.

Every time somebody ask, "Who made the salad?" The peoples yell "Caesar made the salad!" And when they ask "who did your retread on your tires?" The peoples answer, "Chug!" But the fame don't matter now. Since we both got taken out by our friends in our prime. And good as I've tried to be to Hollis over the years. This is the thanks I get. Hollis! You're like a homeless dog that bites the hand that feeds him. You think I won't stand up for myself, don't you? Answer me, Hollis! You yaller-bellied, tic-biting, spineless son of a ballooza! Answer me!!"

"Let it go, Chug," pleaded Hollis. "It was an accident when I stepped on your foot. I ain't meant you no harm or disrespect."

"That's all I want!" said Chug, weaving from side-to-side. "All I wants is some R-E-S-P-T-C-P! That's what I want——and deserve!"

"Chug," interrupted Blookie. "Man…that ain't how you spell 'respect'."

Chug fixed his smoldering gaze on Blookie. "I says I wants me some R-E-S-P-T-C-P! Now Blookie….tell me….is that how you spell respect, or no?"

"That's how we gonna' spell it today," announced Blookie, as he backed away to the outer edge of the crowd, since he had no intention of getting involved in this fight.

"Chug," said Hollis, trying to end this argument in a non-violent way, "Like I said before….I ain't disrespecting you. I never meant to step on your foot. I didn't even know I had touched you."

"Oh!" said Chug, in a course whisper, taking another quick swig from his bottle. He stopped pacing back and forth, shifted his feet, spread them twelve inches apart and glared menacingly at Hollis. "So now you got the nerve to be calling me a *liar*. Who in 'dignation you think you is? You ain't nothing special. You just a piece a reg'lar mail, same as the rest of us. I puts my pants on the same way you do Hollis. Both legs at a time. But no. It ain't enough for you to stomp all over me. Now you gonna' go to acting all biggity and calling your friend a liar! Well I won't stand for none of that fresh talk. Treatin' me like I'm a piece of common trash. Come on over here and fight me like a man! I'm standing here in eye-reach. Pretend you're a grasshopper and hop on over here and get some of this. Answer me this, Hollis! Who's your daddy?! Huh?! Who's your daddy?!"

This last insult evidently touched a nerve with Hollis because he quickly stomped over and punched Chug square on his left jaw. Chug dropped like a load a brick. But, quick as a flash, he sprang back up, scrambled around a bit and punched Hollis in the left ear——hard. Chug shouted "I ain't a-done yet!" And just like that———they were rolling around on the ground, throwing harmless body punches.

"Fight!!" yelled the men. "We got us a fight!! Looks like a good-un' too!!"

The crowd of men yelled encouragement to Hollis and Chug. Then they whipped raggedy dollar bills outta' their pants pockets and started placing bets on the outcome of the fight. The pot quickly shot up to thirty dollars.

Finally, Charlie Lee had seen enough. Charlie Lee jumped up and grabbed Chug under the arms, as he separated them and pulled Chug away. Chug was still kicking at Hollis as Charlie Lee dragged him away off to the side.

"Chug!!" shouted Charlie Lee. "Boy! What is wrong with you?! Stop it! Quit that! If you kick him again, *I'm* gonna' hit you myself! I mean it! We out here trying to socialize and here you are fighting and carrying on. Pull yourself together and set down. I mean it. You hear me? I oughta' whip you myself! Causing all this uproar. And over nothing!"

"Charlie Lee!" screamed Chug. "I can't believe you gonna' hold me so's Hollis can beat me up! And me and you been friends since first grade. It's a shame the way ya'll is double teaming poor Chug this-a-way! And me being the smallest one of the bunch. And here ya'll ganging up on me this-a-way. But you know me. I ain't no quitter. No sireee! I ain't going out like this. I'll fight all of ya'll if that's the way it's gotta' be. But I'm a warning you. You'd better bring a "A" game! 'Cause I may be on the smallish side——but I got the strength of ten men! And you don't wanna' make Chug sad! I mean——mad! I…..I…..I…."

"Hush up Chug!" said Charlie Lee. "Ain't nobody double teaming on you! I'm trying to sit you down before you get yourself hurt. Come over here and sit down! You'd better act like you got some sense. I'm gonna' drive you home if you don't cut it out. Every time you get in your cups you wanna' start a fight. Hush up now! I mean it."

"Hollis," announced Chug grandly, flinging his arms open in a gesture of welcome and good will. "Come on over here and let me pour you a drank of my finest whiskey! You deserve it! And more, Hollis——you the best friend a man ever had. I mean that from the bottom of my heart. And you're the bravest man in this whole passel of low-lifes out here. Ain't a man out here brave enough to tangle with Chug——but you. And I wants you to know….I respects you for your courage. I 'shore do. Hollis…..you're a champion amongst thoroughbreds. A race horse running around with a pack of plow mules. That's you, Hollis. You're a man amongst boys. I saved my finest words…for the finest man….in his finest hour……and I salute you. Boys! Let's drink a toast to my bestest friend….Hollis!"

"Chug," said Hollis as he strolled over and poured them both drinks in two Dixie cups, "I always liked you. I want to say this in front of every man here. I'm so glad we're friends! You're like the brother I never had. If I was in a bar fight, why you'd be the one man I'd want there to cover *my* back. You're a man after my own heart, 'cause you got a lotta' heart. You're one man with hair on his breath…and hair on his chest! Chug….I'll say one thing about you….. you ain't afraid of the devil hisself!"

"Hollis, quit it now," said Chug, glancing bashfully at the ground and kicking up a small tuft of dirt with the heel of his right boot, basking in the praise from his friend. "You ain't got to say that on my account. But it sounds like it's coming straight from the heart. So, I'm a taking it that-a-way. I ain't holding no grudges. All's forgiven. That was some little tussle we had, wasn't it? Here! Here!"

The two men toasted their enduring friendship with their arms wrapped around each other's shoulders, propping themselves up. Everybody relaxed and got back to the task at hand, as the harsh words and missed punches quickly faded from their collective memories, blown away in the cool morning air.

"Hey Chug," whispered Charlie Lee, as he leaned over towards Chug in a conspiratorial manner. "I didn't wanna' say this in front of the others, but Caesar's friend that stabbed him.....his name wasn't no Et Tu. I don't know where Blookie got that foolishness from."

"It wasn't?" said Chug, in a puzzled tone of voice. "Well.....what was his name then?"

Charlie Lee twisted his nose and made a small sniffing sound, as he puffed himself up with importance and whispered, "his name was.....Brute."

"Like that there cologne they sell in the green bottle with the silver label?" asked Chug, obviously in awe of Charlie's Lee's superior intelligence.

"The one and the same," said Charlie Lee, as he took on a look of modesty and flicked imaginary dust specks off the thighs of his blue jeans.

"Charlie Lee," sad Chug, "thanks for pulling my coattail and setting me straight. You know.....you always been the smartest one amongst us. Even back in high school. I should've known to ask you for the answer. I'm mighty appreciative for the way you handled this on the down-low."

"No problem," said Charlie Lee. "I know them classics back-wards and forwards like the back of my hand. Sometimes, I reads 'em just for fun."

Now that they had cleared the air regarding their fight, Chug started telling Hollis and the other men what he was gonna' do to them if they had not stopped the fight.

"I was just about to raise my game," explained Chug. "It's a good thing Charlie Lee pulled me away. It was about to get ugly out here..."

"You're already ugly enough," chipped in Charlie Lee, with a sly smile, as he listened to Chug lying. All of the men roared with laughter, relieved that things were back to normal within their ranks.

Chug basked in the moment, as he rubbed his hands together and continued doing something he was really good at——lying. "I was just about to raise myself up and whip some behinds! Ya'll don't wanna' see Chug mad. It ain't a pretty sight. Hide the wom-enfolks and children. That's all I got to say. I was gonna' take on the whole pack of ya'll! Yes I was. I don't normally tell folks this, but I was once a United States Navy Dolphin. Special operations is what we did——mostly."

"Chug," said Leggs, in a low, conspiratorial tone of voice. "You was a Navy *Seal*. Remember?"

"That's right!" said Chug, fired up with enthusiasm. "I was a Navy Seal baby! I mean to tell you. We fought on the land. The sea. We even fought in the air. I was a mess. I once swimmed across the Sea of Galilee with three injured comrades on my back."

"Come on Chug," said Travis. "That's impossible."

"When Jesus walked on the top of the water in the Sea of Galilee," said Chug. "There was somebody back in Galilee just like you, Travis. Talking about "Jesus, it's impossible to walk on the water. Fess up now. You know you ain't walked on top of no water." The men howled and screamed with laughter at this come-back. Even Travis laughed and waved his hands in mock defeat.

Meanwhile, the pigs seemed darn near paralyzed as they watched these preparations unfolding like a stage crew getting the stage set up before a big production. A feeling of excitement rippled through the air. Anxious anticipation crackled around the pig pens like thunderbolts on steroids, as the whole pig pen felt like it had been hit with a bolt of electricity. Ordinary activities took on new meanings because the pigs didn't know what anything meant anymore. They were operating in an arena that was not like anything they'd ever seen before. The pigs were paralyzed because they didn't know what was going on.

Some of the men commenced to boiling water in giant barrels. Others were sharpening their carving knives. Quite a few of the men were still guzzling whiskey from flat bottles wrapped in brown, crumbled paper bags. They told other outrageous tales and traded jokes, as a feeling of excitement and antsy anticipation sliced through the chilly air. They rubbed their hands together in the cold, brisk air, as they loudly swapped stories, threw their heads back and laughed in booming, knee-slapping outbursts. Although the pigs didn't understand what all the commotion was about, some of them started to feeling like they were taking part in the festivities too.

A rumor spread amongst the ranks of pigs that this party was a joint celebration between humans and pigs to cement their new, harmonious relationship of mutual co-existence. A glow of happiness settled around the pigs, as the feeling of excitement rose to a fever pitch.

Then......a single rifle shot rang out from the direction of a grassy knoll about thirty-six yards away. **POWWW!!!**

So much for the feeling that this might be turning into a celebration of mutual co-existence between humans and pigs.

The sound of the rifle shot exploded like a bomb, as it slashed through the air and echoed throughout the pig pens. The sharp sound of the rifle shot seemed to ricochet through the woods for twelve minutes. Elmer G. and all the other pigs froze in their tracks. Then some of them raced over to where the shot had come from. Others ran the opposite way. The pigs skidded to a stop, as they saw Scruff Daddy stretched out on the ground......motionless and absolutely quiet. He was either dead or doing one heck of a job playing 'possum.

The answer became clear once they noticed a slight trickle of blood rolling down from an almost invisible hole in the center of his forehead. Scruff Daddy had been shot smack dab between his eyes. His limp body was dragged off to a giant oak tree where they tied him up by his hind legs upside down, four feet above the ground. In a flash, his lifeless body was swaying from side-to-side in a solitary death dance.

And then, just when it appeared the scene could not get any more gruesome, Farmer Brown casually walked over to where Scruff Daddy was hanging, flicked his still burning Malboro out behind him onto the ground, exhaled a toxic cloud of cigarette smoke from between his parched lips, ran his tongue across his bottom row of jagged, yellow-stained teeth and slowly drew his carving knife out. As the pigs watched in fascination, he slit Scruff Daddy's throat from ear to ear and let his blood drain down into a large bucket that two of the bystanders slid underneath the lynched pig. When the blood slowed to a drip, several of the men hoisted Scruff Daddy down and carried him over to a huge brown metal barrel of hot water. They unceremoniously dropped him in head-first, where he commenced to boiling like a gigantic, hairy tea bag.

After he'd perculated for thirty-seven minutes, Farmer Brown and his friends lifted Scruff Daddy's body out of the barrel and wrapped him in a pile of course old croaker sacks. Then they poured a gazillion gallons of scalding hot water over the croaker sacks. They left his body lying inside the wet croaker sacks with steam slowly rising, as it drifted lazily skyward, like cigar smoke blowing gently in the balmy afternoon air.

Evidently the hot water worked to soften Scruff Daddy's body hair, because when they snatched those croaker sacks off of him, they got all lathered up with sweat, as they commenced to feverously scraping the hair off his body with their sparkling carving knives by scraping their sharp knives opposite the natural direction that Scruff Daddy's hair grew. They held their knives with both hands, as they gripped the knife handle in one hand and placed their other hand on the blunt edge of the knife above the cutting edge. They scraped from his rear above his tail towards his head. The men got all down on their knees to get better traction, as they scraped the hair off Scuff Daddy. They scraped him until Scruff Daddy's entire body was pink as a white rabbit's eyes. When they finished scraping his hair off, they deftly cut Scruff Daddy up into pieces and dropped the different pieces of his body into gigantic silver-colored roasting pans.

Elmer G. and the other pigs stood frozen in shocked disbelief. They watched as Scruff Daddy was miraculously transformed from a live pig into a red and pink panorama of neatly butchered up display meats. He changed right before their eyes into hunks of hams, slabs of bacon, racks of pork ribs, pig feet, chitlins and a leftover pile of meat pieces that would later be ground into sausage. There were so many piles of meat lying around that Elmer G. thought the humans might say a table blessing and eat Scruff Daddy right on the spot.

The pigs gathered around in a semi-circle to get a close-up gander at what the humans were doing to Scruff Daddy. The pigs on the front row had the best vantage points, since they were there first. The late-arriving pigs in the back row started pushing and complaining that they couldn't see the action.

"Ya'll move along now, so other folks can get a look see," said a pig named Janice. "Ya'll taking up all the best spots! Move! That ain't enough! Move over some more!!! Let me see!!"

"That's right," chimed in Horace. "Ya'll done looked long

enough. Now ya'll hogging up all the prime spots up front. We cain't hardly see nuthin' from way back heah!"

"Horace is right," said Sarah Jane. "Git' your fill a-looking and move on outta' the way. Some of us other pigs wanna' see 'em cut Scruff Daddy up. Won't be nuthin' left of him by the time ya'll finish ooahing and ahhhing up a storm. Ya'll taking up all the prime spots! We cain't see nuthin' back here!"

"Tell 'em Sarah Jane!" shouted Tally, who was standing three rows back and couldn't see a thing except the rear end of the pigs crowed in front of him. "Move along if you done already seen him. It just ain't fair....I tell you. It ain't fair a'tall. Ya'll pigs up front don't care if we miss all the good stuff. Doggone it! We're missing the best parts. We gonna' miss it all for 'shore. I cain't see nuthin'. Not one speck of blood or nuthin'!"

"We got a right to see 'em cut Scruff Daddy up!" screamed Beller. "We wuz' friends with Scruff Daddy just as much as ya'll. I tell you....we got as much right as any of ya'll to see him get cut up. Us pigs back heah' has got rights too! Somebody do something. Ya'll know this ain't fair!"

Their complaints fell on deaf ears. Not a single pig in the front row moved an inch. They all stood transfixed, mesmerized by the scene unfolding in front of them. Meanwhile, as new arrivals cautiously walked by, a pig named Jack started re-enacting the murder of Scruff Daddy for the late-arrivals.

"I saw the whole thing," explained Jack, bursting with excitement. Jack proceeded to do a one-pig play as he acted out the shooting of Scruff Daddy for the benefit of a sizable crowd that had just arrived on the scene. He re-enacted Scruff Daddy's shooting as they gathered around him.

"Scruff Daddy was walking along right about here" said Jack, as he strolled casually across the crime scene, pretending to be Scruff Daddy. "He was walking just like this, minding his own business and out of nowhere...POWWW!! A single shot rang out from over there by that grassy knoll. Scruff Daddy was down and out!"

As Jack made a sound like the rifle shot, he jumped up into the air about twelve inches and plopped down flat as a pancake on the ground just like he'd been shot. He wiggled his body as he pretended to feel the fingernails of death embracing him, twitched a few more times and laid still as a possum in a croaker sack. As Jack laid there, pretending to be dead, his friends walked casually around him, comparing notes on how real he looked, as they praised his theatrical abilities. An admiring murmur swept through the audience when Jack suddenly bounced up and took a bashful bow.

Jack did his introduction and set-up the scene again for another group of late–arrivals. Jack was just getting to the part where he described the crime scene. "Scruff Daddy was walking just like this, minding his own business and out of nowhere…"

POWWW!

Another shot rang out from the 22-caliber rifle. At that instant Jack jumped twelve inches up into the air and plopped down flat on the ground in a dead heap just like before. His body commenced to wiggling and twitching and then he laid still. For a long time. Naturally, his friends thought Jack was acting out the scene when Scruff Daddy was shot. So they exploded in a lingering burst of applause. But Jack did not immediately bounce back up this time to take his bows.

"Jack shore' looks dead, don't he?" asked Teresa.

"Yep," said Amber, That boy shore' can act up a storm."

"He looks so real lying there," said Robert. "I'm amazed at how good an actor he is seeing as how he just discovered his talent today. Ain't that something? Jack had all that talent inside him all this time and the boy didn't even know it. He's pro'bly been dying to be an actor all his life."

"What's that red stuff leaking from his forehead?" asked Aaron, innocently.

"Where?" asked Robert.

"On his forehead," said Aaron.

"Is that——blood?" asked Kay Kay.

Suddenly, three men surrounded Jack and started dragging his lifeless body over to the side near Scruff Daddy. One of the men quickly slit Jack's throat. As his blood gushed out into the same bucket they'd used to catch Scuff Daddy's blood, the pigs were paralyzed by the shock of this second slaughter scene unfolding before their eyes. It happened so quickly they didn't have time to digest the horrific events and be afraid. They watched the men lift Jack's limp body up and toss him upside down into the barrel of scalding hot water. Slowly, the pigs realized the humans were putting Jack through the same orientation process that Scruff Daddy had gone through.

WHOOSH!!!

Pigs lit out running in twelve different directions all at once. Those pigs who had not seen Jack get shot did not break stride to ask why everybody was stampeding in all directions. They lit out running away on instinct, like ancient buffalo herds roaming the western plains so many years ago. The pigs raced around squealing, slipping and sliding, as they rammed into each other, trying to escape the long thunder sticks that shot fire out the end of the cold, grey metal barrel. But they were trapped inside the boundaries of the pig pens and could only run so far.

POWWW! Ben was dead.

POWWW! Theodore caught a 22-caliber bullet between the eyes and popped three feet up into the air before plopping back down on the hard ground with a thump. He laid there in a dead heap, like a croaker sack full of gigantic baking potatoes. He was on his way to join Scruff Daddy, Jack and Ben in the display case at Casey's Sugar Baked Ham Store down on the corner of Buena Vista Road and Sixth streets.

POWWW! Diane was history. She would end up providing flavoring for a mess of collard greens at Sand Hill Military Base in Fort Benning. All of the pigs shuddered in fear each time a shot rang out, until they realized it was a friend of theirs who had been shot......and not them. Then they relaxed and breathed a sign of relief. The hog slaughtering continued all day. By Elmer G.'s count, twenty-three pigs were shot and butchered that cold Fall morning.

Elmer G. thought to himself, "Boy....it 'shore ain't gonna be crowded at the slop troughs tomorrow."

This was a day that each pig would remember forever. In later years, everybody could tell you exactly what they had been doing at the precise moment Scruff Daddy was shot. It was a moment that was burned into their consciousness. Some pigs believed there was a conspiracy and that some of the pigs were cooperating with the humans. Some of the pigs argued for years afterwards about whether a man standing on the grassy knoll shot Scruff Daddy, as though it mattered. Several pigs started a rumor that there were actually two shooters, instead of one. Either way, he was dead and nothing was going to bring him back to life. Others said that's just the way life is. Stuff happened to you in life. Sometimes it was good stuff. Most of the time, at least for pigs....it was bad stuff.

Elmer G. staggered home, weak and exhausted from the events he'd just witnessed. He stayed awake most of the night, as he wandered in and out of a fatigue induced state of semi-sleep. Elmer G. lay there, inside his wooden hog-head barrel, staring into the darkness. As he lay there, he started dreaming about ham, slabs of bacon, ribs, pig feet and dead hogs swinging from tree limbs. He felt so sick that he thought he would never see another sunrise. Black storm clouds were swirling over the pig pens. He prayed for the souls of Scruff Daddy, Ben, Theodore and all of his other friends who were slaughtered that day. Elmer G. prayed that they all made it safely to Hog Heaven, if there was such a place.

"Dear God. I am asking you to give me the proper words to say what I'm wanting to say about my friends. I ain't long on eloquence, so you may need to apply some additional finery to my prayers. Heavenly Father, please swing open the doors of Hog Heaven on this sacred day. Acres and acres of good souls have been killed on these muddy, but hallowed grounds. We humbly offer these solid souls to your loving care. The Bible says that the Lord giveth and the Lord taketh away. And today you have obviously seen fit to taketh away a whole lot more'n you giveth. A whale of a lot more. We will keep our memories of how our friends lived their lives deep inside our hearts. These private memories will serve as living monuments to the sacrifices they have made on this day. From this day forward, we will dedicate our work, laughter, tears, hopes and fears as a reflection of the lives and times of our noble, fallen friends. This way, we can keep their memories alive long after the events of this day and the words offered in prayer here tonight have been erased from the blackboards of time. We ask that you keep them safe from further ham....I mean...harm. In Christ's name....we ask these things. Amen."

"I'm 'shore scared," thought Elmer G. "I just feel so bad. There just ain't no way I'm gonna' be able to avoid the slaughter house. Farmer Brown is not even waiting to take the pigs to the slaughter house any more. Now he's taking a fancy to killing us right here at the pig pens."

He cried and mumbled into the darkness. "God.....it's me....Elmer G.....again. I know I'm sorta' a fair-weather believer. But I ain't got nobody else to turn to. I know I quit believing in you this morning. But naturally....that was before they started killing pigs. I realize you're pro'bly a little put out by my lack of staying power when it comes to keeping a strong faith. But now....Barley...he says you are a forgiving God. Please help me. I'm so scared of being shot and sliced up into mooshu pork. Gives me the shivers like nothin' I've ever felt. I know I ain't nothing but a pig, but please have mercy on me. Remember me Father....'cause I ain't got nobody else. Mama and daddy are dead.

I ain't got nobody but me. I'm just so scared. I don't know what to do. These humans are killing pigs left and right....like we ain't got no feelings at all. Even though sometimes I forget about you.....please remember your new friend, Elmer G."

As Elmer G. sat there on the ground, staring up at the sky, a soft wind blew gently over him. It was just strong enough to dry his tears. The same wind was cool enough to remind him that even colder winter weather was arriving. As the day prepared to shutter its blinds for the night, Elmer G.'s thoughts turned to his friends. He saw visions of salted hog meat swinging in the rafters of the smokehouse, as it was being cured. He prayed, *"Jesus.....please....please....please....build a pig pen fence all around me and protect me every minute of every day."*

Exhausted.....Elmer G. wept.....and finally......slept.

CHAPTER 13

Returning To The Flock

"There is nothing so inspiring as a Christian pig brimming over with new-found faith, returning to the flock bristling with enormous energy after a scathingly close brush with death."

arly the next morning, Elmer G. wandered over to visit Barley. Neither of them mentioned yesterday's events. It was too horrible to talk about. Words were not powerful enough to adequately express their feelings about witnessing their friends' executions. Neither one of them wanted to mention the spectacle of Farmer Brown and his friends hacking Scruff Daddy and the other pigs up into hams, bacon, chitins and pork chops. So they simply let it be.

"Barley," said Elmer G., as he bowed his head. "Let us pray."

And they did.

After they finished praying, Elmer G. announced, "Barley, I've got to go make me a salad. I want to eat early, so that I can take my morning walk. It's a beautiful day for walking. I've got a lot of stuff on my mind."

"I understand," said Barley. "Believe me, Elmer G. I do understand."

Elmer G. made himself a salad out of some vegetables he found in the slop trough. The other pigs scoffed at his strange behavior. Whoever heard of a pig eating salads? Then the rumors blasted out of the starting blocks. Whispers and innuendos raced from one set of eagerly waiting ears to the next group of gossip mongers. "Elmer G. is eating salads and exercising," they whispered.

"What was the point of Elmer G.'s dieting and exercising?" the other pigs asked each other. "Whoever heard of a pig eating salads and jogging? Unless Elmer G. was getting in shape to make an escape."

Soon, a rumor raced through the pig pens that Elmer G. was in training to prepare for a daring breakout. Another hot rumor was that Elmer G. was organizing either a resolution or a revolution. Later, clarification was received that it was indeed a resolution he was organizing. The word on the streets was that Elmer G. was plotting an escape *and* a resolution. An armed resolution at that. He was planning to go live out west in San Diego, California.

Course, Elmer G. knew nothing about any of these fantastic plans and plots. He was simply trying to show up every day when the sun came up over the horizon. The only other thing he focused on was placing one foot in front of the other foot each day and surviving. He'd lost interest in thriving. Now, he would settle for simply surviving.

The next morning, Elmer G. woke up and scrawled another message on the fence. He wrote:

> *"If you want to rush a stray pig back through the front doors of God's Church, let him witness his friends getting shot and boiled in a barrel of scalding hot water."*

As the weeks flew by, Elmer G. continued praying, exercising and eating a salad two times each week. Slowly, but surely, he started to lose weight and tone up his muscles. Elmer G. was looking good. And because he was exercising regularly, he had a ton of energy these days. He had become quite socially active around the pig pens. He was the first one in line to volunteer to do chores. He helped the elderly pigs, like Marion and Jose, build new sleeping quarters. Elmer G. babysat the piglets so their mothers could enjoy some free time. He told lovely stories to old man Weed and Sally Pearl, because they were feeling sickly. Elmer G. even took food to where Big Mama Christie and Granddaddy Sherman lived because they were too old and slow to walk over to the slop troughs. Elmer G. was the caretaker, it seemed, for everyone who needed help. After he finished his fellowship work, Elmer G. walked over to visit Barley.

"Barley, I'm following your program. I quit wallowing in the mud. I don't run away into the woods no more. I'm praying twice a day and trying to live a more spiritual life. But you know the one thing that's bothering me now?"

"What's that?" asked Barley.

"You know I ain't got no family to speak of. Mama and daddy and them are gone on. They were sent to the slaughter house when I was just a child. So were all my brothers and sisters. Since I ain't got no relatives, there won't be nobody at my funeral when I die. I shore' wish I had me a family like the other pigs."

"What funeral?" asked Barley.

Elmer G. thought about Barley's question a few moments, then answered. "The day they send me away in the red trailer truck to the slaughter house will be my funeral, since I won't be coming back. I wish I had a family to see me off. They could holler and scream as the humans take me away. Since I ain't got nobody to mourn me going, it will almost be like I ain't never even lived. Barley......I wish I had me a family."

"But you do have a family, Elmer G. Every pig out here is a member of your family. We will all miss you Elmer G."

"I just don't want to be alone on my last day," said Elmer G. "I don't wanna' die by myself, even though I ain't nothing but a pig. I still don't wanna' be shipped off to die without nobody there to mourn me leaving. I want somebody there with me, Barley."

"God will be with you," said Barley

"Barley...I don't want to offend God...but I was kinda' thinking that I want somebody there......that I can see. You know...somebody to holler and cry and be upset about me going away to be slaughtered. I mean....dying is hard enough on a body...and I at least want a funeral ceremony or something. Otherwise...the whole thing just don't seem right. I want to know that I will be missed. That way...everybody will know I at least lived. Is that too tall an order for me to make?"

"No Elmer G., that's not asking for too much on your last day."

CHAPTER 14

The Last Days

"The last days are the hardest because we don't know which days are the last days."

In late-March Farmer Brown herded a group of pigs into the special pens with the hardwood floors to become Cornmashers. Naomie, Hattie and Elmer G. were in that group. When one of Farmer Brown's hands named Sonny Bob Sweeney, swung his pole to bullyrag Elmer G. into the special pens, he realized sadly...that his moment of truth had arrived. Although he knew this day was coming by-and-by, he was still set back considerably at the suddeness of it all.

Elmer G. poked along real slow-like, as though he didn't know that Sonny Bob was chasing after him. Then he collapsed and slouched down into a corner of the pig pens. He felt a great sadness swash up around him. He tried to will himself into becoming invisible. "Sit little," he thought to himself. "Sit little. I'm invisible. I'm sitting so little they can't see me," he whispered to himself, as he tried to ignore Sonny Bob's swinging pole that was whacking him in the side. Elmer G. squirted away for a moment, but Sonny Bob cornered him and laid into him good with that pole of his. Finally, Elmer G. reckoned he had haggled as long as he could. He shrugged his shoulders and gave up. With a solemn expression on his face, he shuffled slowly into the sparkling pens to become an official Cornmasher. He trudged reluctantly into the pens with a heavy heart. A great number of his friends joined him, as they crowded into the pens, bunched up together. The pigs were nervously stamping around in half-circles, looking excited, but puzzled.

The Cornmashers were usually kept cramped up in the special pens with the hardwood floors for about three weeks. Elmer G. was amazed at how this life-and-death crisis seemed to increase his appetite for praying. During the first few days, Elmer G. prayed two times each day. By the end of the week, he was praying four times each day. Since he had not heard back from God, Elmer G. was tempted to stop praying. But praying provided him his only source of hope, even though it was a long shot.

Elmer G. thought to himself that "I have tried to take a-holt of my own fate and failed. My final reward is gonna' be getting myself raked over the coals, smoked, salted down, rubbed in honey and shipped to Glazier's Honey Baked Ham store where they're gonna' plop me inside a glass display case."

The fact that Elmer G. had no hope of escaping made it worse. The other pigs happily stuffed their snouts with hunks of corn mash and generally enjoyed themselves. After a couple of days, Elmer G. confided in Hattie and Naomie all the things that Barley had shared with him. Now they were mad at him for ruining what had been a pretty good time for them. Hattie and Naomie were not totally shocked when he told them they were going to be slaughtered. Elmer G. thought Barley was right when he said that most of the pigs knew more about their ultimate fate than they were willing to let on.

At first, he was too scared and confused to eat the corn mash, but he was getting weak from hunger. He mulled over his situation a tolerable long time. Elmer G. was dog-tired. And hongry'.

"The delicious smell of this corn mash sure is making my mouth water," Elmer G. thought to himself.

Although he was ashamed of giving in to his appetite, Elmer G. stooped down and smelt some of the corn mash. "It won't hurt nothing by me smelling it," he thought to himself. Then he tasted some. It was so good and he was so hungry, that he polished off two helpings in no time flat.

His third week of captivity ended on Good Friday. As the sun set that afternoon, Elmer G. heard a truck engine in the distance. Bobby Lee Pain's red trailer truck came rumbling up the dirt road.

Bobby Lee Pain stepped down out of the cabin of his truck, standing tall...and casting a long, dark shadow...like a character from an old horror movie. He was a burly truck driver who always wore a faded, black cowboy hat and brown, scuffed-up cowboy boots. After Bobby Lee let his wooden ramps down to the entrance of the pig pens where the Cornmashers were huddled, Farmer Brown gave the signal for Bobby Lee and Johnny B. Elvis to start loading the Cornmashers into the trailer. Bobby Lee poked the pigs with a long pole and began guiding them up the long ramp leading into his trailer bed. As the line of pigs started moving, Hattie turned to Elmer G.

"Elmer G.," said Hattie, "do you believe that this God you're praying to will save you?"

"Yes I do," said Elmer G. "God can do anything we believe He can do."

"If I started praying right now," said Hattie, "do you think He will save me too?"

"Yes He will," said Elmer G. "He doesn't care about how long you've been praying to Him. All you have to do is have faith in His powers. And turn your life over to Him."

"Elmer G.," said Hattie. "Are you sure all God wants is for me to believe in Him and for me to turn my life over to Him. I mean...it looks like I've only got a few hours left. I'm so scared."

"Just stay right behind me," said Elmer G. "We'll face this thing together. Barley says God can work miracles."

As Elmer G. and Hattie began to pray together, Naomie piped up.

"Oh pu....lease!! Give me a break!" said Naomie. "I ain't putting no stock in no imaginary God I can't see. Far as that go, I don't trust my friends I *can* see. If your God is so smart and so powerful, and so wise, then why you up in here with us about to be killed? Elmer G....you ever seen God? I didn't think so. You don't even know if he's real. Up there listening to Barley. What does he know? He's too old to be slaughtered, so he can afford to speculate about God. You ever notice that the most religious pigs are always the ones that are too old to do much more sinning? While we're on our way to the slaughter house, Barley is about to eat slop for supper and go to sleep."

"But Barley is smart," said Hattie. "He wouldn't say things that weren't true."

"Tomorrow, while Barley's still alive," said Naomie, "we'll be keeping cool in cellophane wrapped packages in the supermarket freezers, as folks pick over us. Elmer G., boy....I think eating all them salads done made you a little tender-headed and addled brained. But, you see me....now. Naomie's gonna' take care of herself. I'm not praying to a God I can't see. You all are losing your minds! Praying for God to save you. If there is a God, then he sure don't care nothing for us pigs! If he cared about us, he wouldn't let us be carted off to be slaughtered, sliced and diced. Now would he? I'm glad I've had my fun already. Right here and right now. I have lived my life. My way. And lived it well....I might add."

"Come on Naomie," said Elmer G. "You gotta' believe in some sorta' God."

"I don't believe in no God," said Naomie. "Nothing on earth and nothing in heaven can save us. We're as good as dead. And that's just the way it is. You and Hattie need to shut up and enjoy your last few hours on this earth, instead of praying to a God that don't even exist. I'm sick of hearing all this hogwash about God and Hog Heaven. We was born pigs and we're gonna' die pigs. That's just the way it is. If God wants me to believe in Him, tell Him to save me from the slaughter house first and then I'll believe in Him."

Bobby Lee interrupted their conversation because he was swinging his long pole at Elmer G., Hattie and Naomie, herding them up the ramp. Elmer G. led the way, followed by Hattie. Naomie walked behind Hattie. They were the last three little pigs to be herded into the trailer truck.

All of a sudden, a lightning bolt flashed across the sky. The fiery streak of lightning was so big, it seemed to stretch across Georgia, Alabama and Mississippi, as it raced across the pitch black skyline. Boom! Boom! The sounds of thunder exploded all around the pig pens and the darkening sky was lit up by brilliant flashes of lightning. But the rain did not come down.

It was turning so dark that Hattie had trouble seeing Elmer G., although he was walking right in front of her. As Elmer G. was trudging reluctantly up the ramp, he felt bad because he didn't have nobody there to cry for him. There was no one there to see him off, as he was being driven away to be slaughtered. No family members to grieve for him. His greatest fear was coming true. He was going to die alone. Since there was no one to mourn his passing, it would be like he had never been alive. He thought to himself, "ain't nobody gonna' miss one lowly, ignorant pig."

Elmer G. drew a deep breath, hung his head and kept trudging along. He was feeling hot and fidgety.

"Well, if the truth be known, I've just been a great pretender," he thought to himself. "I've been strutting around these pig pens like I wasn't afraid of nothing, playing and laughing the days away, like I had nothing to worry about. I pretended like I didn't care about not having my family. I'm out here by myself and I'm plain scared. I ain't never died before, so this is new territory for me."

He tried to remember what Barley had said about courage. Faith
was the breeding ground for courage. Having courage meant going
forward when you knew you would fail. Elmer G. tried to hold his
tears inside. But it warn't no use. All of his pent-up emotions from
the last few months came raining down, like water gushing
through a Grand Canyon-sized hole in the water trough. His emotional tank settled on empty, as he stared at the end of his life.

Meanwhile, Farmer Brown and his farm hands had stopped the
loading of the pigs to fix the truck engine, which had sputtered
and died on them. Elmer G., Hattie and Naomie were left standing on the loading ramp, while the men fretted with the engine.

As he stood on the ramp, Elmer G. felt downright mournful.
He could hear a dog howling off in the distance, which unfortunately, meant that somebody was going to die. Then he heard a
rabbit scurrying through the underbrush. It was so quiet that he
heard a bird up in the oak tree rustling around, trying to settle in
for the night. He glanced up at the sky where the stars were starting to twinkle. Ice cold shivers were racing up his legs.
Reminiscences rapped on the door guarding his past. When he
didn't answer fast enough, they pulled back the dusty old velvet
stage curtain, as they trooped out before him like fashion models,
prancing confidently down the catwalk. His life passed before
him. Through the darkening haze of the evening shadows, he saw
Scruff Daddy scrambling to make his escape, as he scooted under
a hole in the north fence. He saw Ben, clear as day....tossing his
massive head back and laughing ever so loud at So-So's jokes. A
video movie seemed to be playing inside Elmer G.'s mind, as his
past came strutting by in all its splendid glory. There goes
Theodore, running like a graceful gazelle during a game of hide-
and-seek. As his past raced down the dirt roads of time to greet
him....Elmer G. started to cry for all his dead friends. He cried for
his mama and daddy, who were taken away from him before he
hardly knew them.

In the mist of all his agony, Elmer G. got to itching in every nook and cranny of his body. He wanted to scratch himself so bad he 'bout couldn't stand it. As he stood there trying to resist that monstrous urge to scratch himself, he rocked from side-to-side and moaned, "Lord. Lord. What shall I do?" He said it in such a sad tone of voice that his moans saddled up on white horses and galloped across the ages, as he cried for his dead brothers and sisters.

"I can't go to Hog Heaven no way 'cause I ain't never even got baptized by getting dipped in no water," muttered Elmer G. to himself. "I did all this work and sacrificing for nothing."

Through the noise of his own sniffling and the crackling "BOOM! BOOM!!" of the thunder in the distance, Elmer G. heard someone calling his name. Naturally, Elmer G. thought it was God.

He turned around and said, "Yes Lord? It's me. Elmer G. You calling me? I'm ready to go to Hog Heaven. I see you finally showed up....and it's about time too. You're cutting it kinda' close, ain't you?"

"Elmer G., this ain't the Lord. It's me."

"Who is me?" asked Elmer G., as he looked frantically through the darkening evening shadows.

"Elmer G....it's me," said the voice again.

Elmer G. peered through the shadows again. It was Barley calling his name.

Looking out through his tears, he saw something else. Pigs. Acres and acres of silent pigs. They were standing there with grim expressions on their faces, in the evening shadows, as brilliant lightning bolts flickered and danced madly across the pitch black sky, before exploding in a crazy cascade of ragged-edged lightning bolts. There were hundreds of pigs in a dazzling array of different sizes and colors. Every pig in the whole doggone pig pens was standing out there.

All the pigs were dead silent, as they stood shoulder-to-shoulder in the driving rain. German pigs. Vietnamese pigs. Black pigs.

Brown pigs. Russian pigs. White pigs. City pigs. Country pigs. Miniature pigs. Giant pigs. Young pigs, old pigs, even sick pigs. Mothers were there with their babies. Younger pigs were helping to brace the older, sick pigs so that they too could stand in formation. They were all staring silently......at Elmer G.

Then Barley spoke.

"Elmer G., I told everybody that you were afraid of dying without nobody being here to see you off. We all talked about it and everybody agreed that we couldn't let that happen. You have a good heart, Elmer G. Lately, you've just been so thoughtful and unselfish. And you always made us laugh, even in our darkest hours. And laughter is a healing thing to share, my friend."

"I did all that?" said Elmer G.

"Yes you did, Elmer G.," said Barley. "You have loved us all in so many little ways. We started off with just a few of us who planned to come and say goodbye. But as word got around, it seems like every pig out here wanted to say goodbye. In some way, you have managed to touch all our lives. We just wanted you to know that you are not alone in your darkest hour. We love you Elmer G. We want you to know that you do have a family. Everybody will know that you did live here. Your life was not lived in vain. God took one family from you...but He has given you a new...bigger family. You have shown a whole generation of young pigs how to volunteer for chores and care for the sick. And we will always remember the laughter you brought."

"But...why ya'll doing all this for me?" asked Elmer G.

"Because you taught us how to appreciate the beauty of our humble surroundings. We will tell our children about a brave pig who dared to be different. You decided to believe in God when it was not a popular thing to do. Keep praying Elmer G. God's powers are great. Hopefully...I'll see you in Hog Heaven. Someday. It don't have to be tomorrow. Or even next month. It don't even have to be next year. Or even the year after that. Obviously......I'm not in a rush to join you up there Elmer G. But I will see you when I do get there. I will see you again on the other side of Glory. Save me some of those humongous cinnamon rolls. You know how much I love 'em."

"I don't know what to say, Barley," said Elmer G.

"You ain't got to say nothing," said Barley. "Look-a-heah. Before you go, we have one more little thing we've prepared for you."

"But you've already done so much," said Elmer G.

"I know," said Barley. "But this is kinda' special. Come on up here Francis!"

A young boar named Francis Scott Lock came walking slowly up to stand next to Barley. He was wearing an old baseball cap that he'd found in the trash pile.

"Francis here is gonna' sing a song to you before you go, Elmer G.," explained Barley.

"Oh good!" said Elmer G. "I love music. Is he gonna' sing *'Peace in the Valley?'* I like that one a lot."

Barley glanced at Francis, who nodded his head from side-to-side. "Francis don't know that one."

"So, he's gonna' sing *'Amazing Grace?'* I like that one even more than *'Peace In The Valley'*," said Elmer G.

Barley glanced at Francis again. Francis nodded his head quickly from side-to-side. "Francis don't know that one neither."

"Ohh! I got it!" said Elmer G. "He's gonna' sing *'Precious Lord'*."

Barley glanced at Francis, who nodded his head frantically from side-to-side. "Francis don't know that one neither."

"Well," said a puzzled Elmer G. "what is he gonna' sing?"

"Francis is gonna' sing *'The Star Spangled Banner'*," announced Barley proudly.

"*'The Star Spangled Banner?!'* said Elmer G. "Don't he know no other songs? Like a nice spiritual? I don't wanna' die to the tune of no Star Spangled Banner."

Barley glanced at Francis, who nodded his head vigorously from side-to-side. "Francis don't know no other songs. He's been practicing this song all week Elmer G. Come on now. Be a good sport. You're gonna' hurt his feelings if you don't let him sing it. This is a big moment for the boy. You're destroying his self-confidence talking like that."

"Alright," said Elmer G. "He can go ahead and sing it. But how about *'Listen To The Angels Sing?'* I can help him sing that one if he wants to give it a go."

Barley glanced at Francis, who nodded his head rigorously from side-to-side. "Francis don't know *'Listen To The Angels Sing'*. He only knows one song. And it's the *'Star Spangled Banner'*. Now, can he go ahead and sing it for you or what? You try to be nice to folks and put together a decent tribute show for 'em and this is the thanks you get. I tell you the truth. Elmer G., the ingratitude and rudeness of you young pigs is just beyond me. Now, you take me. If somebody went to all this trouble to put together a tribute song for my life, I'd be thanking 'em to no end."

"Okay! Okay!" said Elmer G. "Go ahead and sing Francis. I'm all ears."

Francis straightened himself up, stiffened his shoulders, cleared his throat and began to sing.

"Ohhhhhhh……. Sayyyyy!!! Cannnnn….. you seeeeee!
By the dawnnnn's…….. ear- ly lighttttt!"

And as Francis sang, Elmer G.'s thoughts drifted back to his childhood and he saw himself playing happily with his brothers and sisters, as mama and daddy were standing by. Then he saw his family being herded into the Cornmasher's pens and later being loaded onto the trailer truck to be driven to the slaughter house. Then Elmer G. saw himself as a young pig growing up alone without any family to speak of.

And Francis sang on.

"What so proudddd…..ly!

We hail'ddd…. at the twilight's…… lasttttt….. gleaminggggg!

As Francis sang, Elmer G.' thoughts continued to wander around, like a ship without an anchor, pitching and swaying in angry, choppy waters. He saw himself on that fateful sunny day, asking Barley about the fate of the Cornmashers. Little did he know that asking that single question would change his life forever. Then he saw vivid images of Tiny Muffins wolfing down extra helpings of slop so he could gain a thousand pounds. He saw Plumper dying from starvation after falling down face-first on the ground, just inches away from the life-saving slop troughs. Then he saw Scooter, clear as day, coughing up a storm and falling over in a fake fainting spell at Farmer's Brown's feet, pretending to be sick.

As Elmer G. day-dreamed about the past, Francis sang on in a sweet soulful voice, sounding like someone who had practiced, but not nearly enough.

Whoseee…broad stripesssss
Andddd…. bright starssssss,
through the periloussss…. fight,
Ohhh Lordddd!
Ohhh the fighttttt!

Then Elmer G. thought about Oraville and Willobur Right building their flying wings and jumping off the top of the barn. As he visualized the Right Brothers jumping off the barn roof frantically flapping their plywood wings, he saw a Host of Holy Angels helping Willobur and Oraville exit their physical bodies right at the peak of their jumps. The Angels helped them get settled into a golden chariot with wings made of fire. Willobur and Oraville looked so happy. Through the smoky haze of times gone by, Elmer G. saw the Slop Eaters Anonymous members eating slop at their weekly meetings, as they encouraged each other to "think thin". He saw Andy Warthog marching around the pig pens using the Socratic method of teaching to explain the underpinnings of his theory that one day in their lives, every pig would experience fifteen minutes of flame. In the beginning, Elmer G. thought all the pigs that had tried to escape the slaughter house were dumb.

As his mind hiked back through the treacherous trails of the past, he realized the real courage of their actions was their willingness to attempt to change a fate they didn't agree with. Willobur and Oraville were happy because they believed, even while their bodies were giving in to the physical laws of gravity and crashing to the ground, that they were going to escape from the pig pens. They jumped off the barn roof in order to experience their short, but glorious moment in the sun. In a way, even Andy Warthog was almost right. After all, the Right Brothers, Tiny Muffins, Scooter, Plumper and all the other risk takers did experience their fifteen minutes of fame."

And Francis sang on.

O'er   the   rampartssss.....we   watched.......were   so gallant.....lyyyy....yeahhhhh..... streaminggggg.

Andddd..... the rocketssss.... red glareeeee!!!

When Francis hit that high note about the rockets red glare, Elmer G. thought for a brief moment that going to the slaughter house might be preferable to listening to Francis finish singing this song.

And Francis sang on.

The bombssss..... busting.....in airrrrrr!!!

Gaveeee..... proofffff!!

through the night that our flagggggg..... wasssss.....stillllll....... thereeeee.

Ohhh sayyyyy

doesssss...

thy.....Star.......Spangled.....Bannerrrrr...

yet waveeeee!

Elmer G.'s thoughts continued to stroll back into the past, as he recalled Gabriella Guchi hiding under the trailer truck and Pooter hiding under his old green blanket, as he tried to sneak out of the pig pens. And he gave an imaginary tip of his hat to the Mad Cows and the pure boldness of their plot.

And Francis sang on with enthusiasm.

O'er the landdddddd..... of the freeeeee!!!

Then Elmer G. thought about how pink and innocent Scruff Daddy looked on the day they killed him and sliced him up, along with the twenty-two other pigs who were slaughtered that fateful day. Then he remembered how sad the Cornmashers looked on their last day as they were driven away, staring blankly out through the bars of the trailer truck. Elmer G. thought about the good memories in his life too. He smiled as he closed his eyes and saw himself romping through the woods with Scruff Daddy, Ben, So So, Theodore and Skinter. There they were. Him and his boys, wallowing lazily in the length and mellowness of the long, sweltering dog days of summer. Refreshing themselves from time-to-time by rolling around in their nice cool mud pit.

And Francis sang on, as he leaned forward slightly with his eyes squeezed shut and belted out the last stanza with all the emotion he could muster.

And the homeeeeee!!

Of theeeee!

Homeeeee...... of the.... Braveeeee!!!

Ohhh Lorddd!

Elmer G. was speechless. Once again, he looked out over the pigs...just yards and yards of pigs....standing in silent formation...crying...for him. Now that he knew how much they loved him, Elmer G. really wished he could keep living. He was even willing to trade places with one of his friends standing out in the crowd.

"Ain't this something," he thought to himself. "I finally find out that everybody loves me and now I'm gonna' die. If it wasn't for bad luck. I wouldn't have no luck at all."

Elmer G. squared his shoulders and stopped crying. He was ready to start walking with a strut in his step. He felt stronger than he had ever felt in his entire life. While he was not foolish enough to be excited about wherever he was going...at least now he was no longer trembling with fear.

"My life has made a difference in somebody else's life," Elmer G. thought to himself.

"Elmer G., my friend," said Barley. "We're coming down the homestretch. The bad news is that we're in the bottom of the ninth inning."

"And the good news?" asked Elmer G.

"The good news is that God is on the pitcher's mound. He's also pinch-hiting, playing shortstop, center-field......"

"First base," interrupted Elmer G. "Second base, catcher and all the outfield positions. I remember what you told me, Barley. God is all over the playing field of our lives."

"Yes He is," said Barley.

"Barley," said Elmer G. "I ain't gonna' make it."

"It ain't looking real good for you," agreed Barley. "But, why do you say that?"

"I ain't never been born again," said Elmer G. "I didn't get a chance to get myself baptized. I wasn't sure if the mud pits would work, so I didn't even try 'em. Now it's too late."

"Look inside your heart, Elmer G.," said Barley. "Are you a Christian?"

"Barley....I am tonight. I believe in God. My faith is strong." Elmer G. lifted his face skyward as he professed his unabashed love for the Lord. He felt for a moment as though he was standing on sacred ground in a place between Hog Heaven and earth. Then, Elmer G. prayed as he had never prayed before. He called upon the God of Abraham, Moses, David and Joseph to help other pigs and not himself. He asked for forgiveness for his past sins and indiscretions. Hot, scalding tears jumped from the outside corners of Elmer G.'s eyes, as he felt the comfort and security of God's grace descend from Heaven and settled around his shoulders.

At that moment, a magnificent thunderstorm came rolling in over the pig pens. *Boom!! Boom!* The vibrations and sounds of thunder came swooping in off the tops of the swirling giant oak and pine trees, as their branches whipped around in a frantic dance. The wind swelled and rushed up from the ground, creating a crazy circus of tumbling, flying leaves. Jagged streaks of lightning crackled and flickered across the dark skyline. Suddenly...... the clouds that had been hoarding the rain let it go all at once. The sky opened its mouth and started raining, as it violently vomited up buckets of ice cold water.

Elmer G. turned his face upward toward the sky, as his whole body was washed down from head to toe. He felt all of his doubts and fears washing away, as the rain seemed to rinse them down onto the ground.

"Elmer G.!" screamed Barley. "Elmer G.!! This is it!!"

"Barley, what are you talking about?!"

"You said you never got baptized," said Barley. "This is it! This is your baptism!! God sent water for you to be baptized with!!"

"I guess you're right," said Elmer G. "This could be my baptism."

Elmer G. peered into the darkness and the driving rain. He stared at the rows and rows of pigs standing there. He realized they were as helpless about their fates as he was about his own. For one last time, he looked into the faces of his friends quietly standing there, witnessing his death march. And he felt....like he wanted to exchange places with one of his friends.

Then Barley said a simple, final prayer for his friend, *"Lord...open his eyes so that he may see."*

Then Elmer G. saw it. The colors rose from the edge of the earth. A brilliant rainbow as big as a super-sized Hall-Mart department store came creeping up from the edge of eternity and laid itself across the jet-black sky. It was made of a million colors and was so beautiful and perfect that only God, or Norman Rockwell could have created such a wondrous thing. The beauty of the rainbow was itself proof that God existed. Only God could make something so perfect. As suddenly as it appeared, the rainbow faded away.

At that moment, a gigantic streak of lightning raced across the black sky and briefly lit up the pig pens. In that instant, Elmer G. thought he saw the dim outlines of something else through the haze, standing behind the rows of silent pigs. Elmer G. stared harder and saw the dim, faint outlines of white feathers. They seemed to be everywhere. He blinked his eyes quickly to clear out some of the rain and to make sure his eyes were not deceiving him. Slowly, the images took shape, as they came into focus.

Elmer G. saw a solid wall of Angels with white wings, sporting gold armor breastplates. There were thousands and thousands of Angels surrounding the pig pens, standing in silent formation behind the rows of pigs. They were standing in military at-ease positions, shoulder-to-shoulder, holding their golden spears, archery bows and golden-tipped arrows. Some of the Angels were standing in the driver's seats of golden colored chariots, with trailing exhausts of fire, pulled by teams of Clydesdales.

"So, that's why it took them so long to arrive," Elmer G. thought to himself, as he stared at the slow-moving Clydesdales that were hitched to the front of the Angel's chariots. And now he had an answer to his question about whether God was a man or a pig. Barley was right. God was whatever you needed Him to be. The Platoons of Angels were standing there, drinking in the scene as though they didn't have a care in the world. And the most amazing thing is that they were all........pigs. Not a man amongst 'em.

"Barley!!!" screamed Elmer G. "Barley!!! I know you're gonna' think I've lost my mind!! But...look!! Out there!! Can you see 'em?!!!"

"I see them, Elmer G.," said Barley, with a satisfied glow. "Beautiful sight, ain't it?"

"But...but....I don't understand!!" said Elmer G. "Just a minute ago, there was nothing there! And now there are thousands of Pig Angels dressed in breast-plates of golden armor standing in military formation out there."

"Maybe they've been there all the time," said Barley.

"That can't be true!" said Elmer G. "If they've been there all the time, then why couldn't I see them?!"

"Maybe because before...you were looking through the eyes of a pig," said Barley. "And now...you're looking through the eyes of faith."

"Praise God!" shouted Elmer G. "I'll never lose faith in Him again!"

Farmer Brown and his ranch hands had finally gotten the truck fixed and they started loading the pigs into the trailer truck again. Bobby Lee whacked Elmer G. in the side to get him moving up the wooden ramp.

As Elmer G. continued walking up the slippery wooden ramp, Farmer Brown stared at him. Just as Elmer G. lifted his right leg to step into the trailer truck, Farmer Brown hollered out to Bobby Lee. "Hey Bobby Lee! You there!! Turn *that* pig around!!"

Bobby Lee grunted to indicate he'd heard the instructions. Then he swung his long pole in a half circle, as he poked Elmer G. on the side of his neck to turn him around to go back down the ramp. Elmer G. was so nervous and stressed out that he stumbled and fell off the ramp and landed head-first on an old tree stump down on the muddy ground. When he slipped and fell down, Elmer G. bumped into Hattie, who fell up against Naomie. Both of them got tangled up and fell off the ramp too. They landed smack dab on top of Elmer G.

As Elmer G. lay in the mud with the rain pelting down on him, he began to lose consciousness. As his mind continued to fade on him....Elmer G. heard a song blasting through the pig pens. Although Elmer G. didn't know it, the song was coming from the cab of Bobby Lee's truck. In fact, it was a song that had been recorded by Mark Cooke and The Soul Searchers. But in Elmer G.'s mind, he heard a Heavenly Choir of pigs singing *"God Is Standing By Me."*

As he continued his slide into unconsciousness, Elmer G. thought he saw a magnificent Heavenly Choir with thousands of pigs in blazing, blood-red choir robes swaying in perfect unison, as they clapped and sang. At the front, leading the choir he saw his mama, daddy and all his brothers and sisters. Elmer G. saw Scruff Daddy clapping and singing. He saw Ben, Theodore, Glen, So-So and the rest of the old gang, swaying from side-to-side, clapping and singing in the most beautiful voices.

God Is Standing By Me
"When your troubles are too big for you to bear,
Don't you worry, don't despair and don't cry.
The same God that saved Daniel from the lions is
*   standing nearby.*

And if.....all your dreams and plans fail,
Don't give up on yourself.
The same God that saved Jonah from the
*   whale......can surely get your ship to sail."*

CHAPTER 15

Hear The Angels Sing

Johnny B. Elvis was putting in some new fence posts. As usual, he had his boom box blasting. The radio was playing as he worked. Johnny loved Gospel music. Mark Cooke and the Soul Searchers were singing a song entitled *"Hear The Angels Sing"*.

> *Chorus – Hmmmm. Hmmmm. Rupppt*
> *"Every time I feel my faith growing weak,*
> *I ask God to wrap his loving arms around me,*
> *And give me all the strength I need.*
> *Chorus – All the strength I need.*
>
> *Lord! I cry out.*
> *Come see about your sheep! Baptize me.*
> *The same way John the Baptist baptized You!*
> *In the Sea of Galilee.*
> *Give me a shield against the evils of the world.*
> *Chorus - Cover me Lord. Cover me with your loving*
>   *wings.*
> *While I…listen to the Angels sing.*

As the music played, Elmer G. woke up and listened to it. Hog Heaven was gonna' be okay, he decided. Waking up to sweet Gospel music every day was gonna' be nice. He opened his eyes and felt his side to see if they had pasted a plastic price tag on his hams and ribs. He poked himself to see if he could still feel his ribs and shoulders.

He stared at the blood stains on his hoof and screamed "OHHHH! Lorrrd!!! I'm....I'm dead!! I don't wanna' be dead. I'm not ready to listen to the Angels sing!" He was still groggy. He looked up right into the face of Barley.

"Is it still raining, Barley?"

"No Elmer G., the storm is over."

"Ohhh Barley!!! I've been slaughtered!! And they done killed you too!! I'm so sorry!! Poor, poor Barley!! I thought you were too old to be slaughtered! What's that smell? You were right, Barley. Hog Heaven *is* just like home. It even smells just like home. The streets 'shore ain't paved with no giant loaves of French bread. That's okay though, 'cause I ain't eating nuthin' offa' the ground up in here. We're in Hog Heaven now. That's all that matters. And look at us. We still together. Even after death. Barley, we beat the system."

"Elmer G.!" said Barley. "I ain't wit' you!! You wit' me!!"

"What you mean?!" asked Elmer G. "Both of us is dead!! You can call it whatever you want. But what's funny is.......I don't remember a thing about the slaughter house. One minute I was walking up the ramp to get into the trailer truck and the next thing I know....why....I'm here with you in this nice comfortable corner of a pig pen that looks and smells just like home. And here we are way up above the clouds in Hog Heaven. I think I'm gonna' like it here. When are we gonna' meet God, Barley? I've got a few beefs with him about this pig slaughtering thing. I still can't get over how painless it was to die. I didn't feel nothing. Hog Heaven ain't so bad...except for the smell. I tell you one thing. I don't wanna' make God mad 'cause I just got here, but He needs to clean this place up. Get some air freshener or something. God's got a serious choir! Whooo boy! Can they belt out a tune, or what?! I wanna' join the Heavenly Choir and get me a red choir robe. You were right Barley. Hog Heaven is just like home. You seen Scruff Daddy and them? How about Hattie and Naomie? How they all doing? Can we eat some of them apples that are the size of basketballs?"

"ELMER G.!!!" screamed Barley. "You ain't dead!!! You're still at home!!"

"What?!" said Elmer G. "Barley, what are you talking about? I'm 'shore dead. And so are you. Look at this blood from the slaughter house on my shoulder. If I'm not dead…then where this blood come from?"

"You cut your shoulder when Bobby Lee turned you around on the ramp to herd you off of the trailer truck. You slipped and fell off the ramp. That's when you scraped your shoulder. You got knocked unconscious when you fell off the ramp and landed on your head on the ground below."

"But why would Bobby Lee turn me around and herd me back down the ramp?" asked a puzzled Elmer G.

"Because Farmer Brown told him to do it. You were just about to step into the trailer truck when Farmer Brown yelled for Bobby Lee to turn you around. When Bobby Lee poked you on the neck with his pole, you slipped and fell. That's when you cut yourself on the shoulder."

"Thank God!!" exclaimed Elmer G. "But what about the Angels singing? I heard the Angels singing when I woke up. What's up with that?"

"That was Johnny B. Elvis' radio," said Barley. "You know he carries that boom box of his everywhere."

"It's a miracle!" screamed Elmer G. "God done outdid hisself this time. You told me about how this man that walked on the water on the Sea of Galilee, saved Daniel from the lions and raised Lazarus from the dead. All that may be fine and well....but for my money.....today was His Oscar winning performance. I mean......saving me from the slaughter house and not a minute too soon. But poor Hattie and Naomie!!" cried Elmer G., with tears brimming up to the rims of his eyes. "They're both dead!!! And they were so young."

"They're fine too," said Barley.

"What do you mean, they're fine?" said Elmer G.

"When you fell backwards, you bumped into Hattie," explained Barley. "Hattie fell backwards into Naomie. Both of 'em fell off the ramp too and landed on top of you."

Elmer G.'s euphoria was short-lived. He was silent for a moment, then he spoke.

"Now we got to go through all this slaughter house business all over again," he said. "Barley...do me a favor. Kill me right now. Here, just grab me 'round my neck and choke me to death. I can't stand going through the experience of being a Cornmasher again. Just kill me right now and put me out of my misery. Puuu...lease help me."

"Elmer G.," said Barley, "if you don't shut up, I will choke you. What I'm trying to tell you is that you don't have to worry no more about being slaughtered."

"Why not?" asked Elmer G.

"Farmer Brown got plain tickled after seeing the three of you spattered on the ground with Hattie and Naomie crying, thinking they had killed you when they landed on top of you. And you laying there eagle-spread, unconscious, looking like you were about ready to receive your last rites. Bobby Lee was trying to herd Hattie and Naomie back up the ramp into the trailer truck when Farmer Brown told him that the three of you were to be let loose. He said that you all were never to be slaughtered. He thinks the three of you are the funniest pigs he's ever seen. He and Bobby Lee were both laughing so hard, that they are telling all the humans the funny story about the three pigs that fell off the ramp and escaped the slaughter house. Farmer Brown views the three of you as pets now. He likes you all too much to slaughter. He thinks you three are good luck charms. So there you have it. Looks to me like your prayers were answered after all."

"You were right Barley," said Elmer G. "God does answer our prayers. But he don't arrive early...does he. I mean...He's a fella' that believes in taking things down to the wire. I'm telling you....He cut it close to the vest this time. Whew boy!!"

"Since all of the pigs in the pig pens heard how you were saved, everybody is praying now. Naomie is even leading the prayer group."

"Wow!" said Elmer G. "And to think...Naomie didn't even believe in God. And she got saved from the slaughter house."

"It just goes to show you," said Barley, "that even if you don't believe in God, you can receive a taste of His blessings by standing close to somebody else that really deserves it."

"Life is amazing Barley. I have been through so much these last few months that I am just plain whipped. Even though I didn't go there, I still believe that there is a Hog Heaven. When I thought I was dying, I saw a Heavenly choir with mama and daddy, my brothers and sisters, Scruff Daddy and the rest of the gang all swaying, clapping and singing a song called *"God Is Standing By Me."* It sent chills down my spine."

"I don't wanna' rain on your parade Elmer G., but that song you heard was playing on Bobby Lee's radio when you slipped and fell off the ramp. But whatever you think you saw is a real possibility because for you....the storm is over."

"Yep, Barley. I guess for me.....the storm is over. And I found out I do have a family right here. I felt so good when I looked out and saw all the pigs standing there to see me ship out."

"And you did not disappoint us neither," said Barley. "Boy, you sure put on a show. Falling off that ramp and laying out there like you were dead."

"Now Barley. You telling me the truth? I ain't really dead am I. I mean…this is not one of them there rookie pranks you're playing on me…..is it? You know….where I relax and think I'm still alive and then later you break the news to me that I'm really dead. This is not no trick like that…..is it?"

"Elmer G.," said Barley, in his most solemn tone of voice. "I don't know exactly how to tell you this one last thing, but….you're really dead."

"I knew it!!" screamed Elmer G. "I knew all the time I was dead! They done kilt me! And I ain't never done no harm to nobody. Now I'm laying up in the supermarket in a giant cooler. Barley, you know I don't like to be cold!"

""I'm joking Elmer G.," said Barley, laughing so hard he could hardly talk. "I just couldn't let this opportunity pass by to play a little joke on you. You're not dead boy."

"Why you wanna' play with me like that, Barley? That ain't funny."

"Well," said Barley, "after all the trials and what-not we been through lately, I thought we could both use a good laugh. Ain't been much laughter around these pig pens in a long time Elmer G. I'm sorry if I scared you. But seriously, everything I just told you earlier is true. You can relax now and live a long, natural life without fear of ever being sent to the slaughter house."

"Then the storm is over," said Elmer G. "And I'm 'shore hongry. What time they bringing slop?"

CHAPTER 16

The Liar's Club

"As a story is told over the years, the hurdles, enemies and dangers grow to gigantic proportions. Naturally, the Storyteller adds a flourish here and tosses in a speck of garnish over there. These spices are added to give a little seasoning to his story. In the process of seasoning his story, the truth gets smaller and smaller, as the Storyteller's heroic role grows larger and larger. Over time, we convince ourselves that the events really happened the way we are telling them, no matter how far we wander away from the truth. The difference between a joke with a punch-line and a great story is that jokes have a shelf life of three days at best. A great story, properly told.....is like a lie...in that they both live forever."

As the years passed, Elmer G., Hattie and Naomie became famous among pigs near and far. They were the only pigs known to have been saved from the slaughter house by almost killing themselves. The other pigs, both young and old, came and sat at their feet, listening to them re-tell the story of that glorious and epic event that took place on Good Friday. According to the story, God himself rode down to earth from Hog Heaven in a teal blue chariot with customized rims and personally saved the three of them from a trip to the slaughter house.

Barley was sloshing through a large crowd of pigs, as they lazed around listening to Elmer G., Naomie and Hattie telling them for the zillionth time, how events unfolded that fateful day. Although Barley was way up in years now, his recollection of what happened that day did not match anything that Elmer G., Hattie and Naomie were describing. He was astonished at their stretching of the truth. In order to get a feel for whether he should put a stop to this tall-tale telling before it got too far out of hand, Barley paused out at the edge of the crowd to listen. The younger pigs loved this story. They all sat up in the front of the group, with their eyes propped wide open.

Johnny B. Elvis, another one of Farmer Brown's farmhands, came down to mend some of the pig pen fences. He brought along his boom box and the radio was playing a song called "*First Love*".

"*The first time I saw you my whole world stood still, as you smiled,*

I wanted to walk inside your eyes and close your eyelids from the inside,

I'd done a million things before we met and thought my life was a blast,

But I had no idea........That God had saved the best for last."

Elmer G. was holding court that day from on top of a slight mound of leftover red clay that Farmer Brown's men had dumped there to use one day for road repairs.

"The whole thing started in March of that year," said Elmer G., warming to the task, as he told his stretcher of a tale. "Farmer Brown was rounding up a group of pigs to herd them into the Cornmashers' pens. He didn't pick me to go because he could look at me and tell I wasn't up for that mess. By this time....I'd seen enough of how humans were treating pigs. I was flat out tired of the way he was bully-ragging us around from pillar to post. I mean...ya'll tell me if I'm outta' line here. But while Farmer Brown and his family were eating their meals in comfort at their nice wooden kitchen table, he had us eating out of troughs on the ground. While the humans were bathing in a bathtub, what did we get to bathe in?! Mud pits! Ya'll pull my coattails if I'm snorting up the wrong tree here, but to my way of thinking, Farmer Brown was treating us wrong."

"Now Elmer G., old chap," said Jules, an English pig, "I do believe that you would have to be some kind of Super-Hero type pig to beat these humans at their own game? Don't you think, mate? A regular government inspected pig wouldn't stand a chance against those kind of odds. How'd did you cope my boya? I've just got to know what's up with that, old bean."

"Jules...I'm glad you brought that up," said Elmer G. "Mind you...I was just a regular pig...at that time. I wasn't no Super-Hero type a pig, although I did save some folks from a fire once in a high-rise building, but that's another story."

"Thank God and the Queen Mother for that. At least I don't have to hear it now..." muttered Jules under his breath.

"What'd you say?" asked Elmer G.

"Nothing, dear boya," said Jules. "I didn't say anything. By all means proceed with your story. You're doing a splendid job, I say. Absolutely splendid."

"Like I was saying," said Elmer G. "Although I reckon I had potential....I was not famous. I did not want to be famous, or great. I did not seek fame. Fame found me. I just did what I had to do to survive. Ya'll know what I'm saying? Do ya'll feel me?!"

"Yes!!" screamed the young pigs in the audience. "We feel you Elmer G.!"

"Well....like I was saying," said Elmer G., shifting in his seat, as he sparkled and glowed, basking in all the attention being thrown his way. I cocked one of my eyes directly onto Farmer Brown's face. I stared at him. Daring him to touch me. And I did not blink. And I did not shy away from his gaze. I was a pig that....had been pushed too far. So I says to him, 'Hey you! Farmer Brown! Don't you stand over there pretending like you don't hear me. I am talking to you Mister....and I want some solid answers.'"

"What happened then?" asked Corinne, a pretty young sow sitting up front, blushing every time Elmer G. glanced her way. "You are just so brave....Elmer G.," she said in her softest voice, batting her eyelashes one thousand times per second. Corinne was batting her eyelashes so fast that Elmer G. stared at her and thought to himself that if she'd had a little less body weight, she would have blasted off in flight like a hummingbird.

"Well....Miss Corinne," said Elmer G., as he amplified his voice, trying to look important and sound real serious-like. "You 'shore is looking mighty pretty today. Mighty pretty...if I do say so myself. Hog Heaven is 'shorely missing an Angel today, 'cause you must've fallen outta' the sky. You're too pretty to be from this plain old earth of ours. Now.....let me axe you something Miss Corinne."

"Ain't you something with all your fancy talking. What is you wanna' axe me, Elmer G.?"

"Are your legs tired, Miss Corinne?" asked Elmer G.

"Naww," said Corinne, shyly. "Why you axing?"

"Well," said Elmer G., "they oughta' be tired————'cause you've been running through my mind all day."

"Quit it Elmer G.!" said Corinne, smiling from ear-to-ear. "You just a sweet-talker. You pro'bly tell all the young sows that same old line."

"Can I axe you one more question, Miss Corinne?" said Elmer G.

"Go ahead," said Corinne. "You know you gonna' axe me anyway."

"Is that perfume you wearing?" said Elmer G. "Miss Corinne....you smell so good. If your sweat was gravy....why.....I would sop a hot buttered biscuit offa' your back and swallow it whole. 'Cause to *me*......you smell 'bout as appetizing as a bucket of country fried brown gravy."

"Elmer G....you oughta' be ashamed of yourself," said Corinne, laughing softly under her breath. "But you're right. I *do* smell like brown gravy. Earlier today I slipped and fell into a pile of brown gravy down by the feeding troughs. Crowds of these hongry' pigs have been following me 'round all day. I tell you...it's downright embarrassing. I need to go waller in one of these mud pits later and clean myself up all nice and fresh. Wash that gravy smell offa' me."

"Well...Miss Corinne...my affections for you are about more'n that there brown gravy. Everything I said earlier is true. I stand by it all. Why Miss Corinne....I would drank your dirty bathwater, just to be close to you. I would do it in a heartbeat."

"Elmer G.! Quit talking like that and get on with your story. You're so bad!"

"Miss Corinne," said Elmer G., "I've been noticing you sashaying yourself 'round here like you ain't got a care in the world. I been meaning to tell you this for some time, but the right moment never seemed to show up. You just got so much class. I mean...you just look so...sophisterated."

"Why...thank you Elmer G. That's such a sweet thang' to say. By the way, you look sophisterated too. And you're so brave. Standing up to Farmer Brown and his men the way you did. I'm so proud of you. Your girlfriend is one lucky sow."

"Girlfriend?" said Elmer G., obviously puzzled at her comment. "Who said I had a girlfriend? Miss Corinne, you know I ain't got nobody special I'm courting. At least......not yet."

"Is that right?" asked Corinne.

"Yes ma'am," said Elmer G. "That's the truth. Are you seeing somebody special these days, Miss Corinne?"

"I'm seeing somebody special right now," said Corinne. "I'm staring right at him."

"Awwww shucks now!!" said Elmer G., all beside himself with excitement and hope. "Go on now Miss Corinne! Don't tease me like that. You know you ain't hardly interested in me. Ummmm....is you?"

"That's for me to know and for you to find out," answered Miss Corinne, in her most alluring tone of voice.

"Miss Corinne," can you please, pu....lease fetch me a cup of water? All this talking has made my throat mighty parched. Would you do that for me, please? I'd be most grateful."

"Alright," said Corinne, as she got up and sashayed over to the water trough, with brown gravy dripping offa' her sides. She poured Elmer G. some water into a tin cup.

Elmer G. watched her prance delicately back across the pig pen yard and just swooned at her beauty. "My beautiful Corn," he muttered softly under his breath. She returned and delicately handed him his cup of water. "I just met the sow I'm gonna' marry," he thought to himself. "Every time I set eyes on Miss Corinne I feel like my heart is going 'Boom!' 'Boom!' Maybe I'm falling in love. Or, as Barley might say, I'm getting twisted up in the game."

"Miss Corinne," said Elmer G., "just plop yourself right on down here next to me, so you can hear better. Come on now. I ain't playing. Sit down right here. You 'shore do inspire me. And besides being a sight for my sore eyes, you got the nerve to be smelling like brown gravy. Girl....I'm twice blessed! There you go. Just sit right here, so I can keep my eyes on you."

"Elmer G., quit it now! With all your insincere compliments," said Corinne, trying to pretend like she was mad at him. "Now go on and finish telling us what happened to Farmer Brown after you started staring at him."

"What happened is that I just glared at him," said Elmer G., trying to switch his thoughts from matters of the heart back to the heart of his story. "I rared back and dared him to make the first move. To tell you the truth, I wanted him to start something. I was standing there wishing for just part of an excuse to lay into him. I was so mad I was getting ready to thrash his behind right then and there! It makes my blood boil even now thinking about it. I'm still lugging emotional scars around."

As Elmer G. described his emotional turmoil, Miss Corinne leaned over and gently patted his brow with a dirty rag she'd been using to wipe gravy off of her shoulders. Course, now they both smelled like brown gravy.

This was almost too much for Elmer G. to digest. "Thank you Miss Corinne," said Elmer G. "You 'shore is thoughtful. Mighty thoughtful. But anyway….like I was saying, I was waiting on Farmer Brown to make the next move. Suddenly… it seemed like the Heavens opened up. I felt like I could fight for days on end without rest. Now….I still needed my daily ration of slop, mind you….but I did not need any rest."

The audience could not help themselves, as they exploded in a thunderous round of applause and laughter.

"Surely," I thought to myself, "God is working through me. Am I lying, Hattie?"

"He's not lying," chipped in Hattie, right on cue. "I told him I had his back. I said Elmer G…..if you become a Corn-masher…..why….you're gonna' need some backup. And I'm the right sow to watch your back."

"What happened then, Uncle Elmer G.?" asked Troy, a young pig, who was sitting on the front row.

"Why…I jumped up and volunteered to become a Cornmasher, so I could join my brothers and sisters in this glorious battle between good and evil. A raging battle that pitted humans against pigs! A battle for our freedom to live! In order to really live, a pig must find a cause he believes in so deeply that he is willing to make the ultimate sacrifice for that cause. And what my friends…is more sacred than slop…..I mean…life? Looking at

Miss Corinne over here, I'm beginning to think that love may be a bigger sacrifice than life....but I'm wandering offa' the subject."

"Tell it like it is Elmer G.!!!" screamed the crowd. "This is your world, Elmer G.!! We just live here!!!" shouted his friends in the audience.

"After they herded us into the Cornmasher pens," said Elmer G., "I refused to eat corn mash. I did not drink one sip of water for the three weeks they held me prisoner. But the humans force-fed me corn mash through tubes. That must be why I gained weight while I was being held prisoner."

"None of the three of us ate or drank a thing," chipped in Naomie, as Elmer G. gave her a disapproving look. He was irritated that she had the audacity to interrupt his story. His thoughts turned dark, as she kidnapped his story and held it hostage.

"I mean.....the nerve of her.....trying to bring attention to herself in such a shameless manner," thought Elmer G. to himself. "That little hussy is trying to bogard her way into my spotlight. Why.....there is absolutely no reason for her to go and start stealing my best lines. Some folks just loved to hog the limelight for themselves. Naomie is just too selfish."

"Did you get weak?" asked Josephine, a teenaged pig sitting on the second row.

"Oh yes," said Elmer G., as he snatched his story back from Naomie's clutches. "I got weak, hongry, hot and tired. But I could not quit. And I could not afford to let myself be afraid. I felt weak from hunger, but, my hunger to be free was greater than the hunger caused by any lack of food. I was hungry....for food. But I was starving.....to be free! And in the mist of my troubles, I never forgot God. I becha' I prayed six times a day."

"I prayed seven times a day," said Hattie, as Elmer G. shifted deeper into his seat on the ground and slowly shot her a dark and dangerous look from under his eyebrows. The daggers he shot at her were meant to shut her up.

He thought to himself, "between her and Naomie chipping in their two cents worth....I can't hardly get a word in edge-wise."

"I prayed eight times a day," said Naomie. This comment was tossed out there so casually that it made Elmer G. and Hattie take deep breaths, as they both glanced sideways at Naomie. They were surprised at her comment, since Naomie didn't even believe in God at the time all this stuff happened.

Not to be outdone by the facts, Elmer G. plowed right back into the story and put it back on track with his two cents worth. "What I meant to say," said Elmer G., "before I was interrupted......is that I prayed seven times in the mornings and three times each evening."

The crowd exploded in an outburst of laughter and shouts of encouragement for Elmer G., Hattie and Naomie to continue telling their story. Elmer G. grinned from ear-to-ear in a bashful sorta' way, as he finally joined in the laughter. Meanwhile, Naomie and Hattie strutted around the crowd, high-fiving with friends. Shouts of encouragement and agreement came rolling in from the audience, like waves rolling towards the shoreline, rising and ebbing and rising again in a hypnotic dance.

"That's right!" they shouted. "Preach Elmer G.! Preach Brother!! God *is* the way!!!"

After sipping on this scene for as long as he could stand it, Barley couldn't bear it any more. He became indignant at Elmer G.'s outlandish stories about his slaughter house adventure. He started walking towards the clay mound where Elmer G. was sitting. He was planning to break in and set the record straight as to what really had happened that memorable day. As he walked towards Elmer G., he looked into the glowing faces of the pigs in the audience. Barley slowed down, looked around the audience and observed the pride, hope and pure joy the pigs were feeling as they listened to Elmer G., Naomie and Hattie re-hash their greatest adventure. Suddenly, Barley realized that the pigs needed some heroes who were regular, every-day pigs like themselves, to believe in and look up to.

Somehow, Elmer G., Naomie and Hattie had stepped into the role of providing a beacon of hope for all the other pigs. From the pigs' perspective, Elmer G., Hattie and Naomie were living proof that from time-to-time, God did intervene in the affairs of pigs. Although most of the time pigs lived awhile, were fattened up and slaughtered…. their adventures had proven that sometimes, even pigs received salvation.

Meanwhile, Elmer G. pressed forward with the rest of his story. "On the day they made us walk the plank, I said my prayers early. Then I squared my shoulders for the ugly task that lay ahead of me. That's when God decided to get in on the action. Out of nowhere….God showed up. He was riding in a customized, teal-blue chariot with fire flaming out of the sides."

"What did God do?" asked Curt.

"God looked around something fierce-like, as He swung his staff 'round his head a circle so big, it stretched from Georgia to Ohio," said Elmer G. He whacked a bushel of clouds with that giant wooden staff of his. Those clouds got a taste of that whirling staff and started crying up a storm….a rainstorm, that is. A bunch of Angels scooted around with wheelbarrows collecting the clouds' tears. Then the Angels dumped those wheelbarrows of tears down outta' that sapphire sky right smack in the middle of our pig pens and created a rousing rainstorm."

"Elmer G.," said Sherman Hutchinson, a very learned pig who read a lot. "I thought that rain was formed by the sun evaporating water up from the earth into the sky. Then the warm air mixes with the cool air and they both get mixed in with dust particles. Next, the moisture condensates on the dust particles and clouds form. Then, the water drops inside the clouds get too heavy and fall down to earth in the form of raindrops. And then….."

"Sherman!!" yelled Elmer G. "Hush your mouth boy! Don't nobody wanna' hear all that techno-scientific mumbo jumbo jabbering. Pigs wanna' know what happened in simple language they can understand. Boy...be quiet and let me finish...."

"Elmer G.'s right, you know," said Naomie, busting in on Elmer G.'s story. "It was a terrible rainstorm. And it happened just the way Elmer G. said."

"It commenced to raining like I ain't never seen before," said Elmer G., as he rescued his high-jacked story back from Naomie.....again. "Like Professor Sherman was saying, the hot air and the cold air got to boxing with one another. They started to mixing and mashing together and started condensating up a storm. It rained by the acres. It was raining so hard that the U.S. Coast Guard ordered all boats and fishes to get outta' the water. It was just too dangerous. While the fishes were checking into the Holiday End Motel, the thunder commenced to rolling in across the pig pens. The sky lit up like a Christmas tree flashing by its lonesome out in a dark forest. BOOM! BOOM!! Roared the thunder."

"How loud was it?" asked Otis.

"The thunder was so loud that it broke all the window panes in every house in Georgia," said Elmer G. "But none of these shenanigans could stop me. I was a pig on a mission. One giant tree was struck by a hundred mile long strip of lightning bolt. Why....that monstrosity of a tree fell about two inches from my head. Darn near killed me. But I never flinched, I tell ya'. Because I was on a mission.....from God."

Barley, upon hearing this whopper of a tale, immediately started walking up to the front of the crowd to interrupt Elmer G. and set the record straight. But, as he saw the crowd of pigs collapsing in laughter, he stopped and turned around, shook his head, smiled slightly.... and strolled away towards home. "Elmer G. is quite a storyteller," he thought to himself. "Quite a storyteller....indeed."

As he walked away, he heard Elmer G., Hattie and Naomie in the background, laying it on….thick as syrup on a cold day, trying to crawl outta' a plastic bottle.

"And when Bobby Lee stepped outta' his truck," said Elmer G.

"He looked twenty feet tall if 'in he was an inch!" chipped in Hattie.

"And he carried a pole with a steel cutting edge that was thirty feet long," added Naomie, not to be outdone.

"Was you scared?" asked Floyd.

"Not one bit!" roared Elmer G., puffing up his chest and a-swelling himself up, as he stole a glance at Corinne, to make sure she was paying attention. "I never even hesitated. When Bobby Lee, that giant of a man…stepped down outta' his truck, a cold blast of wind whipped up around his shoulders, as it followed him around. Blocks of ice crashed down offa' his shoulders and snow whirled around his head."

"Snow?" said Kevin. "In Georgia?" "In April?"

"Well," mumbled Elmer G., in a small voice. "Maybe it wasn't snow. But it 'shore looked like snow."

"They were clouds," said Hattie, as she jumped in to help Elmer G. out of his bind. "White clouds."

"White Clouds?!" asked several pigs in unison, as they tried to figure out why white clouds were swirling around Bobby Lee's head.

"Yep!" said Naomie. "I seem to remember that there were white clouds swirling around Bobby Lee's head."

"Why were white clouds swirling around Bobby Lee's head?" asked Lula.

"Because Bobby Lee was a giant!" said Elmer G., finding a thread to hang his story onto, as he jumped back into the action. "He was so big. And so tall….that his head stuck out through the clouds. That's why there was white clouds swirling around his head!"

The pigs erupted in howls of laughter and whoops of joy. They slapped each other on the back and marveled at this ripper of a tall tale that seemed to get bigger and better every time Elmer G. told it. Naturally, you needed to take some of it with a grain of salt, they whispered to each other, with knowing glances. But even with the added stroking and seasoning by Elmer G., it was all and still a magnificent story.

"Why…if I wasn't a Christian, why…I'd a thrashed Farmer Brown, Bobby Lee, Sonny Boy and any other human that had the audacity! The nerve! To mess with us pigs!" shouted Elmer G., as he jumped up and started dancing around in a circle, crouched down low, bobbing and weaving, punching the air, doing his best imitation of the Ali Shuffle. Elmer G. was in his favorite place, in front of his friends telling them his version of his great adventure.

The crowd erupted in a frenzied roar of approval, as Elmer G. raised both his clenched hoofs in the air like a boxer who has just been declared the winner by a knockout.

"And I was right there to back him up," chipped in Hattie. "I told Elmer G., there were too many of 'em for him to handle alone. Even a brave pig like Elmer G. still needed some backup."

"And don't forget me," said Naomie. "I was there too. 'Shore as day. I was the backup to the backup," explained Naomie. "I had a tough job though. Because although Hattie was watching Elmer G.'s back. I had to cover….both their backsides. You might call it….double duty!"

Again, the audience roared its approval with another rousing round of laughter. They howled with pure, unrestrained laughter, slapping their thighs and clapping their neighbors on the back. Some of them laughed so hard at this outrageous story that they started coughing and couldn't stop themselves from hacking and almost choking on their own laughter.

"Elmer G.," said Henry Handlemore, "ya'll oughta' start charging folks to tell 'em this story. I mean really. This is 'bout the funniest thing I ever heard."

"This ain't no story," said Elmer G. "This is all the truth," he said, making a mental note to add "stop lying" to his growing list of spiritual goals. "As I whipped around and dropped down into my fighting stance, Farmer Brown shouted out to Bobby Lee. Bobby Lee! We got ourselves a problem. This Elmer G. ain't no regular pig. He's a back-alley, bare-footed, barrel-chested, brass-knuckled brawler with a conscience the size of a miniature flea! This feller's got lightning quick moves like I ain't never seen before. But it was too late for 'em, 'cause I was already mad. After an hour of me whipping up on those old boys, Bobby Lee was begging for mercy. Ohhh Mr. Elmer G.....I will leave you alone. If you let me up...all I want is for you to give me back the keys to my truck. And I'll leave. I swear I'll leave ya'll pigs alone! Naturally.....I felt sorry for the boy. So I decided to show a little mercy."

"What did you do?!" asked Sam, excitedly.

"I stared at Bobby Lee for a minute....that seemed to last an hour," said Elmer G. "Then, I casually tossed his keys across on the other side of the fence and told him....Go fetch those keys boy. And get yourself outta' my pig pens. Now! You shoulda' seen the dust clouds that boy kicked up hightailing it outta' here, snatching up his keys on a dead run."

Once more, the crowd tossed their heads back and erupted in a trembling wall of laughter that came from deep down inside their bellies. Barley couldn't help himself, as even he involuntarily cracked a smile. Barley glanced back at his friend Elmer G. For a brief instance, their eyes locked. Each peered deeply into the other's soul. Their quest was over and they were at home. Only a few pigs were safe from slaughter, but it was a start. Elmer G. stared back at Barley. Then, with an air of quiet confidence, he returned to telling the story about his greatest adventure.

Elmer G. turned slightly and braced his face against the spectacular sunshine that was exploding across the powder-blue afternoon sky, as is came crashing down upon his regal shoulders in his finest hour. Although he wore no crown, he felt no less regal than any other King, as he surveyed his realm. Elmer G. breathed deeply, as he drank in the scene in his small, luxuriant world of modest pig pens, black mud pits, slop barrels and faded-brown slop troughs. Even though he had not won his battle against the slaughter house for the other pigs...he had survived. And there was something to be said for simply surviving. The school bus yellow, splendid sunlight seemed to crackle with a life of its own, as it beamed down on Elmer G. and his drowsy pig pens, bathing him in flickering rays of blazing sunshine like his final benediction.

For a brief moment, it seemed like God had taken His fountain pen and placed a giant comma in the mist the pig pens, as their world seemed to pause, stand still and reflect on itself. Once again, memories from the past came raining down from the skies to greet Elmer G. He looked up and peered through the cobwebs that were wrapped around his memories. He saw mama and daddy playing hide and seek with him and his brothers and sisters on a lazy Sunday afternoon. Then, he closed his eyes and saw Scruff Daddy, Ben, Theodore and all his other friends racing against each other to see who could run the fastest.

Elmer G. looked around, took a deep breath and reflected on all of the events of the last few months. He had traveled a lot of miles to get to this point. Yet, he knew there were many miles to go before he could rest. He decided that for now, he was going to have some fun. Tomorrow, with its sorrows and joys was an unhatched day. Then Elmer G. turned back to his audience and plowed right back into his story without missing a beat.

"But I haven't even got to the best part yet......" said Elmer G. "Ohhh nooo. We're just getting started. Like I was saying....my friend Barley was the first pig to give me the low-down that something wasn't right about Bobby Lee taking them Cornmashers for a little joyride. I told Barley I did not believe that humans were slaughtering and eating pigs. That's disgusting! But you know being a pig ain't all bad. Now….you take those turkey gobblers….they got a really bad situation. They're worse off than pigs. Ya'll ever heard about Thanksgiving? Well, let me explain about Thanksgiving. When you learn about Thanksgiving, ya'll will be glad God made us pigs, I can guarantee you that! But wait! Wait! Who wants to be a lobster?"

"I do," said Wanda Wilson. "I'll be a lobster instead of a pig. I could swim all day."

"Not hardly," said Elmer G. "If you were a lobster…girl….the folks at the Orange Lobster Restaurant would stick a blinking red and yellow neon sign on your back, put you in an aquarium at the front door of the restaurant….and the customers would pick you out to be boiled and served with melted butter. That's why we oughta' be glad we're pigs. Being a pig is not as good as some other folks' situation, but then again it is better than some other folks' situation. Who wants to be a gorilla? Naw! Wait! Wait! Who wants to be an elephant?!"

Six pairs of hog's hoofs shot up in the air, as the pigs started becoming active participants in Elmer G.'s explanations about life and death.

"Does anybody know what it means to have faith in God?!" asked Elmer G., deftly shifting the tone and content of his storytelling. "I didn't think so. Let's talk about faith. Having faith in God means believing in someone that you can't see."

"What is God?" asked one of the pigs, as the crowd quieted down at this serious question that many of them had wondered about. "Is God a pig or a man?"

After a slight hesitation, Elmer G.'s voice seemed to change and drop down an octave, as he said in a vibrating baritone, "God is whatever you need Him to be."

A satisfied murmur swept through the crowd at this concise, yet decisive response. Barley found himself refocusing on Elmer G. and blinking in surprise, as he listened to his response.

"All of the world and all the creatures in it are pieces of paint," continued Elmer G. "We are created from the dust and shall return to dust upon our death. The space of time between birth and death is a large, blank, sparkling white canvas propped up on a new easel. We are untouched paint lying in our paint cans waiting for God to dip His brush into our souls and paint something worthwhile on the landscapes of our lives. We have free will to become the best pigs we can be in our daily activities. When God observes us striving to be the kindest, most faithful and loving pigs we can be, He jumps in and finishes painting these landscapes of our lives. In some lives, the paint starts out looking marvelous, but later dries out and peels away. In other lives, the paint thins out, runs down the walls and messes up the linoleum floor. But, the landscapes of some of our lives are beautiful. A few, like the masterpieces of Raphael and Michelangelo were inspired by God's hand pressing down extra hard on the clay when He molded them and their works in His own image. In essence, God's hands mold all of us. He just presses harder on the clay when he molds some of us. With others...it seems like He may have gotten in a bit of a rush and flung a bucket of paint at a blank canvas........and hoped for the best."

"What about me?!" shouted Angelo. "I ain't even got no talents. God's not gonna' wanna' take no credit for making me."

"Yes He will take credit, Angelo," said Elmer G. "Remember, God don't make no trashy artwork. In some way, whether you can see it or not, God's hand has been placed on all of our lives. It is up to us to unlock the secrets of our own destinies. I'm here to tell you all that...I'm not worried anymore. I'm not fearing...any man! I'm not dodging the slaughter house. I don't know what will happen to me in the days ahead. But I can't stop painting on my life's canvas because I'm spending too much time worrying about dying. I'm living my life every day and I encourage you all to do the same. I have walked the plank up to the slaughter house trailer truck and stared death in the face. And it was then..."

"Tell the truth Elmer G.!!" shouted one of the pigs in the crowd, overcome with emotion.

Elmer G. continued. "I have walked the plank up to the trailer truck. I have been to the top of the plank and looked over on the other side, as I stared death in the face. And it was then......in my darkest hour...that the Master answered me. I proclaimed my faith in God on that night. I believed for the first time. Then I looked out over the crowd of pigs staring at me. And through the rain...through the mist and through the darkness of the night...I saw them. I saw thousands of Angels dressed in golden coats of armor, standing by chariots of fire."

The audience erupted in shouts of approval and yelled for Elmer G. to continue preaching. "Go ahead Elmer G.! Tell the truth now! I feel you!!"

Elmer G. squared his shoulders and continued. "God's mighty Army of Angels seemed to stretch through eternity and back again. A rainbow danced across that same dark sky.....kissed me and blew hope into my tired and discouraged heart. I remembered I was not baptized and again———I worried. We all worry about something, even as we face the end of our days. We are always racked with worry. That night, as I stood trembling on the top of the plank preparing to step into the trailer truck, I cried out to God that I had no water for my baptism. Evidently He heard me because He sent me water for my baptism in the form of a rainstorm. God snatched me from the impending gory of the slaughter house and bathed me in His Glory. With a God this strong...I don't have time to walk around fearing———nothing! Man nor beast! Nor the ravages of death. I'm alright now. I have been to the top of the wooden plank and God...has allowed me...to gaze out.....over the ages——on the other side———and I have seen———the Promised Land!! I may not get there with you. But we, as an animal group....will get to the Promised Land!!"

The crowd erupted in howls of joy, excitement and encouragement.

Elmer G., was standing there, bathed in a stream of golden sunlight, talking in a slow, pleasant drawl, as he continued giving his Sermon on the Red Clay Mount.

"I'm here to tell the truth today, my friends. We face many difficulties as we continue to be raised for sale to the slaughter houses. But I have a dream today. It is a dream as deeply real and committed as any human's dream. I have a dream that one day the human race will raise its moral bar and learn to live in peace with us pigs. It is written in the timeless laws of Nature that all of God's creatures are created equal. Today, we are living in violation of this natural law. I have a dream that one day on the wheat filled, brassy-brown, open fields of Nebraska, among the smoky, curvaceous mountains of Tennessee and even on the rolling red hills of Georgia, that man and pig will one day be able to sit at the Table of Fellowship and share......a tossed salad, instead of ham, spare ribs, bacon and pork chops. Instead of choosing selections from a menu filled with meats to nourish the body——we will be choosing from a menu laden heavy with morsels of morality in order to nourish our famished souls."

"But, I'm worried about my piglets," said a sow named Cheryl.

"I know you are," said Elmer G. "We all worry about our young ones. I am hopeful that one day Corinne and I will marry and have piglets. I have a dream that my little piglets will not be judged by the size of their shoulder hams, but by the depth and breath of their intelligence and by the strength of their moral fiber. If we remain faithful in the power of God to move the hearts of men, then we will change today's bleak slaughter house option to an oasis of hope for a brighter tomorrow."

"The problem don't seem to be with us pigs," said Durwood. "The problem is 'Man'." Several pigs quickly agreed with him.

"This issue of salvation is not just about saving pigs," said Elmer G. "Somebody needs to save man too."

"Save him from what?" asked Emmit.

"From himself," said Elmer G.

"What does that mean?" asked Emmit.

"Today, Mankind is struggling with grave issues of life and death all over the world," said Elmer G. "The issue today is not one of war or peace. Instead, the issue faced by mankind is mutual co-existence, or ultimate destruction of the human race. Today, in every corner of the world, men engage in wars, murders, terrorism, bombings, random killings and general strife. Holy temples are destroyed, airplanes are flown into buildings, buses filled with children are blown up and entire ethnic groups are murdered and maimed in the cause of religious, political and ethnic purgings. Most of these destructive acts of violence are done in quests for power, disguised as parades for peace."

"Elmer G.," said Bixby, "you are really carrying on today! Go ahead, with your bad self!"

"Everybody," continued Elmer G., "both pigs and men, worry about the world we will leave our offspring. We are at a dangerous intersection at the crossroads of life. The issue is no longer the quality of life we leave our children. It is a bigger question we are faced with today. The issue is no longer war or peace. The issue is not race, religion, height, weight or place of origin. The issue is peaceful co-existence or total destruction of the world as we know it. These are the times we live in."

"Go on, Elmer G.!" said Roxy. "You're making sense."

"In addition to the world order being at risk, we also struggle with other equally solemn quality of life issues on an individual level," said Elmer G. "For example, we all grapple with the issues of quality educational opportunities, protection of our young, caring for the elderly, safe food, solid shelter and a sense of security. When we have these things under our belts, we are then free to engage in the pursuit of happiness. But it's hard to pursue happiness——if you're hongry'. It's hard to pursue happiness, if you ain't got no proper public housing...."

"But Elmer G.," interrupted Tidwell, "we ain't got no public housing. We all sleep outside, or in stray barrels."

"Doggone it, Tidwell!" said Elmer G. "Now you done gone and interrupted my flow here. But you do have a point. Skip the public housing issue. Where was I? Oh yeah. It's difficult to pursue happiness if you're looking over your shoulder every time you hear a truck pull up, thinking they're coming to haul you away to the slaughter house."

"Now you're talking about something I can relate to," said Tidwell, with an approving nod of his head.

"Who's gonna' be able to solve all these problems?" asked Roxanne. "I'm exhausted now just from sitting here listening to you tick 'em off like that."

"You're right, Roxanne," said Elmer G. "It is a long list of ills. That's why we must turn them over to God and then help Him out. The answers to these great issues can not be solved by man, nor pig. God is waiting to be called onto the battlefield of life. Most of these immoral acts are done because people lack a God-inspired, personal sense of moral responsibility."

"And how are we supposed to fight these problems?" asked Roxanne.

"In these ominous times of public violence and private indifference," said Elmer G., "we need to start standing up and engaging our enemies with weapons forged in the fires of love and non-violence. We must remain morally bigger than our enemies in order to give them something to live up to. We must engage in public displays of our private moral conscience. It is all good and well to give God credit for waking us up in the morning and blessing us with material things, such as thick, fresh slop. But God has enough credit. What He needs now is some help to counter-balance the forces that are afoot in the far and near corners of the world."

"I still don't understand how we can help?" said Lucy.

"We have to move away from 'group thought' and stroll with confidence towards the banner of individual morality in everything we do," said Elmer G. "Many of us are not equipped spiritually to resist the pull of 'group-thoughts'. When a pig has a predetermined set of moral values, he can say "no" and walk away when asked to violate the eternal laws of God and Nature. Each of us must find some noble cause that he believes in so strongly that he is willing to die to preserve it. This is the ultimate price of a well-lived life."

"If we don't do what the dominant group tells us to do," said Robert, "then what other choice do we have?"

"We must return to a state of individual moral and spiritual accountability," said Elmer G. "Instead of relying on somebody else to instruct us about what is right and wrong, we must decide for ourselves in our private hearts. If we move in this direction, we will one day have a world where all of God's creatures, pigs, cows, birds, rabbits and men can all join hands and sing the words of that old spiritual "*Peace In The Valley*". But remember.....there can be no peace in the valley until there is peace on earth."

"Did Jesus leave us any guidelines to go by, in terms of how we should live?" asked Cathy. "Otherwise, how will we know what to do?"

"Elmer G. don't know the answer to that," said Clarence. "He ain't never met Jesus. Elmer G. ain't even met nobody else that ever met Jesus."

"I haven't met Him," said Elmer G. "but I've read about His life. And yes, Jesus did leave us some Commandments to live by. When Jesus preached His Sermon on the Mount, He taught the gathered multitudes, saying, "Blessed *are* the poor in spirit: for theirs is the Kingdom of heaven. Blessed *are* they which do hunger and thirst after righteousness: for they shall be filled. Blessed *are* the pure in heart: for they shall see God. From these teachings we can see that we must start our moral revolution on a small scale."

"What does that mean?" asked Eric.

"It means that we have to do good acts in our daily lives," said Elmer G. "Honor your father and your mother. Be kind to friends and strangers. Although it is hard to do, learn to love your enemies. And most importantly.....love yourself because you are created in God's image. If you can't stop a war between nations, then avoid starting a fight with your neighbor. If you don't know anybody that you can reform from being a thief, then stop stealing yourself. Don't feel good because you only listen to gossip. Get up and walk away from the gossiper, especially if it's some gossip you've already heard. In all things big and small, seek to live your life on a higher moral ground."

"But, I'm only a pig," said Eric. "What if I slip up and fail?"

"That's okay, Eric," said Elmer G. "Even if you fail in your efforts, you will still be failing at a higher moral level than before you started. The sin is not in failing, but in not trying to be better."

"But if I follow those rules, some other pigs may get mad and freeze me outta' stuff," said Franks. "They'll start to bad-mouthing me for sure. You know how they are."

"I understand where you're coming from, Franks," said Elmer G. "If you seek to follow God's Commandments in your own life and other pigs scorn you, or persecute you, then remember Jesus' other teaching. He said, "Blessed *are* they which are persecuted for righteousness' sake: for theirs is the Kingdom of Heaven." God's Commandments are simple and easy to understand. What's hard is remembering to follow them. Since there is never a wrong time to do the right thing, the fear of what others will think should not hold you back. The question on Judgment Day is not what others thought of you, but what God thinks about the things you chose to do——and the things you chose *not* do."

"Elmer G.," said Hoke, "I understand what you're saying. And I'm the first to admit that these are some mighty powerful ideas you're tossing around. But to tell you the truth....these principles you're talking about scare me near 'bout to death. There's so much new stuff to learn. I'm flat-out scared, Elmer G. And I don't mind saying it."

"We're all scared, Hoke," said Elmer G. "The first time Barley told me about the horrors of the slaughter house, I got so scared I almost fainted. When Barley first told me about God, I was scared. When I couldn't understand what it meant to have 'faith' in a God I couldn't see, I was scared. Sometimes, I'm scared now. Especially in quiet moments when I'm by myself. But remember, to go forward in certain situations when you know you will win is not a display of courage. That is ambition. But to go forward and attempt an endeavor, even though you are afraid and know that you may fail.....that is courage of the highest order."

"I'm still scared Elmer G.," said Hoke.

"That's okay," said Elmer G. "It's hard to shake off our fear of the unknown. We spend so much time and effort worrying about tomorrow's imagined horrors that we can't enjoy today."

"But there's just so many changes involved in this stuff you're talking about," said Hoke.

"There is a lot of change involved," said Elmer G. "But change can be good if you participate in the change-making process. Every time the winds of change blow through our lives, we get scared because changing things upsets our routines. But we have to change in order to grow. Otherwise, we will die at the same spiritual place that we started out at birth. And that would mean we didn't absorb any of the rich experiences we have lived through. And who among us wants to live an unexamined life? Enough of this serious talk. Let's have some fun! Who wants to be a lion instead of a pig?! Who thinks they'd be better off as a lion?"

Several trotters shot up into the air, as the pigs laughed nervously in anticipation of Elmer G.'s answer.

When Barley recovered from his shock at the eloquence and wisdom of Elmer G.'s words, he wondered if God had touched

Elmer G.'s heart that night as he stood on the ramp. He thought to himself, "Nawww. No way. Not Elmer G. Not with all the pigs in the world to choose from. Surely God would not pick Elmer G. to spread a message of hope to other pigs. But then again, you never know. After all, Moses had a stutter. And God chose him to lead the Israelites out of bondage in Egypt. Surely God is not training Elmer G. to be a Disciple. Nawww! It couldn't be. Then again, stranger things have happened. One thing was for sure. Elmer G. did sound different these days. And obviously he's been reading the books Barley had loaned him. It would be ironic if Elmer G. did get a shot at the one job he'd always wanted.......a Disciple. Nawww. No way. Not Elmer G."

Barley walked slowly towards home, chuckling to himself, as he realized the truth could never rival Elmer G.'s exaggerations. Barley thought about telling Elmer G. that he'd read in the newspaper that humans needed even more pigs now for their new experiments. According to the newspapers, the humans were cloning pigs to kill them and transplant the pigs' body parts to use as replacement body organs in humans.

"If they keep eating pigs and cloning us to use as replacement for their own body parts," thought Barley to himself, "one day you won't be able to tell humans from pigs. 'Course, this might be a step down the food chain for us pigs."

Since Elmer G. was enjoying himself so much telling stories, Barley decided to tell him later about this new pig cloning development. Sometimes you just have to let things be.

Barley smiled slightly to himself, as he paused and glanced back at his friend, who was in rare form telling his stories. Pigs from neighboring farms were streaming in to sit in the fields and hear Elmer G.'s Sermon on the Red Clay Mound. For the first time, Barley realized that Elmer G. was indeed spreading the Gospel, which was wrapped up in his outrageous stories. Elmer G. was reaching more pigs than Barley ever could hope to convert into believers. Evidently the Lord did work in strange ways. Sometimes, it seems like God picks the most unlikely messengers. Elmer G., a lowly and not terribly learned pig, was bringing new believers into the fold by wrapping the message of "faith" up in shiny new wrapping paper.

"I guess entertainment and the Gospel must be merged in order to get and hold the attention of your audience," he thought to himself. "Human preachers evidently discovered this connection many years before. I guess a sincere spiritual message taught to an empty classroom is not nearly as effective as an outrageous story told in a colorful manner to a packed house. And I have to admit...that Elmer G. does include a solid spiritual message every now and then. Even if he is a tall tale-teller."

As Barley walked towards home, he glanced around his pig pens and saw life pulsating everywhere, as Elmer G. entertained the crowds and pigs roamed listlessly about the place. He smiled slightly to himself, as he decided to wallow awhile in his sublime purpose and wait until tomorrow to talk further with Elmer G. about their past adventures and coming challenges. But, for the moment, he decided to just "let things be". After marinating overnight, things tended to have a different flavor the next day.

He thought to himself, "I'm gonna' go home, prop these tired dogs up awhile and get a good night's sleep. I've gotta' get ready to show up tomorrow. After all, the way life is these days, with all the changes and what-not.......there's a lot to be said.......for simply showing up."

Looking in from the outside, life at the pig pens was pretty dog-gone good.

It is finished.